IT'S NOT A SECRET ANYMORE . . .
MELISSA SENATE'S *THE SECRET OF JOY*
IS WINNING RAVES!

"A wonderfully heartfelt story about hope, possibilities, and the yearning for real connections. *The Secret of Joy* will take you on a much-needed vacation, while sneaking vital life lessons in when you're not looking."

—Caprice Crane, international bestselling
author of *Family Affair*

"*The Secret of Joy* is a heartwarming story that hits all the right notes. Senate has you cheering for more."

—Cara Lockwood, *USA Today* bestselling
author of *I Do (But I Don't)*

Critics adore the bestselling novels of
Melissa Senate

"Smart, funny . . ."—*USA Today*

"Warm, witty."—*Booklist*

"Endearing."—*The New York Post*

"An absolute delight."—*The Daily Buzz*

"Tantalizing . . . entertaining."—*Publishers Weekly*

"Cheeky."—*Newsweek*

"Fresh and lively."—*The Boston Globe*

The Secret of Joy **is also available as an eBook**

THE SECRET OF JOY

A NOVEL

MELISSA SENATE

DOWNTOWN PRESS

New York   London   Toronto   Sydney

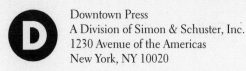

Downtown Press
A Division of Simon & Schuster, Inc.
1230 Avenue of the Americas
New York, NY 10020

First Downtown Press trade paperback edition November 2009

DOWNTOWN PRESS and colophon are trademarks of Simon & Schuster, Inc.

For information about special discounts for bulk purchases, please contact Simon & Schuster Special Sales at 1-866-506-1949 or business@simonandschuster.com.

The Simon & Schuster Speakers Bureau can bring authors to your live event. For more information or to book an event contact the Simon & Schuster Speakers Bureau at 1-866-248-3049 or visit our website at www.simonspeakers.com.

Manufactured in the United States of America

10 9 8 7 6 5 4 3 2 1

Library of Congress Cataloging-in-Publication Data

Senate, Melissa.
    The secret of joy / Melissa Senate.—1st Downtown Press trade pbk. ed.
        p. cm.
    1. Sisters—Fiction. 2. Maine—Fiction. 3. Chick lit. I. Title.
PS3619.E658S43 2009
813'.6—dc22   2009020034

ISBN 978-1-4391-0717-1
ISBN 978-1-4391-6659-8 (ebook)

For my mother

acknowledgments

I wrote this book during one upside-down year and have many to thank for their support and good cheer. (Wow, that was unintentionally Seussesque.)

First, to my editor, Jennifer Heddle, for *everything*, including that amazing editorial letter, the perfect title, and the cover of all covers.

To superagents Kim Witherspoon and Alexis Hurley of Ink-Well Management, for assuring me (and quite rightly so!) that I'd find a happy new home.

To my family, for their willingness to drive eight hours to Maine with dogs and small children—and extra thanks to my mother, for journeying with me to Wiscasset one beautiful summer day.

To my friends Lee Nichols Naftali and Elizabeth Hope, for all the coffee and Indian food and *talking*.

To Adam Kempler, for always giving me the extra time I needed to write.

To the administration, staff, and teachers at my son's school:

ACKNOWLEDGMENTS

Catherine Glaude, Raelene Bean, Jen Beaudoin, Cheryl McGilvery, Meg Pachuta, Valle Gooch and Margi Moran. Your above-and-beyond kindness and generosity enabled me to know my son's heart, mind, and psyche (and hip) were being well cared for during a very tough year of wheelchairs, casts, braces, and sitting out. I could not have lost myself in a fictional world and written this novel without that comfort.

And to Max, who inspires me every minute of every day. You are the definition of a great kid.

THE SECRET OF

JOY

prologue

When Rebecca Strand was five years old, she saved her money—quarters from drying dishes, a dollar bill for the one tooth she'd lost so far—to buy a sister. She had in mind someone like her best friend Charlotte's nine-year-old sister, Olivia, nice enough to French-braid their hair and teach them how to play Miss Mary Mack, yet tough enough to chase down the block bully who twice tried to pee away their chalk-drawn hopscotch board.

Rebecca had brought her Curious George piggy bank to her parents for help in counting what she had. "Do I have enough?" she'd asked. "Grandma Mildred said kids cost money."

Her mother, unaware that Rebecca *did* have a sister (no one knew, except Rebecca's father, of course), sat Rebecca on her lap and told her about the birds and the bees. That yes, kids cost money, but the reason Rebecca didn't have a sister—or a brother—was because God hadn't blessed them with one.

Now, more than twenty years later, Rebecca tried to remember if her father had looked pained as her mother explained what God and biology had to do with each other. If he'd excused himself from the room. Or if he'd just stood there, smiling as always.

one

The moment Rebecca did learn she had a half sister she never knew existed—a twenty-six-year-old half sister—she was twirling (just one twirl, really) in a hand-me-down wedding gown and her beat-up Dansko clogs in her father's hospital room. The dress wasn't hers. It belonged to Michael's mother. And though Rebecca wasn't entirely sure she loved Michael Whitman, her boyfriend of two years, she adored his larger-than-life mother with her *Real Housewives* overly long blond hair, showy jewelry, and supersized heart. According to Rebecca's married friend Charlotte, being fond of a man's mother ranked high up on the pro side for marrying him.

Glenda Whitman had driven close to two hours from Connecticut today when she heard that Rebecca's father had taken a turn for the worse. She'd whisked Rebecca off for a quick bite because "I know you need your lunch hour to see your dad," then mentioned that the dress bag she was schlepping around was for Rebecca, that maybe it was time she and Michael got serious about being serious. Rebecca had unzipped just the top and saw something very white and very satiny.

"I'm making a statement," Glenda had said, laying the garment bag over Rebecca's arm before kissing her on both cheeks and dashing off on her heels with a tossed back, "I've always wanted a daughter just like you."

I once had a mother just like you, Rebecca had thought. In your face in a good way. Funny, kind, bighearted. A know-it-all who really did know it all. *"She was a menschy yenta,"* her Jewish father always said of her Christian mother. *"The best kind."*

Her mom would have loved Glenda Whitman. Michael, not so much.

With the garment bag weighing a thousand pounds on her arm, Rebecca went to NewYork-Presbyterian to see her father. The hospital was like a palace, all atriums and marble and glass-enclosed wings overlooking the East River. She hated the place.

"Fancy shindig tonight?" her father whispered, eyeing the dress bag. His voice, once so radio-announcer strong, was now nothing more than a hoarse whisper. He lay in the standard-issue cot, IVs and poles aplenty, beeping constant, a Mets cap covering what was left of his sparse brown hair. There were flowers in vases everywhere, so many that they lined the wall underneath the window.

"Michael's mother is making a statement," Rebecca said with a bit of a smile, a bit of a shrug, smoothing the down comforter over her father's slight form. "She thinks it's time we got engaged." She rolled her eyes, then pulled a pair of

SmartWool socks from her tote bag. "I got you the best socks, Dad. They are so warm."

He smiled and tried to kick his feet out from under the comforter, but the lightweight down barely moved. That was how little strength he had left. As she slipped the thick blue and white marled socks on her dad's skinny feet, he said, "Try on the dress for me, Becs. This'll be my only chance to see my baby girl in a wedding gown."

She kept the *Oh, God, do I have to?* to herself. Her father had days, maybe a week, left on this earth, and if he wanted to see his only child in a long white dress, so be it.

Days left. The relentless truth of it made Rebecca burst into tears everywhere since she'd gotten the news of his collapse three days ago—at work with clients, in the supermarket while checking eggs for cracks, on the subway, and this morning while watching a man she barely knew from her apartment building hoist his two-year-old daughter onto his shoulders as they headed out.

"Be right back," she said, tears pooling in her eyes. There was no "Be right back" with stage 4 pancreatic cancer. She could be right back in a split second and he could be gone.

She went into the small bathroom and took off her Whitman, Goldberg & Whitman–approved gray pantsuit and slipped into the wedding gown. It was one size too big, but beautiful, simple, perfect. A strapless princess dress, not too poufy, not too plain. She stepped back into her comfy commuting clogs to make herself a little taller (she was only five feet two) so that the gown wouldn't trail on the well-worn tile floor.

She stared at herself in the mirror above the sink, almost

surprised to see she looked exactly the same. Yup, there was the same shoulder-length, wavy, chestnut-brown hair. Same pale brown eyes. Same fair skin, paler these past few days, since her father had been admitted and would not be discharged.

She felt like the gown was getting tighter, squeezing her.

"Becs?" her dad called.

I do, I don't, I do, I don't, she thought as she came out. She should want to marry Michael Whitman, handsome young partner at Whitman, Goldberg & Whitman (not that he'd asked). But every special occasion, holiday, and birthday, she held her breath until she opened his gift and breathed a sigh of relief at the doorstopper edition of *How to Be a More Effective Paralegal* or the charm bracelet with charms that made no sense to her. A tiny silver tennis racquet? Rebecca had never even held a tennis racquet. Last month, for her twenty-eighth birthday, she'd almost hyperventilated over the small jewelry box he'd handed her until she'd opened it to find exquisite diamond stud earrings, a half-carat each.

"You're beautiful, Becs," her father whispered, but then his gaze strayed over to the wall, his attention on the little poster of fire-safety rules. He turned back to her. "You should know that you're—" He clamped his mouth shut, then let out a deep breath. "That you're not going to be all alone when I go." His voice cracked, and he coughed, and Rebecca sat down on the edge of his bed and took his hand.

"Michael's a good guy." Her dad didn't need to know about her ambivalence. Michael *was* a good guy.

"I don't mean him." He burst into tears and covered his face with his hands. "Rebecca—I . . ."

"Dad?"

"I'm okay, I'm okay," he said, dabbing at his eyes. "I'm just so damned emotional. Pour me some eggnog, will you?"

Rebecca headed over to the minifridge. It was only mid-September, but eggnog had started appearing in the supermarket along with the giant bags of Halloween candy that Rebecca easily ignored. As if she could pop fun-size 3 Musketeers bars in her mouth when her father was dying.

He wanted to be surrounded by certain favorites, ones he'd whispered in her ear. And so every day she brought something he loved, from the eggnog to strawberry cheesecake, from Junior's (his beloved original on Flatbush Avenue in Brooklyn, even though a Junior's had opened close to her office in Grand Central) to a greasy, no-good Steak-umms sandwich piled high with fried onions. The cuddly down comforter she'd bought him for Hanukkah last year. And Neil Diamond's greatest hits on repeat on his iPod, her present for his fifty-ninth birthday last week.

He burst into tears again. She hurried back to him, then realized she'd forgotten the eggnog and spun around, the beautiful white dress swishing at her ankles. The one thing her father hadn't done since he'd been admitted this time around was cry. Daniel Strand was tiny for a man, only five feet four like Michael J. Fox, and he'd told Rebecca he'd learned in first grade that *never* crying and being very funny was the way to make up the inches with the other kids. Rebecca could think of only two times she'd seen her father cry: when he'd told Rebecca her mother had died and then again at the funeral.

"There was a baby," he whispered.

She set the plastic cup of eggnog on the gray swivel tray over his bed. He'd been doing a lot of this these past few days: throwing out the odd reference to events big and small. Big like her mother, who'd died when Rebecca was nineteen. Medium like Finn Weller, who'd broken Rebecca's heart during her senior prom. Small like Cherub, Rebecca's childhood guinea pig, who'd lived a short, uneventful life in a cage on her pink and white dresser. *"We had a dog,"* he'd said last night. *"What was its name?"* His brown eyes had twinkled with memory, but then he'd turned and stared out the window, his expression heavy and sad. *"Bongo, was it?"* Rebecca had held his hand and reminisced about their dear little beagle, Bingo, reminding him of how he'd taken her to the ASPCA on her sixth birthday and let her pick out any pet she wanted, from the biggest dog to the tiniest kitten. She'd chosen the sad-faced beagle, and every morning and every night, she and her father would walk Bingo together, singing funny versions of the old song—that first year, anyway. *"Was a chicken, laid an egg and Bingo was its name-o . . ."*

"Is a baby," her father said. *"Is. Is."* Tears pooled, and he turned his head toward the wall, his gaze on the poster of fire-safety rules again.

Rebecca tried to think what her father was referring to, hoping to fill in a blank for him. Perhaps her mother had lost a baby and they'd kept it a secret from Rebecca?

"I never wanted you to know, Rebecca," he said, his voice cracking again. "Your mother never knew."

Whoa, Rebecca thought, her shoulders stiffening. Wait a minute. *What* was he talking about?

"Dad, what baby?"

"She called her Joy."

"*Who?*" Rebecca asked.

Tears streamed down her father's face. And for the next half hour, between sobs and "I'm sorry," Rebecca slowly learned the story of a baby named Joy Jayhawk. Of an affair, a summer affair in Wiscasset, Maine, where the Strands had gone for vacation. There'd been a woman named Pia Jayhawk, an artist.

Rebecca had a half sister. A *twenty-six-year-old* half sister.

This made no sense. Her tiny, hilarious father, the kindest person she'd ever known, had a secret life?

"Don't hate me, Beckles," he whispered. "Please just don't hate me. I can't go with that. But I had to tell you. I couldn't go without telling you."

Beckles. He'd started calling her that when she'd come home complaining that she didn't have freckles like the reigning queen of first grade, a girl named Claudia. And when he'd been calling her Beckles, somewhere in Maine was a four-year-old who was probably starting to ask where her own father was.

"I have a half sister," she repeated. "I can't believe this." Rebecca stood and paced the room, stared out the window at the stretch of gray water. A hot shot of anger slammed into her stomach, but at the effort it took him to take a deep breath, the sadness returned, the grief.

He took another deep breath, then another, and told her about the phone calls he'd received from Pia Jayhawk when the family had returned to New York. There were two: the first to alert him to the pregnancy, the second to the birth. A girl, six pounds even, named Joy.

"When she called to tell me she was pregnant, I didn't say anything. Not one damned word," he said, staring up at the squares of ceiling tile. "She'd said, 'Daniel, are you there?' And I didn't say anything. I just held the phone, not breathing, afraid to move a muscle. And she said again, 'Daniel?' And finally she said, 'Okay,' and hung up."

Rebecca stared at her father, unable to process this. The words were just building up on top of each other.

"Every day I expected the phone to ring again, expected your mother to answer it, expected her to come ashen-faced to find me with '*I know.*' But weeks passed, and months, with nothing. I think I was in some kind of denial. It just went away and I didn't think about it."

Didn't think about it? This couldn't be right. This couldn't *be.*

"Until she did call again," her father said on a strangled sob. "The day the baby was born. I thanked her for informing me, then hung up and went back to the Sunday crossword. I finished the entire puzzle, Rebecca." He covered his face, then let his hands drop as he stared up at the ceiling again. "And then I suggested to your mother that we take you to the Central Park Zoo and maybe the carousel. We never made it to the carousel because you couldn't bear to leave the polar bears. You screamed every time we tried to wheel your stroller away. By the time we were back at the apartment, it was as though the phone had never rung."

He explained it was why they moved a few weeks later to the Westchester suburbs. Why their telephone number was never listed. Why he dared never make another false move.

Her mother's face, the sweet doe eyes and long, strong

nose, her wavy auburn hair, floated into Rebecca's mind. Norah Strand had died almost ten years ago, three days before Christmas during Rebecca's freshman year in college. A speeding cab at the corner of Lexington and Sixtieth, right in front of Bloomingdale's, where her mother had bought a pink cashmere hat and matching gloves that Rebecca still used every winter. Rebecca, a dazed, grieving mess, hadn't gone back to Cornell. Despite a complete lack of interest in the law, she'd worked for her dad's law firm for a while, not wanting to take her eyes off him for a second, then commuted to Hunter College to finish her degree (psychology) and earn a paralegal certificate for its structure and security, its "you are now *this*" quality. She'd lived with her dad in the too-big Westchester colonial through college and her postgrad work. He'd been so devastated by her mother's death. *Seemed* so devastated.

"So the reason you didn't cheat again was because you were afraid of another phone call like that?" she asked, the anger building again.

"I had a vasectomy," he whispered. "Right after I found out. I was so ashamed, Rebecca. I didn't deserve another child with your mother."

So much for God and biology.

"Please don't hate me, Rebecca. I couldn't—"

A large, squishy lump made its way from her stomach to her throat. "I couldn't hate you."

She was about to ask if he'd loved the woman, this Pia Jayhawk, but then realized she didn't want to know.

"Rebecca, come close," he said, and she hesitated, but sat

down on the edge of bed. "In my desk drawer at home, in a red leather case, there's a key to a safety-deposit box at the Citibank on Lex near my office. There's more in there about all this. It'll explain better than I can now. Go there now, Becs."

No. No, no, no. She didn't want *more*. And she couldn't bear the idea of being alone with this crazy story. As long as she was in this room with her father, the man she'd always known, always loved and adored, things were as they always were. He was still the same man, the same father. There was no lie. No baby named Joy. No *more*.

But the moment Rebecca walked out of room 8-401, cold, gripping reality would knock into her knees.

There was a baby.

Is *a baby.*

"I want to stay with you, Dad."

He shook his head. "Please, sweetheart. I want you to get what's in the safety-deposit box. I want to know, be sure, that you're going to the bank. Please, Rebecca." A wheeze came from his throat, and her heart clenched.

"What's *in* the box, Dad?"

"I'm so tired, honey. So, so tired. Just promise me you'll go today. I know you always keep your promises."

"I promise," she assured him. Suddenly, she *could* imagine leaving, could imagine walking out of this room, could imagine going to the bank with the key—as long as she didn't open the box. "But, Dad, what do I do with what's in the box? Do you want me to bring it back here?"

"No," he said. "Not here. I know you'll know what to do."

He closed his eyes and she sat there in the wedding gown, afraid to move.

"A half sister?" Michael repeated. Rebecca had flung out the story in a rush of words and wasn't sure she'd made any sense. *"What?"*

Michael Whitman wasn't easy to surprise. As a divorce lawyer, a specialist in mediation, he'd been there, done that, and heard it all. From affairs to hidden assets to secret children. Last year, he'd had a case involving a man who juggled two families at the same time, a wife and two kids, and a mistress and a daughter, but the mistress hadn't known about the wife either. She'd believed him to be an international businessman when he really lived less than thirty miles away half the week. Still, Michael had managed to work his mediation magic on the couple—the married one—and they'd avoided a long and nasty divorce battle.

An unacknowledged baby? A secret safety-deposit box containing who knew what? Business as usual around the law and mediation offices of Whitman, Goldberg & Whitman.

Michael shook his head. "I can't believe it."

Rebecca nodded. "Me either. I have a half sister. I've known about this for almost an hour and it's still not sinking in."

They stood at the windows in Michael's office. If Rebecca looked left, she could make out the cluster of buildings that the hospital comprised. She'd almost gotten off the bus when she saw her father's Citibank branch on the corner, but she hadn't been able to move, lift her herself up. She'd stared after the Citibank logo as if bypassing it would make this all go away, temporarily anyway. She would go to the bank after work. She would find out what was in the safety-deposit box, then be able to go home. Michael would make her his famous Irish chai latte and she could try to think.

There was a tap at Michael's door, and Marcie Feldman, the senior paralegal who reported to Michael, poked in her shellacked blond bob. She sneered at Rebecca. "I was looking for you. The Frittauers are here." She made a show of glancing at her watch.

"I'll be there in a minute," Rebecca said. From her father's bedside to *this*. To smug Marcie and Rebecca's interminable case files of divorcing couples. For the past several months, walking through the front doors of Whitman, Goldberg & Whitman had required three strong cups of coffee. Because Michael was there? Or because her job had become so un-bearable?

Or both?

"And as an FYI," Marcie added, "per HR, if you're going to be out of the office past allotted lunch hours between noon and two, you need to clear it with me first."

If my father dies at 2:01, I'll be sure and call you first to ask if I can stay by his side, she felt like shouting. Talk about not sucking up to the boss's girlfriend. Rebecca almost had to give Marcie credit for that.

"She cleared it with me," Michael said. He was always way too kind to the superefficient automaton that was Marcie Feldman. Granted, the office would fall to pot if it weren't for Marcie, but still. "I was so busy I forgot to mention it to you."

Marcie smiled her tight smile at Michael, then looked at her watch again before the shellacked blond bob withdrew from the doorway.

"Forget the Frittauers," Michael said. "I'll have Marcie cover it."

"She'll just hate me more. I can do it. And I like the Frittauers. They'll distract me from thinking about my dad and I'll be able to focus on them. I think I can keep them on track." Unlike the Bergerons or the McDonough-Pages, the last two sets of clients who'd had to be physically pulled apart—and not because they were hugging or had rediscovered their love at the eleventh hour. Marian Bergeron had flipped out over something Rebecca had said (seemingly in favor of her husband) and had pushed Rebecca so hard against a credenza that Rebecca had gotten a whopper of a black-and-blue mark on her thigh. And Jeffrey Page had thrown the contents of a water pitcher at his wife—and the pitcher at Rebecca. At least it hadn't been a glass pitcher.

And Rebecca was just a paralegal—she wasn't even the mediator.

She'd once actually thought she'd enjoy working in divorce mediation. Boy, had she been wrong. The result was always the same: a divorce. *Divorce with dignity* (the firm's tagline) or not.

"No one could hate you, Rebecca Strand," Michael whispered, and then pulled her into a hug. For a moment she actually felt that she *could* do it, sit down with the feuding Frittauers and go over the few remaining unresolved issues in their case. A hug from Michael had that power. Another addition to the pro column.

She and Michael had been a couple from her third day at the firm. On that third day, Rebecca had entered conference room 1 to attend to new clients, Mr. and Mrs. Plotowsky, and the moment she sat down she smelled Chanel N° 19, her mother's signature scent. Her mother had been gone for years then, but it was the first time she'd smelled that scent since she'd put her mother's clothes in storage, unable to give them away or put them in her own closet. Chanel N° 19 wasn't popular like Chanel N° 5. And so she'd smiled at Mrs. Plotowsky and said, "Your perfume reminds me of my mother. It was her favorite."

And Mr. Plotowsky, who'd sat staring at the cherrywood table until that moment, jumped up and yelled, "No fair! No fair! Disqualified!" He'd run screaming into the hallway, yelling that Rebecca had sided with his wife and couldn't be impartial.

Mr. Goldberg had sent the senior paralegal (the smug Marcie) to "write Rebecca up" and go over protocol, which included no personal comments. Ever. That afternoon, Michael Whitman, the young partner at the firm (the elder Whitman and Goldberg were in their sixties), asked Rebecca to lunch, and she'd assumed it was to fire her.

"Actually," he'd said at their little table in a crowded Chinese restaurant around the corner from the office, "I asked you to lunch because I think you're beautiful and smart and kind and I wanted to know if I had a chance."

A chance. Michael Whitman, six feet two, eyes of blue, a smart, compassionate, if uptight, thirty-two-year-old attorney-mediator in a three-piece suit and an expensive briefcase, thought she was beautiful and smart and kind, even though he himself had had to spend over an hour calming down Doug Plotowsky. She'd recently had her heart bruised, if not broken, by an effortless liar, and Michael Whitman's romantic intensity, especially given her mistake with the Plotowskys, had done something magical to her spirit. She'd explained how she thought her years of experience as a paralegal, her psychology degree and interest in counseling might serve her well in the field of divorce mediation, and Michael had been so encouraging. Her entire life she'd been the go-to girl for friends with problems, which was why she'd chosen to study psychology in the first place.

People had been telling her of their tragedies and triumphs since preschool. With pinky promises and crossed hearts and swearing on various boyfriends' lives not to tell (and Rebecca never did; she was a supreme keeper of secrets), she would hear stories of parents divorcing, of older sisters getting pregnant, of letting a boy unhook a bra. When she'd started working, she'd spent her lunch hours listening to all sorts of family dysfunction, of boyfriends, fiancés, and husbands who wanted this or didn't want that. But then her mother had died and Rebecca had lost her way and trailed along in her dad's career as a real-estate attorney—for too long. She'd started at Whitman, Goldberg & Whitman with such high hopes, and as she'd realized very quickly that she hated the job, she'd fallen for one of the partners, which had made coming to work a lot more enticing. For a long while, anyway. Michael had told her often in the beginning that she had a gift for paying supreme attention without judging or validating, which allowed the other person to unload and reach his own conclusions without even realizing it. He sad it was why divorcing couples responded so positively to her style.

"Sweetheart," Michael said, "if you really think you're up to dealing with the Frittauers, go ahead, but if you need to just let all this new information percolate, I understand."

What he really meant was: Don't screw things up with the very prominent clients. Like you've done several times in the past few months. If she weren't Michael's girlfriend, she would have been on probation and fired by now.

New information. Rebecca hated when Michael spoke to her as though she were a client. But the words lit up a light-bulb over her head. "Michael, I just realized I'd better find this Joy Jayhawk fast. Before my dad—" She burst into tears and covered her face with her hands.

Michael leaned his head down on hers. "Becs, listen, honey. One thing at a time. Just focus on your dad right now."

"But there's no time left," she said, wiping her eyes. "If I track her down and let her know, she might want to come. At least meet him before—"

Michael tipped up her chin and shook his head. "Rebecca, I strongly advise against that. Keep in mind that you are oper-ating under an informational deficit. This woman, whoever she is, is *not* your sister. She is a total stranger who will feel entitled to half of your father's estate."

Depending on the circumstances, Michael was sometimes more attorney, sometimes more mediator. Right now, be-hind closed doors in his office, the corner office he'd worked eighty hours a week to get (the elder Whitman did not believe in nepotism and grudgingly made Michael a partner only when he had to concede the old adage about the chip and the block), he was both of these things, when what Rebecca wanted, needed was more *boyfriend*.

"Straight talk here, Rebecca. Your dad is worth over *a million dollars.* You want to see half disappear into the hands of someone you know nothing about? She could be mentally unbalanced. Or a junkie. Or just a greedy bitch. You wouldn't be wrong to excise her from your mind. Like your father did."

Rebecca could not seem to do that, not that she was trying. She already had a picture formed in her mind of the half sister. Despite her own brown hair and her father's, she saw blond hair. Yet brown eyes, like hers and her father's. A sweetness in the face. A need for an older sister.

Rebecca, the classic lonely-only, hadn't stopped asking for a sister. Every birthday, every Christmas, every Hanukkah, until she was old enough to understand about God and biology and luck, she asked. She'd received pets instead. A betta fish, a guinea pig, a white rabbit, the sad-faced beagle named Bingo. All that time, all these years, she *did* have a sister. A sister walking and talking and breathing the air.

"Take the rest of the day off," he said, hugging her. "Go be with your dad. He needs you more than the Frittauers right now."

Leave the Frittauers in the hands of Marcie Feldman? No. They were hers. They were the one couple in the past several months who seemed to truly calm down in Rebecca's presence. At the tail end of the mediation process, the Frittauers had been married for six years and separated two months ago over Edward Frittauer's admitted and ongoing affair with an administrative assistant at his firm. An administrative assistant who was now pregnant with his child. Gwendolyn had been willing to overlook the affair until Edward mentioned he now had an extra mouth to feed and that perhaps little Angelina could attend a summer camp for less than ten thousand next year. When Edward Frittauer came to pick up their five-year-old daughter for scheduled "Daddy time," the fighting and screaming and accusations between Mommy and Daddy in the doorway of their co-op led little Angelina Frittauer to hyperventilate. She was rushed to the hospital, where the ER doctor, a former client of Whitman, Goldberg & Whitman, handed the Frittauers Harold Goldberg's card.

Rebecca had done much of the preliminary work with the couple, sitting across from them at the large square table in conference room 1, gathering information to see where they stood on the major issues: division of property, child support, and visitation. During the first five minutes of their first meeting, both Frittauers said that nothing mattered more than their daughter and her well-being; they wanted to divorce as calmly and as amicably as possible. That sentiment lasted for another minute, until Michael Whitman walked into the room with his briefcase. Suddenly, Edward wanted to sell the co-op, which Gwendolyn Frittauer wanted to keep. Suddenly, Gwendolyn wanted every-other-week visitation for Edward, and Edward to split the week. Suddenly, they were screaming again.

Until Michael left Rebecca to "redirect the tension." She'd so appreciated his trust, his faith in her, when everyone else in the office had started expecting very little. In less than ten minutes, she had the couple quiet and verbally agreeing that Gwendolyn would live in the co-op and Edward would have weekends with their daughter. Something about Rebecca, something in her looks or her manner, seemed to appeal to Gwendolyn Frittauer. Apparently, she reminded Gwendolyn of her favorite cousin, who'd moved to California years ago. And when Gwendolyn was calm, Edward was calm.

Because of the Frittauers, Rebecca had gotten back some of her standing in the office. She wasn't the "screwup" anymore.

The Frittauers would have been Rebecca's parents had her mother known about the affair. Norah Strand had been such a proud person. She wouldn't have stood by her man. She would have kicked him out. Rebecca was sure of it. It was clearly why her father had protected his secret.

The Frittauers were here for their final meeting to draw up the separation agreement. Rebecca would lead them through it before Harold Goldberg came in to finalize everything. Then she would go find that red leather case containing a key to a safety-deposit box she wasn't sure she wanted to open.

two

Gwendolyn Frittauer reminded Rebecca of a younger version of Glenda Whitman. She was forty, yet had past-bra-strap-length bouncy blond hair. She wore heavy makeup, including iridescent lipstick and bronzer. Her eyes were remarkably close together, giving her the look of a ferret, yet there was a sweetness in her face and a sadness Rebecca had picked up on right away. Gwendolyn sat across the square table from her husband, who alternated between staring out the window and glancing at his watch.

"Afraid you'll miss an ultrasound appointment?" Gwendolyn snapped at him. "Oh, wait a minute—that's right. You don't go to those things."

Okay. This was going to be a long session. Rebecca sat down at the head of the table and opened her case file, the one that had accompanied her on the subway to Junior's last night for her father's cheesecake. But instead of making a quick review of what was already in her head, she envisioned Pia Jayhawk, vampish-looking, a man stealer, a home wrecker, lying on the obstetrician's table, no one waiting with her to see the heartbeat, the tiny growing form of a baby. *Focus, Rebecca,* she reminded herself. *Stop thinking about Dad.*

Mr. Frittauer was examining his nails. "You won't bait me, Gwendolyn. So don't waste your bad breath."

"Would you like some coffee?" Rebecca rushed to say. *Redirect the tension.* "I recall you both liked the French roast."

Gwendolyn snorted. "Bad breath. Is that the best you can come up with, Edward? Sad."

"I'm dying for a cup of coffee," Rebecca said. "Why don't I have our receptionist bring in a carafe and a tray of pastries, and we'll get started on the last few items." She picked up the phone to buzz Jane.

"Fine, whatever," Edward said to Rebecca, then turned his attention to his wife. "I repeat: You won't bait me, Gwen. I've been attending Buddhist meditation classes." Edward did look less . . . buttoned up. He usually wore wire-rimmed glasses and precisely combed hair; today, the glasses were gone, the red hair showed signs of gel, and the Rockports had been replaced by Italian black leather.

Sometimes divorce had that effect.

Gwendolyn laughed. "Hilarious! I'm wondering what the karmic repercussions are for adultery. And, hmm, you fought me for years on having a second child, yet your skanky girlfriend is knocked up. Trust me, the kid will be born with eleven toes. Or worse."

"Shut the hell up, Gwen," he practically spat.

Welcome to divorce mediation. Sometimes the couple was so grateful to be splitting up they fell over backward to get their agreements in order. "No, *you* take the one-hundred-inch plasma TV!" "No, *you!*" Though those couples were rare. There had been only three in the past two years. And sometimes the couple needed help in seeing what was fair for both.

And then there were Gwendolyn and Edward, both of whom had been determined to avoid the kind of divorce that would clearly affect their daughter's well-being. Their lawyers were not present and would not advocate for their clients during the mediation sessions. They would vet the agreements, of course, but at the table would be the husband, the wife, and the mediation team, who worked for the end result: a divorce agreement both parties could live with.

That was both the positive and negative of working in divorce mediation. In the end, you were dealing with the dissolution of a marriage. That result never changed. Very rarely did Rebecca ever see the flicker of love in a client's eyes for their soon-to-be-former spouse. When she first started working at Whitman, Goldberg & Whitman, she used to think it possible that discussing what was fair for both parties would reignite some spark, some not-too-distant memory of love, of vows, of happily ever after. But the couple usually sat glum-faced and resigned, the only resolution signatures on an agreement to part.

Because the nature of the work was in itself positive, no miserable divorce battle, no custody fight, no throwing vases at each other's heads (just the occasional water pitcher), Rebecca had slowly learned to accept that there *was* something called a good divorce. That was how Michael put it, anyway, whenever she would talk about leaving, about going back to school for graduate work in counseling or clinical psychology. *"Why waste your paralegal certificate by going back to school?"* he'd say. *"We can put that money toward a trip to Aruba."* And then he'd actually surprise her with tickets to Aruba and she'd have a great, relaxing time away from New York, where everything moved so fast, and away from the office, where everything moved so . . . meanly, and she'd be rejuvenated for about three weeks. And then Michael would buy her something fancy. Deflection was the name of the game.

She knew one thing for sure. She did not want to be a paralegal in a divorce mediation firm. She did not want to be a paralegal. The only thing she knew she *did* want, even just once, was for the divorcing couple to agree to go back to the start, take everything they'd been through and start over with their experienced heads and hearts.

"Well, then we wouldn't be a divorce mediation firm." Michael had said. As if that helped.

"That whore isn't getting a cent of what should go to me and Angelina," Gwendolyn said as calmly as if she'd mentioned it had started to rain.

"Give it a rest," Edward said, rolling his eyes. "For God's sake, just shut the hell up! We've been through this over and over."

Focus them on the good ending, Rebecca told herself. *Before they lose control.* "Hey," she said, setting out some documents. "Let's go over the few areas left unresolved. You're so close to reaching a resolution that's good for both of you and for Angelina. Let's focus on that, okay?"

"Do you know what *I'm* focusing on?" Gwendolyn said through gritted teeth. "Do you know what we *haven't* been through over and over? That his skanky slut had the nerve to show up on my doorstep yesterday to 'talk woman to woman.' First of all, she's not a woman—she's a dirty slut. Second of all, I wouldn't give her two seconds of my life. And third, she's not getting a goddamned penny extra that should be allotted to me and my child."

Edward crossed his arms over his chest and turned toward Rebecca. "I'm not speaking directly to her."

Gwendolyn picked up her water glass and flung its contents at her husband. It was time for an office memo about not allowing beverages in the conference rooms.

Edward leaped up, flailing his arms and shrieking, "You bitch!"

Rebecca rushed to the credenza in search of a roll of paper towels, but only found a box of tissues. The tissues left a sheddy residue on Edward's jacket.

Restore order. Restore order. Restore order, Rebecca chanted to herself. "Gwendolyn," she said. "I understand how difficult this is for you. But you are so close to a peaceful resolution. That's what you wanted most of all—for Angelina's sake."

Gwendolyn glared at her husband. "I want additional child support for the extra therapy that poor Angelina will require from having an illegitimate half sibling. An additional one thousand."

"I have another child to support," Edward yelled.

"I don't care about your other child. I care about *my* child. That slut's spawn can rot in the street for all I care."

You should *care*, Rebecca wanted to yell in her face. *It's not the kid's fault.*

She wondered about Pia and how she'd managed, an artist in Maine left to raise a child alone. Perhaps Pia Jayhawk had had a trust fund. Or, very helpful, rich parents. Perhaps she hadn't been a struggling single mother, which was what Rebecca envisioned: Pia sitting at a kitchen table in a small one-bedroom apartment, the flip-out couch open in the living room, a pile of bills that would leave just enough for one new shoe but not two.

"Gwendolyn," Rebecca said, "Edward is taking responsibility for his child—"

Gwendolyn stared at Rebecca, her cheeks bright red. "So now you're on his side?"

Rebecca held up a hand. "I'm not on anyone's side. I'm here to help both of you reach agreement."

"But you're saying I'm right, right?" Edward said, his beady eyes suddenly bright. "I can petition for less child support now that there'll be another baby?"

"You stupid bitch!" Gwendolyn screamed at Rebecca.

The door opened and Marcie entered, Jane at her heels with the tray of coffee and pastries. "Rebecca," she whispered through gritted teeth. "We can hear you all down the *hall*." She smiled from one Frittauer to the other. "May *I* be of assistance?"

Gwendolyn lunged for Rebecca's folder and began ripping papers in half and tossing documents in the air. "I want Harold Goldberg in here right away! She's fired!" she added, pointing at Rebecca with her long red fingernail.

This was not the good ending Rebecca had envisioned. Then again, maybe it was.

• • •

Rebecca arrived at the hospital just as it began drizzling again, the heavy gray sky and distant crack of thunder warning of a downpour. She stood outside and lifted her face up and let the intermittent raindrops pelt her until someone bumped into her with a *"Lo siento, señorita."*

The *"I'm sorry"* did her in and tears pricked her eyes. People rushed by her in both directions, and a taxicab driver slammed on his horn so hard that Rebecca almost jumped. She stared at the taxi driver, blabbering into his cell phone and making angry hand gestures out the window at the cab that had stopped short in front of him to let out a passenger. *You could be the lunatic driver who killed my mother,* she thought, tears streaming down her cheeks. And in that moment she was filled with a hatred of New York. Of the speeding taxis and the noise that never stopped, even at three in the morning. Of the cancer that was taking her father from her, eight floors up.

As she stood there letting the rain soak her instead of dashing under the hospital's overhang, she realized she was in trouble. There was no haven anymore, now that her father was lying on the cot, attached to those tubes, barely able to bite into the fancy chocolates she brought him. Her best friend Charlotte was married and wrapped up in her career. Her mother was long gone. And Michael . . .

She desperately wanted to blink herself away to Aruba again—without Michael.

"I told you to go home!" he'd said in his office after the big blowout with the Frittauers. "I wish you'd listened. Take the rest of the day off, Rebecca. Go see your dad. I'll see what I can do to get this fixed. Don't worry, okay? Everyone knows you're up against a wall."

Up against a wall. When she was younger, Rebecca would bargain with God. *If you let me pass this test I will never not study again. If you make me more popular this year, I will think kinder thoughts about Claudia Herman, of whom I am deeply jealous.*

There was no bargaining now. No *If you let my father live by some miracle, I will be a better daughter, a better person.* She knew because she'd tried that on her way over to the hospital that first day, before she'd known just how sick he was. And she'd tried when the oncologist had explained to her that she should start thinking about arrangements.

The tears pricked again, but as she headed inside, the anger rushed up inside her. Her father had had an affair. And he'd let his own child grow up without him. Without being acknowledged in the slightest. How dare he! He wasn't who she'd thought he was. Not from the time she was two years old.

She pushed back the wet hair stuck to her face and closed her eyes and counted to five. As she passed the nurse's station, Rebecca nodded at the kinder of the two nurses who attended her father during the day, then took a deep breath and headed inside room 8-401. Her father was still. She moved closer, checking the telltale sign of his chest rising and falling. He was sleeping. The anger abated, then returned with a rush a moment later. He'd slept through his child's entire life.

She had so many questions. *Did you ever think about the baby? As she was growing up? Did you send money? Did you ever see her? Did you love her mother?*

And the biggest: *How did you just turn your back on them?*

"I don't understand," she whispered. And she didn't want to learn the whys from whatever was in that safety-deposit box; she wanted answers from her father, the man she loved more than anyone else on earth.

"How could you?" she whispered so low that if he were by chance awake, he couldn't have heard. She kissed his forehead and watched him for a moment, then took the long way out of the hospital and walked uptown in the rain to his apartment building. He'd downsized from the house Rebecca had grown up in when she'd moved to the city to be on her own with a roommate from work. They lived in the same neighborhood, and Rebecca always liked the surprise of running into her dad in The Food Emporium or in Barnes & Noble or on the subway platform.

She let herself in with the key that was always on her key chain. His third-floor one-bedroom was spotless, thanks to his weekly cleaning service. She stood in the small living room and felt his presence so strongly. Her dad was a collector, and his apartment was like a scrapbook and photo album of his life. His fossil collection from an excavation trip to Belize lay on the long windowsills. Shells from every beach he'd ever walked on were strewn across the top of the upright piano against the far wall. And a self-portrait Rebecca had painted in seventh grade was hung above it.

Family photographs graced every spare space. Of Rebecca at every age. Had her father looked at those pictures and wondered, every day, what Joy Jayhawk was doing, how she was doing? How could he not?

She forced herself to move over to the small desk by the windows. In one corner was a picture of her and Michael and her dad, from her father's birthday party last week. The desk had only one drawer, so finding the key wouldn't be difficult. But she was frozen.

Oh, just open it already, she told herself. And so she forced her hands forward, and there it was, the red leather case with the key, an ordinary, ugly gold key. She zippered the case shut and dropped it in her bag, then glanced at her father's papers and folders and files, his checkbooks and ledgers. What of a baby he hadn't acknowledged twenty-six years ago would she find in the safety-deposit box? In these papers? The idea of her father carrying this secret for all these years seemed preposterous. *"Ask me anything!"* he always told her when she was shy about asking questions, about boys, about her mother. It had never occurred to her to ask if he'd ever had an affair. She wouldn't have thought it possible. Not with the way he'd looked at her mother, right until the end.

You don't know, really know, anyone, she thought, then hoped it wouldn't stick. She'd never been cynical, never a pessimist. She was strictly glass-half-full.

The ugly gold key in her tote bag, off she went to Citibank with twenty minutes to spare before closing.

The vault of gold safety-deposit boxes looked like P.O. boxes. Rebecca showed the key to the clerk, he verified access and then pointed to box number 1232.

"Do you want a private room or cubicle, or is this okay?" the clerk asked, upping his chin at the long table in the center of the room.

"This is fine," she said. She didn't want to be alone with whatever was inside.

What was inside was a black leather box that flipped open with a tiny silver latch. Inside the leather box was a batch of letters, held together with a large blue rubber band. Rebecca flipped through them; there were twenty-six envelopes, each addressed to Joy Jayhawk. Just the name, no address. No stamp. No return address.

So he hadn't turned his back emotionally, she realized. That was something. Almost.

There was another letter, a single one, addressed to Rebecca in the same chicken-scratch handwriting as the rest. She'd always been able to decipher her dad's handwriting, even as a kid. *"What in the world does this say?"* her mother would ask when her dad left notes under magnets on the refrigerator. *"Went to have a swim, be back at six,"* Rebecca would proudly read for her mother. That she could read his illegible scrawl made her feel closer to him, that they shared a special bond.

She glanced at the stack of letters. Twenty-six letters for twenty-six years. She took off her trench coat and slipped it on the back of her chair, wishing she had time to stall. She glanced up at the round clock on the wall. A quarter to four. She had fifteen minutes.

She sucked in a breath and opened the one addressed to her.

Dear Rebecca,

If you're reading this, I'm in bad shape. Right now, it's

May, and I've just been diagnosed. But I've been told the end will come fast and furious.

My Beckles, how I love you. I hope you'll forgive me one day for keeping this secret from you, for having this secret in the first place.

The letters will tell you something of the story. I don't know what you'll do with them, but I leave that up to you. I think she should know that I did care. In any case, I want you to know that I did.

I'm so sorry, Rebecca. Know that I loved you—and will always love you—with all my heart.

—All my love, Dad

She stared at the letter and then eyed the banded others. Then her gaze moved up to the clock, at the second hand ticktocking, ticktocking its way very slowly, very surely around and around. If she watched the little ticking arrow long enough, the big hand would eventually get to the twelve.

"Miss?" a guard said, appearing at the doorway. "The bank is closing."

She let out a deep breath and nodded. She wasn't ready to read the letters, even one. She stood up, slightly dizzy, and dropped back down on the chair. She'd had coffee for breakfast and then had picked at her crepe at the French bistro Glenda had taken her to. She needed more coffee and something in her stomach to get rid of the churning acid. She put the letters back in the little leather box and stuffed the box in her tote bag.

Good old Starbucks provided her with bracing coffee and a

cinnamon raisin bagel, which she brought with her to Central Park. The rain had stopped, and the pale blue sky was heavy with clouds. She sat on one of the still-damp benches lining the walk to the zoo, suddenly aware of all the young children in strollers and skipping around, their little hands in bigger ones.

What had it been like to grow up never having met your own father? Rebecca watched a little girl, three years old, maybe four, chasing after a pigeon intent on a discarded hot-dog bun. She imagined the girl asking her mother where her father was, who her father was.

Jesus. What was *that* conversation like?

She took a long sip of her coffee, wrapping her hands around the warm paper cup. She'd screwed up today at work with the Frittauers, but she hadn't been wrong. She'd just said it wrong. *"Don't screw up the screwing up,"* her dad used to say all the time when Rebecca worried over a mistake like not handing in a high school assignment or saying something mean to her mother. *"Own up to it."*

Her father had never been a "Do as I say not as I do" type of person. When she and her friend Charlotte had experimented with cigarettes at fifteen, her father had caught them, his own cigarette between his fingers. He'd quit that day. Rebecca had never smelled smoke on him again. He'd always walked the walk.

Or maybe just talked the talk. *How in hell could you have done it?* she screamed in her head. *You cheated on Mom and you got some woman pregnant and then said nothing as she told you. And then you did nothing. How in hell could you have done that? And now you're dying and you're leaving me with this? Bastard.*

She felt so guilty that she immediately closed her eyes and sent a *Sorry* through the airwaves. *Oh, God.*

She took another long sip of coffee, then balanced the cup on the slats of the bench and reached into her bag for the letters. She had to know something, anything, that would help, that would make sense of what she'd been told. She slid a random letter from the pack and held it, a picture of Joy Jayhawk as a teenager forming in her mind. Long blond hair down her back, and a pink bikini, and flip-flops with flowers between the toes. She was with friends, all with the same long, pretty hair. She wore a gold necklace that sparkled in the summer sun, a heart locket with a *J* engraved on it.

Okay, she told herself, pulling out the letter from the envelope. Just start with this one.

Dear Joy,

    In the very first letter I wrote you, which took me a good seven months from hearing the news of your birth, I told you I liked your name, that it was a good name. Now you're twelve and I suppose everything is starting to change in your world. Puberty, boys, friendships. I hope you know that you are your name, that you can find solace in it whenever times get tough. Take Rebecca, for instance. She was named after my grandmother, the kindest person on the planet, and my girl Rebecca Strand is pure kindness. Just like I'm sure you are pure joy. . . .

Rebecca felt sick to her stomach and put the letter back, probably out of place. She knocked over her coffee by accident, scaring away the pigeons. She stared at them, their fat gray bodies and spindly little legs, unable to focus on any one piece of information—that her father had cheated on her mother, or that it had resulted in a pregnancy, or that her father had turned his back on the baby and child's mother, including, she assumed, child support, or that her father, who she'd thought until that morning was so perfect, was dying.

She stared up at the overcast sky and whispered, "I'm sorry," to her mother, then called Michael on his cell phone. She couldn't speak, though; all that came out was a sob and that she was sitting on a wet bench by the zoo. He said he'd meet her in twenty minutes.

And then there he was. She told him about the letters, showing him the stack.

Michael tucked them in her bag. "Honey, I think you should go back to the hospital and let your dad know you read the letter he wrote you and that you need time to digest. He'll understand. All he needs to know is that you got the letters, you read his to you and one of his to her, and that you don't hate him for the affair. These letters are for *you*, Becs, not her. He wrote them to assuage his guilt to you."

"I think he wrote them to her, for her," Rebecca said. "To assuage his guilt for not being there for her."

He shook his head. "If your dad felt that guilty, he would have tracked her down at some point over the past twenty-six years. It's a deathbed confession, Rebecca. It's to ease his heart. It's so he can die in peace."

A pain, so sharp, sliced through Rebecca's chest and she let out a wail and the tears started falling. A little kid walking past with his mother stared at her.

"Trust me, Rebecca," Michael said, sliding his arm across her shoulders. "This is what I do. Guilt makes people do all sorts of things at the end. It's one of the reasons mediation works at all. It's why Edward Frittauer signed the separation agreement an hour ago. He gave Gwendolyn the co-op and all its contents, including the Peter Max."

The drizzle started again, and Michael, always prepared, held his large black umbrella over their heads as he led the way to Fifth Avenue and hailed a cab. He took her home, to the apartment they shared. It was a one-bedroom on the twenty-third floor and had a great, sweeping view south. Rebecca would often sit at the tiny dining-room table next to the windows and stare out at the dizzying array of buildings, of lights. She could easily see the Empire State Building. She thought she'd go sit there now, in her view chair, and just stare, but Michael led her to the couch and gently patted the pillow, then covered her with the chenille throw. She heard him opening and shutting cabinets in the kitchen, then the microwave beep, and then he returned with a mug of tea and buttered toast. She loved when he was like this, when he was being her boyfriend instead of a lawyer. When she felt he *was* a haven.

"So do you think I should just send the letters?" she asked him. "I guess all I need to do is Google her name with Maine and her address will probably turn up."

He stared at her. "I think you should just let it go, Rebecca.

You've got enough to deal with right now. Just put aside the letters, this Joy person, for now. Focus on your dad."

She liked this advice; it gave her something to do that made sense *and* let her forget the letters—for now. She sipped her tea and closed her eyes for a half hour, then went back to the hospital and sat at her father's side while he slept until the nurse told her it was time to go.

Her mind was blank; it had clearly short-circuited. Now there was nothing but *numb*. With the little leather box in her arms, she kissed his wrinkled forehead and went home to Michael, who took her to bed and made love to her with a tenderness she hadn't experienced from him in months.

And when she arrived at the hospital in the morning, her father was gone.

Since Rebecca's father was Jewish, the funeral was immediate. Michael made the arrangements. There were distant relatives in North Carolina who flew in, and friends of her father's, some coworkers, and a few clients from his private law practice. His secretary, a tall, thin fifty-something woman named Barbara, cried so constantly that Rebecca wondered if she'd been her father's girlfriend. He'd never introduced Rebecca to a "ladyfriend" in the years since her mother's death. Rebecca told Barbara to take anything she wanted from the apartment. With tears in her eyes, Barbara asked if she could have his watch, the twenty-dollar Timex he'd worn every day for the past twenty-three years. Rebecca had given her father the watch for his birthday with her piggy-bank money when she was a kid and he never took it off. She still wasn't sure if Barbara and Daniel Strand had been a couple, but if all Barbara wanted was the watch, she must have loved him. Rebecca gave it to her.

The day after the funeral, she sat shiva in her father's apartment, on one of the hard kitchen chairs. She chose the kitchen because the one window overlooked the brick wall of the apartment building across the street. She stared at the brick, at the tiny, frosted hallway windows in a vertical row. She sat and sat and sat, her father's ancient Columbia sweatshirt not doing anything to take the constant chill from her skin, her bones. If a snake slithered out of the kitchen drain and came toward her, she probably wouldn't flinch. She was that numb, that bone tired.

Her dad was gone. Her mother was gone.

When her mother died, Rebecca's boyfriend at the time, a jerk philosophy major named Laird who hadn't bothered to show up for the funeral, told her it was a shame her father wouldn't be able to join her mother in heaven, since he was Jewish. That had been the end of Laird. Her father *had* believed in heaven, which was a great comfort to Rebecca ten years ago, and now she imagined her father's soul, the part of him she still knew was very, very good, making its way to where her mother was. Her mother would know now, of course, and forgive. Perhaps her mother would help her father work through it all.

At around three in the afternoon, the distant relatives, a second cousin and his family, came over to pay their respects. Rebecca was tempted to tell him there was another Strand out there.

"She's not a Strand," Michael said that night as he and Rebecca lay in bed, the shiva candle burning on her bedside table. "She's just some stranger."

Not to Rebecca. For the past few days she would be walking down the street or washing dishes or trying to read the book on loss that her best friend, Charlotte, had given her, and she would see a flash of blond hair. Brown doe eyes. She would see Joy as a child, maybe five years old, spinning around, then stopping to say, *"Daddy? Do I have a Daddy?"* That morning, while Rebecca stirred Sweet'N Low into the terrible coffee Michael had made (always too strong), the little blond girl stopped spinning again and stood still, her face in shadows, and said, *"Hello?"*

"Hello," Rebecca had whispered back. "I am cracking up," she'd said to the coffeepot.

She pulled the blankets up to her chin. "The point is, Michael, she's not *supposed* to be a stranger. I'm going to track her down. It's what my dad would have wanted me to do."

He turned on his side to face her, his dark blue eyes full of sympathy. "Rebecca, from what you told me, I don't get the sense he wanted you to find her. It's not like he said that outright. And remember, he's *nothing* to her. And he can never *be* anything to her because he's gone. She's just going to want the money. And because of all the documentation he left, she'll very likely win half the estate."

"So?" she said, consumed by the urge to push Michael out of the room and shut the door. "She *should* have it. If only for back child support."

"Honey, that half million you're so willing to give to some

stranger, some very likely trashy loser, is our future. If we get married one day, it's a down payment on a house. It's our kids' college education."

She bolted upright. "She's my father's daughter. She's not a trashy loser. Don't say things like that, Michael."

"Sweetheart, it's the truth. Or the potential truth, anyway. I can't sugarcoat it for you. That's not who I am. My job is to help people understand the truth, find the best in the truth, in the real circumstances. I know you just lost your only living parent, Becs. And I know how close you and your dad were. But this person isn't part of your father. She's just some stranger he wanted nothing to do with."

"Because of the *circumstances*," Rebecca said. "He didn't want my mother to find out. The circumstances are now completely different."

"Really? How are they different now than they were ten years ago when your mother died? It's not like your father tracked down this illegitimate daughter after your mother's death. And speaking of your mother, Rebecca, how do you think she'd feel about this? Do you really think she'd want you to go find her husband's bastard daughter?"

Rebecca moved over to the windows and looked out onto Second Avenue, cold in her thin T-shirt and underwear. She focused on a cab squeezing past double-parked cars. *Deep breath, Rebecca.* "Don't twist this around on me to suit your argument." She had no idea how her mother would feel. No idea at all. But this wasn't about her mother or her father or even Rebecca, really.

"Fine," he said, coming up behind her. He wrapped his

arms around her. "You'd be opening a can of worms. You have no idea who she is, what her family is like, if they'll come after you for money. Maybe she has three little kids and no husband. Maybe she's a junkie. Have I proved my point?" he asked with a condescending kiss on the back of her head.

"I need to find her," she said in such a low voice she wasn't sure he heard her. "I just have to. She has a right to those letters."

He turned her around, his blue eyes intense. "Rebecca. I'm giving you excellent free advice. And I strongly advise you to take it. I'm sorry you lost your dad. I love you and I don't want to see you lose everything else, too."

Such as yourself? she wanted to ask, but she turned around instead and stared out the windows at the twinkling lights of the city.

Rebecca didn't have parents anymore. But she had a sister, somewhere in Maine. And she was going to find her.

three

The next morning, after Michael left for work (Rebecca was on bereavement leave and pretended to be asleep until she heard the key locking the door), she typed the name Joy Jayhawk into Google, then stared at the name and deleted it.

She needed reinforcement. She called her friend Charlotte, who said she'd be over in twenty minutes with coffee and bagels. By the time Charlotte arrived, in her uniform of pantsuit, silk scarf, and bun-controlled wildly curly brown hair, Rebecca had typed the name and deleted it five more times.

"I'll do it for you," Charlotte said, beating Rebecca to the desk chair. She hit Enter and peered at the screen. "She has a website!"

Rebecca's hands shook slightly around the cup of coffee. Just like that. A website. Instant information she wasn't so sure she was ready to have.

"And there's a picture of her," Charlotte said. "She's so young. And pretty. And blond. She has the Strand round brown eyes. And a much bigger chest than yours. She operates singles tours in Maine."

Singles tours? Rebecca stood behind the chair and peered around Charlotte.

JOY JAYHAWK'S WEEKEND SINGLES TOURS

Join your tour guide and host Joy Jayhawk for fun, informal weekend tours of Maine's tourist towns, beaches, state parks, lighthouses, and attractions.

Make new friends and maybe meet that special someone as you spend Friday night to Sunday afternoon exploring the Pine Tree State.

For more information, phone Joy at
(207) 555-2515

SEPTEMBER TOURS:

9–11: Bye Bye Beaches

16–18: Portland

23–25: Winslow Park, Freeport
(Note: This is our Rocky Relationships Tour)

**And coming in October:
Ogunquit and Kennebunkport**

TESTIMONIALS!

"I met my fiancé during Joy Jayhawk's Weekend Singles Tours getaway to Sunday River!"
—Elizabeth P., Portland

"I didn't meet the love of my life on the Camden tour, but I did have a blast, made two new amazing friends, and can't wait to take another tour!"
—Maddie R., Freeport

"Annie and I are going on our third date tomorrow night . . . all thanks to Joy and the Ogunquit tour."
—Jack M., Gorham

"My boyfriend dumped me and the next day I signed up for Joy's Old Port tour. I flirted all weekend, got my groove back, and came home happy. Thanks, Joy!"
—Carlie W., Pittsfield

There were more testimonials, fee ranges, a What You Need to Know section, disclaimers, and a small photograph of Joy. Rebecca looked for an About Joy link, but there wasn't one.

Joy was barely higher than the WELCOME TO MAINE sign she had her arm wrapped around. She stood on the side of the highway, an orange minibus parked behind her.

She looked remarkably like the girl Rebecca had

envisioned, down to the blond hair, a rich sunlit sandy shade, and brown eyes.

She didn't look anything like Rebecca or her father, except, as Charlotte noted, for the round shape of her eyes. Her hair was just past her shoulders and pin straight, the kind Rebecca, with her dark waves, had always coveted. Joy looked like a nature girl. She wore a white sleeveless button-down shirt and low-slung jeans with a belt that looked like a real daisy chain. She was very pretty, yet there was a no-nonsense glint in her eyes.

This is my sister, Rebecca thought, unable to take her eyes off the photo. *My sister.*

"You're my sister," Rebecca said to the small photo. "We have the same father."

"I like the looks of her," Charlotte said. "She looks like a nice person, a good person. And she's a matchmaker."

Rebecca stared at the photo. "I have a sister. I still can't believe it, can't wrap my mind around it."

"Do you think she knows about you, that you exist?" Charlotte asked, taking a sip of her coffee. She stood, wrapping her hands around the white takeout cup, and gestured for Rebecca to sit.

Rebecca shrugged and sat down in front of the laptop. "I have no idea." Joy's mother must have told her something about her biological father. Pia Jayhawk clearly knew his name and had been able to call him at the Manhattan apartment. Had she known the man she'd been seeing was married? Had a child? Or had Daniel Strand lied, pretended to be single?

"Do you even know your father's name?" she asked the

photo. "That you have a sister?" Surely Joy could have tracked down her father if she'd wanted. But then Rebecca remembered the unlisted number, the move to Westchester. Perhaps Daniel Strand hadn't been so easy to find.

Rebecca typed her dad's name into the search engine. Thousands of hits. She entered the name into Manhattan White Pages. Hundreds. No, he would not be easy to track down.

"She is my sister, right?" Rebecca asked, turning to face her friend. "Michael is wrong, isn't he?"

"She's your sister," Charlotte said. "Michael is dead wrong. And you're going to change her life. One hello and her life completely changes."

"She might already have a sister," Rebecca said.

"Not a sister of the father she never knew," Charlotte pointed out.

Charlotte, who Rebecca had known since preschool, had the kind of intact family that held reunions every summer at state parks. Her parents had been happily married for thirty-four years and still held hands. She was very close to her older sister and her two brothers. A sister was a sister. Michael, on the other hand, had become a divorce mediation attorney because of his own parents' hateful divorce trial, which he'd been subjected to for almost a year at age thirteen. He barely spoke to his own brother, who at sixteen had sided with their father over their mother. A brother was not a brother to Michael; a brother had to earn the title.

Rebecca picked up the phone and called Michael. "She has her own business," she told him. "She hosts informal singles tours."

"I know," he said. "I Googled her last night. Sounds a little trashy, Rebecca. She operates singles tours? Out of an orange minibus?"

"Sorry I called," she said, and hung up on him.

He didn't call back and neither did she. Operating a singles tour bus sounded sort of enterprising to Rebecca. And fun. And, well, romantic, which she could not say for her own relationship with Michael.

On their one-year anniversary of dating, he'd handed her a small velvet jewelry box and she'd almost fainted—and not from happiness—as she opened it. She would not have said yes to forever with Michael Whitman. She would not have fallen into marriage the way she'd fallen into becoming a paralegal. But it hadn't been a diamond ring in the little box; it had been a silver key—to his apartment. That was a year ago. She'd said yes to moving in because she had loved Michael then. How had things changed between them so much in a year? In much less than a year, actually. A few months ago, Rebecca started realizing that she was making plans after work with Charlotte or visiting her dad a lot more often. She went to the movies alone. Joined a gym.

She'd been avoiding going home. And Michael had been doing the same thing, though it had taken her a while to see it. Something was wrong, but neither of them was ready to acknowledge it or even name what it was. They *liked* each other, that had always been there—a fondness, a connection. But something had happened when they moved in together, something cloying and claustrophobic that neither of them had expected. When right felt so wrong for reasons not so readily apparent, you could end up in a holding pattern, waiting for something to become clear. But that had never happened. Instead, things had became cloudier.

Sometimes she did think she still loved him. But lately, she wasn't so sure. She knew only that she was content enough to live with him, to not break up with him. For the time being. That was a favorite phrase of Michael's, actually. *"It's fine for the time being."* The problem was that Rebecca's time being had lasted a long, long time.

And now the time being felt interminable. After her gaffe with the Frittauers, Marcie had once again "written her up" by filing a memo with Michael and the partners detailing her continual errors:

> *Rebecca is a paralegal, not a mediator or an attorney. She has overstepped her bounds on numerous occasions, this previous occasion almost resulting in the loss of a client and potential new business from the Frittauers' friends and associates. It's my experienced opinion that Rebecca take the refresher course in paralegal studies offered by several schools of continuing education.*

Michael had told her to forget about it, that it would blow over during Rebecca's bereavement leave, but that Marcie wasn't entirely wrong—*"but don't think about that now, honey."* Rebecca had stiffened; she knew Michael was trying to make a point, that *she* didn't know it all, that she wasn't the mediator here, and perhaps she should listen to his advice about chasing after a stranger who ran a matchmaking service out of a minibus. A stranger who could go after her father's estate.

"Want to know what I think he's so afraid of?" Charlotte asked, taking out her compact and dusting her unshiny nose. Rebecca knew Charlotte really meant what her husband, a therapist, thought.

Rebecca nodded. She'd never shared her ambivalence about Michael with Charlotte for fear that Peter would be full of *why*. Rebecca wasn't ready for *why*.

"I talked it over with Peter, and we think he's afraid of losing control over you. Michael has a very strong personality. So now he's afraid your sister will influence you."

Possibly, Rebecca thought. "But to do what?"

Charlotte adjusted her pink and red scarf around her neck. "Not be such a devoted girlfriend, maybe. Break out. Maybe he's worried she'll convince you she deserves the entire estate. And since he knows about her business, maybe he's even more worried she'll have all sorts of men to fix you up with."

Rebecca laughed. "Michael Whitman, worried about a rugged Maine lobsterman? Doubt it." Michael didn't lack confidence.

Charlotte smiled. "You never know."

Rebecca stared at the photo of Joy. "Should I call her first? I can't decide which would be less shocking to the system— getting a call from a long-lost sister or a knock on the door. I mean, she's going to hear that her father is dead. She very likely has held out hope that one day she'd get to meet him."

"I'd just go," Charlotte said. "Especially because she still lives where the affair took place. That is where she was conceived and born, and just being there might help you come to terms with the affair."

"What terms?"

Charlotte shrugged. "I'm just repeating what Peter said."

"Maybe I'll just go right now," Rebecca said, the idea not seeming so crazy. She needed to get out of the apartment, Michael's apartment, with its black leather and chrome furniture, if only for a day or two. "Just up and rent a car and drive to Maine right now."

Charlotte smiled, then wrapped Rebecca in a hug. "You'd better. It's Wednesday. She's gone Friday through Sunday, remember."

And before Rebecca could even think of changing her mind, Charlotte was on the phone with Budget Rent A Car, booking a compact.

She left a note for Michael, that she was driving to Maine and would be back on Friday. But Rebecca packed practically all her clothes, not that she had many. Instead of two days' worth of clothes—a pair of jeans, her favorite green cashmere sweater, her old cowboy boots that Michael hated, and a pair of nice shoes, maybe some black pants and a dressier top—she'd packed it all. All her shoes, including both pairs of sneakers. Her red suede loafers, her black T-strap heels, brown ankle boots, tall black boots. A stack of sweaters and shirts and camisoles, several pairs of pants and jeans, and four dresses, one fancy. Piles of underwear and a tangle of bras went into another suitcase with all her toiletries.

On her way out, she picked up a small framed photograph of her and Michael, one taken at last year's firm holiday party. Rebecca in a red dress, Michael in his customary gray suit. Both with big smiles. She meant to put the picture back down on the hall table, but it went into her tote bag instead. Then off she drove in a silver Honda Civic.

She should have flown. The drive was endless with pockets of traffic and construction and accidents and rubberneckers. Eight hours later, she passed the sign her half sister had leaned against: WELCOME TO MAINE: THE WAY LIFE SHOULD BE.

The sign seemed like her fortune, her horoscope, her Magic 8 Ball answer. Her life was not the way it should be, and she knew it, had known it for a while. She liked the idea that simply passing the sign meant she was working on that.

An hour later, she couldn't bear another minute behind the wheel and ended up checking into a hotel in the tourist and outlet mecca of Freeport, forty minutes or so south of Wiscasset. The hotel was a bed-and-breakfast, a white clapboard New Englander on Main Street, just a couple of blocks from the famed L.L.Bean, which according to a brochure in the hallway was open twenty-four hours a day, seven days a week, Christmas included. As she headed back out to the small parking lot to lug in her suitcases, she took a deep breath and was surprised by how different the air felt and tasted. Clean, calm, with the scent of grass and flowers. Rebecca had expected to smell the ocean, especially because Freeport was right on the coast. But the grass, the flowers were good enough. It was barely seven o'clock and still light out, and both sides of narrow Main Street were packed with people swinging shopping bags. The streams of people, the cars, reminded her of home. Except there were no speeding taxis and, oddly, no noise. The quiet was like a soothing balm. It wasn't Aruba, but it was good.

In her cozy single room with its wide-planked wood floor and round braided rug and fluffy down comforter, Rebecca changed into yoga pants and a tank top and slipped into bed with her tote bag. She took out the leather box and a manila envelope of keepsakes she'd taken with her from home—pictures of her mother and father, a copy of their marriage license, a copy of her birth certificate, every report card she'd ever gotten. On her third-grade report card, her teacher had written: *"Rebecca is a smart, sweet girl, but she needs to become more of a leader, less of a follower."* Rebecca had hated that critique. She'd always had just one best friend, a few different ones over the years due to moves or school changes, and she'd always been the less vocal, the less sure, the less everything. She liked that, though, felt safe within that. Like with Michael. Her mother's response to the teacher's scribbled line had been, *"You are who you are, and I like you fine."*

Rebecca's heart squeezed at the thought of her mother, and again those doe eyes floated into her mind. "I don't think you'll mind my doing this," she whispered to the ceiling. "I would like to be more of a leader of my own life, less of a follower. Michael is wrong about so many things." She took the pack of letters from her father and pulled one out at random.

Dear Joy,
You're five years old. I'll bet you love kindergarten.
Rebecca was so shy at five, but blossomed in kindergarten

and made friends. In fact, she's still friends with one of the girls, Charlotte is her name. I keep forgetting that I should focus on you in these letters, not Rebecca, but I suppose it's natural for me to think you're alike. You're sisters, even if neither of you knows about the other. I've often wondered about nature versus nurture, and I think nature accounts for more than half. I'll bet you like robots instead of princesses, like Rebecca. And I'll bet you love chasing after frogs in muddy creeks, like Rebecca.

You're now at the age where you are likely wondering where your daddy is. I've never spoken to your mother since the phone call she made alerting me to your existence. I made sure she'd never be able to track me down. I was afraid, afraid of what it would do to my wife, afraid she'd leave me and take Rebecca from me, too. I'm sorry for that. I had a big hand in bringing you into being and then I just—I don't even know a word strong enough to write down. I've rationalized my absence by assuring myself that your beautiful, interesting, funny mother, with that raucous laugh and incredible face and figure, found a father to step in, someone deserving of her and a daughter. I didn't know Pia Jayhawk very well; we only spent a couple of weeks together before I left for New York and told her it had to end and stay ended. But I know she was dignified and strong.

I think of you swinging on a tire swing at a playground or sounding out words like Rebecca used to. She's seven— almost eight—and reads at a middle-school level. Sharp like her own mom. I'm sure you're every bit as wonderful

*as your mother, too, Joy. That's one of the reasons I don't
worry about you.*

—*Daniel Strand*

Rebecca didn't think a cast-off daughter would appreciate
that last line—or be able to read any of it, anyway. "*. . . alerting me to your existence . . . ?*" To a five-year-old? Perhaps the
letters were more for her father than for Joy. But most of the
letter *was* kind. And tomorrow morning, the recipient would
be reading them.

She slipped out of bed to get her laptop and brought it back
into bed with her. She wanted to see Joy's picture again, to
somehow prepare herself for tomorrow. But the inn had no
Wi-Fi and she hadn't saved the website with Joy's photo to her
desktop.

She thought about calling Michael, but it bothered her that
he hadn't called her once today. To apologize for last night. To
tell her he'd support her no matter what she decided. He was
likely just getting home now, reading her note and muttering,
"*Fucking Rebecca*" under his breath.

What she should be thinking about was tomorrow. Showing
up unannounced at Joy Jayhawk's door. She wondered how Joy
would react. With shock. With surprise. And then she'd throw
open the door and pull Rebecca into a fierce hug. "*I've always
dreamed of meeting you, my long-lost half sister!*" Joy would say,
tears of happiness running down her cheeks. And they'd sit in
the kitchen and talk for hours over coffee, then celebrate their
reunion—if that was the right word—that night, over a bottle of
wine. They'd talk and talk and talk, like sisters did.

With a smile on her face, Rebecca pulled the blankets up to her chin and closed her eyes, drifting off to the very nice fantasy of sisterly bonding she'd concocted. Next thing she knew, the sun was streaming through the filmy white curtains.

In the bright light of day, she imagined driving to Joy Jayhawk's house, knocking on the door, and saying, *"Uh, hi, you don't know me, but I'm actually your half sister. We have the same father."* But she suddenly couldn't imagine saying that and knew she wasn't getting out of bed so fast.

four

According to the welcome sign at the town line, Wiscasset was the prettiest village in Maine, and Rebecca had to concur. Downtown was picture-postcard material, a small collection of charming shops and restaurants and cafés, with the Sheepscot River behind it with a beautiful, long, narrow bridge across it. The streets, so clean, were dotted with antique farmhouses, New Englanders, Victorians, and stately Colonials, mostly white, on lots big and small with manicured lawns and white picket fences. In one half-mile stretch, Rebecca passed four white clapboard churches. In another direction, at least ten antiques shops. Flowers, trees were everywhere. And the blue, blue water of Maine's coast, which would suddenly appear behind a curve, through a thicket of evergreens. She felt like she was in Candy Land, minus the lollipops on the trees.

She'd waited an extra day before leaving Freeport. She'd walked along Main Street, buying gifts—a red Shetland sweater for Charlotte from the J.Crew outlet, an army green messenger bag for Michael from the Timberland outlet. She'd bought herself a pair of ridiculous red and pink plaid rain boots, the kind that went up to your knees. She had thought about buying Joy Jayhawk something, but couldn't think of the occasion. *Welcome to the family?* Or maybe just *Hello?* The leather box was for Joy. That was Rebecca's offering.

Her mind had been so blessedly blank as she'd shopped, as she'd had an organic veggie hot dog from a stand outside L.L.Bean, that she might have even waited another day. Another day to gear up, plan what to say and how to say it, but if she hadn't gotten back in that little silver car this morning, she'd have lost the entire weekend. Rebecca knew from Joy's website that she had a tour leaving tonight. It was today or else.

She couldn't find 52 Maple Lane and had to drive back to town to ask directions. She was given landmarks to turn at: a weeping willow, the pink gingerbread Victorian. She finally found the road; the sign, which she'd passed earlier, was completely obscured by the leaves of an oak.

As she drove slowly down Maple Lane, which turned out to be over a mile long, looking for numbers on houses or mailboxes, she passed two sets of joggers and a mother wheeling a baby stroller. The quiet was startling. Birds chirped. A lawn mower whirred. There was a complete lack of car horns or car alarms.

Number 52. There it was. The house, the last on the dead-end road, was tiny, a Wedgwood blue Cape Cod with a red door. It was the smallest house Rebecca had ever seen, yet had at least an acre of property. The road, which had no sidewalk on either side, was lined by several other little houses, all of them cute and welcoming with colorful doors.

At number 52, JAYHAWK-JONES was in sticky-taped letters on the mailbox.

Jayhawk-Jones. She was married, then. Or had a roommate. There was a green Subaru Outback in the driveway. And an orange minibus.

She wondered if this house had been Pia Jayhawk's, if her father had been here. If this was where they would have their little trysts. It didn't look like a love nest.

She glanced at the bay window of the house for signs of life, but couldn't see through the curtains. *Go,* she told herself. And after pulling down the visor mirror to make sure she didn't have sauerkraut in her teeth, she said, "Okay," to her reflection and got out of the car with the leather box in her hands.

The path was lined with purple and pink impatiens in small ceramic pots, a good sign.

She took a deep, deep breath of the clean air, then rang the doorbell. No answer. She waited a minute, then rang again. Finally, the door opened, and there she was. Joy Jayhawk.

Rebecca's knees wobbled and she grabbed hold of the doorframe. *Say something,* she told herself. But for a moment, all Rebecca could do was stare. She saw her father's face in this woman's. In the shape, in the nuances, in the lips. She had the same color eyes as her father, that lovely driftwood brown.

Joy looked exactly like her photograph, but prettier. She wore jeans and a white button-down shirt and red suede clogs. Rebecca stared down at the clogs for a second, then looked back up at Joy, who was clearly waiting for Rebecca to say something.

She was clobbered in the stomach by something—fear? This person, this Joy Jayhawk, was a complete stranger. A stranger, like Michael had said.

"Are you needing directions?" Joy Jayhawk asked, staring at Rebecca as though she were in need of psychological help.

She had a nice voice. The voice of a kindergarten teacher. Kind, hopeful.

The kind and hopeful steadied Rebecca. "My name is Rebecca Strand," she finally said. She waited to see if the name meant anything, and in a moment, a slight change of expression, of guarded wariness, came over Joy's face, but she didn't say anything. "I'm very sorry to just barge in on you like this, but I didn't know how to do this, so I just decided to drive up from New York City and knock on the door."

Still Joy said nothing. Her features tightened.

Rebecca's words came in a rush. "My father, Daniel Strand, passed away from cancer several days ago. The day before he died he told me that he had an af—a relationship with a woman named Pia Jayhawk and that Pia called to tell him she was pregnant with his child and—"

"Why are you here?" Joy interrupted.

"Um, well, my father wanted you to know that he did care about you," she said, feeling like an idiot. "He wrote you a letter every year." She held out the box. "I have them here. Twenty-six of them."

"I'm sorry for your loss, but—" Joy stared at Rebecca's pointy high heels for a moment, then glanced back up. "I think you should just go. I'm sorry." She began to close the door.

"But—we're . . ."

Sisters, she finished silently as Joy closed the door in her face.

• • •

Rebecca couldn't find her way back to a main road and drove in circles until she spotted a jogger, whose big smile and "Ooh, I see from your plates you're from New York! We have tickets to Radio City for Christmas. I cannot wait!" almost made her cry.

Did you really expect Joy Jayhawk to throw her arms around you with a "My long-lost sister!" and launch into her life story, ask all about yours, then announce you'd never be separated again?

Maybe. If she were very honest.

The jogger finally stopped talking long enough for Rebecca to ask directions to Route 1. Rebecca made her left, then right, then left at the pink Victorian, then right at the picket fence with the ornate trim, and found herself back in the center of town, the road out stretching in front of her.

She had no idea where to go. She couldn't leave, but she couldn't stay, either. What was she supposed to do? And why hadn't she considered that Joy Jayhawk might close the door in her face?

Should she try again? Go back to Joy Jayhawk's house and say, "Look, I realize this must be quite a shock, but we *are* sisters"? There had been nothing in Joy's face, not a hint of *Oh my God, I know who you are!* Just a dulled anger.

She was about to turn the car around and go back, but go back and what? Ring the doorbell like a lunatic until Joy answered? And then what?

For starters, for an immediate plan, she pulled into the parking area of a small white restaurant—Mama's Pizza, according to the sign featuring a cartoon of an old woman in a chef's hat tossing a pizza in the air. She could sit and think, decide what to do, over a slice and a Diet Coke.

She headed inside, the jangle of a bell on the door announcing her arrival. The place was cozy and sweet, and reminded Rebecca of an old-fashioned candy shop. The long counter was lined with jelly jars full of penny candies and chocolates, and silver scoops hung from a post on the wall. There were pastries—cannolis, Rebecca's favorite—neatly wrapped whoopie pies with red-and-white-polka-dotted ribbon ties, and baskets of green apples and yellow-green pears. Ten or so round tables covered with red and white cloths dotted the room. The walls were lined with paintings for sale by local artists, of lighthouses, the ocean, houses, lobster. There was no one in the restaurant—or behind the counter.

"Can I help you?"

A tall woman, about fifty years old, with remarkable green eyes, appeared from a doorway and stood behind the counter. Her hair was much longer than Rebecca's and completely gray, but appeared to be lit from within by different shades of gray, from a pale charcoal to silver to almost white. She wore a fabric sling around her body, and if Rebecca wasn't mistaken, there were two furry gray-and-black-spotted ears poking out. A cat? Or maybe it was a tiny dog, like Charlotte's toy Chihuahua. Was the woman attachment-parenting a pet?

A hand with silver and gold rings on every finger patted the furry head. "Poor baby is recovering from surgery. Her right ovary almost exploded. If I hadn't brought her to the vet just when I did, poor kitty would have died."

Rebecca burst into tears. She had to stop doing that. She covered her hands with her face and tried to stop, but she was hundreds of miles away from home, and home suddenly seemed a nebulous nowhere.

The woman came around the counter and patted Rebecca's shoulder. "There, there, dear," she said. "Suzy will be just fine. Won't you, Suzy." The woman nuzzled her nose into the gray fur, then led Rebecca to a table, under a painting of a yellow house. "Sit, dear. I just made a pot of Earl Grey."

Which was how Rebecca came to be drinking Earl Grey tea, real lumps of sugar and all, in the kind of old-fashioned china cup she'd inherited from her mother's mother. As the woman went back and forth between the kitchen and Rebecca's little table, bringing a silver cup of cream and a plate of tiramisu, she learned the woman's name was Arlene Radicchio, and she was German, but had married an Italian man.

"I assume you're not in tears over Suzy," Arlene said, setting a box of tissues on the table. "If you want to talk, I'm known for being a good listener."

Rebecca thought of telling this woman everything, but this wasn't a city of eight million; it was a town of six thousand. She was in Joy's territory. "My dad died last week. We were pretty close."

"Ah. I'm very sorry. I lost my dad some years back. I found myself crying all over the place. Once I burst into tears while placing meatballs and onions on a pizza. That was my father's signature order."

"I'm sorry," Rebecca said.

Arlene patted her hand. "Time makes it easier. So does

fresh, hot pizza. Lunch is on the house. What would you like, hon?"

Rebecca loved being called "hon." Jane, the Whitman, Goldberg & Whitman receptionist, called everyone "hon," even Marcie, who wasn't hon-like at all. The only time Marcie Feldman had ever made a personal statement to Rebecca, it was to complain under her breath to Rebecca that she was "no one's 'hon.'" No doubt there, Marcie.

"I appreciate that," Rebecca said. "I'll have a slice with green peppers and spinach. And a Diet Coke. With lime, if you have."

"A slice?" Arlene repeated. "We only serve whole pizzas. We have an individual size, which is about four slices, medium, which is six slices, and large, which is eight. Extra large is twelve."

"The individual pie, then. With peppers and spinach."

Arlene smiled. "You must be from New York. I've heard that New Yorkers call pizzas *pies*. I've always liked that."

Rebecca nodded and was about to say something when a singing baritone interrupted her.

"'When the moon hits your eye like a big pizza pie, that's amore.'" A teenage boy poked his head out from the back room. The smile on his comical young face was so bright, so contagious that Rebecca laughed.

"Hi there," she said. The teenager tipped his baseball hat at Rebecca, then pulled his blond head back.

"That's my son, Matteo, the cello player," she said. "He's a senior in high school. But every day he comes home for lunch for Mama's pizza. He was accepted to Juilliard, isn't that something? He starts next September."

THE SECRET OF JOY

"Juilliard! That's very impressive." The kid could sing, too.

Classical music, and the beautiful sounds of a cello, soon followed, and Arlene began twirling around, her hands held up as if dancing with an imaginary partner. The bell jangled on the door. Rebecca turned around. A good-looking guy in his early thirties walked over to Arlene and said, "May I have this dance?"

Arlene beamed and gave the man her hand. They did something of a waltz until the teenager stopped singing and shouted, "Bye, Mom!"

"Bye, hon," she called out.

"I'll take the usual," the man said. He turned to Rebecca and smiled a polite smile, then picked up a local newspaper and thumbed through it.

"This young lady is from New York City," Arlene told him, gesturing her chin at Rebecca.

"Rebecca Strand," she said, surprised that his good looks even registered, given how crazy everything was right now. He was fine featured but rugged at the same time, with great hair, dark sandy blond and wavy. And brown eyes, like Rebecca's. He wore jeans and a navy T-shirt and had a tool belt slung low around his waist. Construction worker? Handyman?

"Theo Granger," he said with a smile.

He was eye candy, but no match for the painting above her table, which Rebecca couldn't take her eyes off of. It was of a sweet little house, pale yellow with white shutters and a blue door. It also reminded Rebecca of a candy shop. There were flowers everywhere and wind chimes, and a white picket fence. It was so charming. She could see herself living in that little yellow house, learning to be herself.

She had no idea where that thought came from.

"I like it, too," Theo said.

She shot him a smile.

"Your pizza's ready, dear," Arlene said, bringing it over on a tray. "Enjoy."

She could feel Theo watching her. But when she glanced at him, he was flipping through the newspaper. Then Arlene handed him his pizza in a box, he said a throwaway "Nice to meet you," and was gone. Rebecca stared after him through the windows.

"Hot, huh?" Arlene said. "If I were twenty years younger . . . And he's single, too, by the by. Are you just visiting?"

Just visiting. Rebecca nodded, her momentary glimpse of spirit sinking, her shoulders slumping. She wouldn't be able to stay in this little dream of a restaurant all day and night. She'd have to decide what to do. In the meantime, she took a bite of pizza. "This is exceptional," she told Arlene.

"It's the fresh Maine air. When I toss up the dough, it mixes with the air. That's why it's so good. That's the secret ingredient—not the sauce."

Rebecca smiled. And believed it.

The bell on the door jangled.

"Hey there, Joy," Arlene said. "The usual?"

Rebecca glanced up. There was Joy Jayhawk, staring at her.

"Actually, no, Arlene," Joy said. "I just came to find—" Her cheeks pinkened.

"Rebecca," Rebecca finished for her.

"Rebecca." She stared at Rebecca, expressionless. No, that wasn't quite accurate. There was a bit of anger. And sadness.

But something else, something that could be both good and bad: resignation.

Rebecca had seen that expression on the faces of so many couples in mediation. *"Fine, you take the furniture. I take the dog. No, you take the goddamned furniture. I'll take Jo-Jo."* And then the mediator would work his magic. Michael was much better with strangers than with his girlfriend. *"Tell me about the furniture,"* he'd say to the husband. *"Which pieces do you love?"* And the husband would say, *"I don't even know what we have. Well, I guess I like the big leather chair in the living room."* And then the wife would cut in with, *"Yeah, you sat in it enough, doing nothing."* Which would lead to a thirty-second argument that Michael would allow, then handle. *"So you won't miss the chair, right?"* he'd say to the wife. The wife would shake her head, then burst into tears, then say he could have the chair and the stereo system and the Wii. But that she needed Jo-Jo, that the husband could have visitation rights for the dog. And the husband would agree. Done.

Joy did not look particularly agreeable. But this wasn't a co-incidence. Joy had gone looking for Rebecca's car in Wiscasset's small downtown.

Joy sucked in a loud breath and pushed her blond hair behind her shoulders. "Okay, I'm sorry I shut the door right in your face. I'm not usually a rude person. I'm sort of having a bad day. Bad week, really. Bad few months, if you must know." She bit her lip and glanced at the floor. "I'm leaving in a few hours for a weekend singles tour of Portland with a small group of people. You're welcome to come, but it'll cost you three hundred dollars since I had to book you a single room at the inn."

Rebecca was so pleased, so relieved, that she rushed over to her and took Joy's hands. "Thank you so much!"

Joy, regardless of the tight smile on her pretty face, was studying her. *Aha,* Rebecca thought. *She's curious, too. She's looking at my face, at my features. Looking for herself. She wants to* know.

Joy pulled her hands away and took a giant step back.

"Although, I guess you should know, I'm not technically single," Rebecca rushed to say. "I mean, I'm not married, but I'm not single. And, oh my God, do I know from bad weeks."

Joy was once again expressionless. "Four o'clock in my driveway."

Rebecca smiled and nodded, and Joy turned and left, the little bell jangling after her.

I did it, Dad, she thought toward the ceiling. *Contact has been made. More than contact has been made.*

"Are you a friend of Joy's?" Arlene asked from behind the counter.

"Not really," Rebecca said.

"Complicated?" she asked, sprinkling dough with flour.

Rebecca nodded.

"The best things in my life are," Arlene said, tossing the dough high in the air.

five

In the backseat of her car, parked in the lot at Mama's, Rebecca took everything out of her suitcases and stacked her clothing and toiletries on the seat, then repacked a pair of jeans, her favorite black pants, a couple of sweaters and her two favorite shirts, the heels and cowboy boots, and zipped up the suitcase. She put the leather box in her tote bag. All packed and ready for Joy Jayhawk's weekend singles excursion to Portland, Maine.

She'd actually once gone on a singles getaway, at the constant begging of her friend Charlotte back in their single days. It had been a weekend camp of sorts for professionals in their twenties and thirties. Rebecca hadn't been remotely attracted to any of the guys, so she'd ended up with her nose in a novel most of the time, their group leader popping by way too often to remind her she had to be "in it to win it!" Charlotte had slept with the guy she'd been ogling on the bus ride up, who'd ended up sleeping with at least three other women in two days. On the ride back, Rebecca had assured Charlotte that she'd meet her Mr. Right in a less forced environment. Charlotte nodded tearily, then stared out the window and didn't say a word for three hours, until they'd arrived at Port Authority. "We should do this again!" she'd said with "You gotta be in it to win it!" determination. And then she'd met her husband the next day.

Rebecca wondered how many singles could fit in a minibus. Six? Three men and three women?

She supposed she would be an extra, paired with Joy, sort of.

This time it was easier to find her way back to Maple Lane. She pulled up in front of Joy's tiny house just as a Land Rover did. A good-looking man in his late twenties, maybe early thirties, opened the backdoor and then a little boy hopped out and raced up the path to the front door shouting, "Mommy! Mommy! I's going to be miss you this weepend!"

Joy came out, a breathtaking smile on her face. She scooped up the boy and held him tight, then her gaze slid to Rebecca's car, and Rebecca smiled, but Joy turned her attention back to the child.

So Joy had a child. She assumed the man was her husband. The Jones on the mailbox.

If Joy had a child, then Rebecca had a nephew.

A nephew! And a cute one at that. The boy, three, maybe four years old, had dimples in both cheeks and a mop of wavy brown hair, lit with gold. He wore a red T-shirt with a huge 3 on it and blue jeans and red sneakers. He was absolutely adorable.

"Mommy, look what I made you!" The boy turned to the man standing by the car. "Daddy, where's the apple tree I made Mommy?"

The man produced a green piece of paper from the back-seat. Joy could see a brown tree (well, it was more like a brown line) and red dots. He walked over and handed the paper to the boy, who thrust it at Joy. She set him down and kneeled next to him. "I love it!" she said. "Let's hang it up on the art wall."

The boy beamed and followed her into the house. A minute later, they were back. "I'm going to miss you, but I'll see you very soon, okay?"

He wrapped his tiny arms around her. "'Kay, Mommy."

"Okay, champ," the man said. "We stopped home to say good-bye to Mommy and now we're off to ice cream." He put the boy in the car seat in the backseat of the vehicle.

Rebecca waited for him to walk over to Joy for their good-bye, but he didn't. He got in the driver's side, pulled the door shut, and left.

Well. It looked like Mommy and Daddy didn't talk much. Or hug good-bye. Or say good-bye. Or kiss good-bye. Were they divorced?

Again Joy's gaze settled on Rebecca's car, and Rebecca saw the spark of anger flare again. *I have enough shit in my life, and now you're here,* it seemed to say.

They stared at each other, and then Rebecca got out of her car. "Thanks for asking me to come. I can't tell you how much this means to me. And I know it probably wasn't easy for you."

"I really don't know why I did ask you to come," Joy said, pulling a tube of Burt's Bees lip balm from her pocket and slicking it on. Rebecca could smell a mixture of vanilla and raspberry. "Crazy thing to do, really. You could be a psycho killer for all I know."

Rebecca laughed. "My boyfriend said the same about you."

"Men and what they know wouldn't fill a—" She stopped abruptly as if she realized she was talking too chummily with a total stranger. Or the potential enemy. With a gesture at the minibus, she added, "I'm picking everyone up. They're either local enough or on the way down to Portland."

"You have the Strand eyes," Rebecca blurted out, unable to take her eyes off Joy's face. "Round and light brown, like our father's."

The hint of anger returned. "Like *your* father's," Joy corrected. "Look, Rebecca, I'd appreciate if you didn't say things like that, okay? I don't know why I came after you. I really have no idea why, considering that I don't want to talk about Daniel Strand. It just seemed wrong to be so rude, I guess. You traveled a long way."

"Well, I can understand your reaction. I mean, having a half sister you've never met show up on your doorstep . . ."

The minitruce declared, Joy headed to the minibus, and Rebecca trailed along, carrying her bags. The little orange bus was exceptionally clean inside. There were three rows of three seats. And one bucket seat next to the driver's seat. Rebecca opted for that.

"You can put your stuff on the back row," Joy said.

Rebecca did, then sat down on the passenger seat. "Your son is beautiful. What's his name?"

Her features softened for just a moment. "Rex."

"Rex. I like it. He's what, three?"

"Three and a half." Joy glanced at Rebecca's ringless fingers. Joy wore a wedding band and a beautiful diamond engagement ring.

"I don't have kids. Yet. I live with someone, but we're not married. I'm not even sure if we're still a couple, actually," she added, staring at her hands.

"I know all about that," Joy said as she backed out of the driveway.

"Are you and your husband having—"

Joy held up her right hand. "First rule of singles tours is that the host does not talk about her pathetic love life, separation, and possible impending divorce, even though her husband still lives in their house, albeit in the basement."

That sounded very hard. "Well, I'm not really on the singles tour," Rebecca pointed out. *And I want to know everything about you.*

"But we've just pulled up in front of Maggie's house," Joy said, "so from here on in, they lead the show with what's talked about. We maintain a positive attitude, especially when it comes to discussing romantic relationships, okay?"

"Got it," Rebecca said with a smile. She looked out her window at the pretty blue Cape. Someone waved at Joy from the screen door. Maggie, presumably.

"Victoria, the Love Bus is here!" the woman called behind her.

The Love Bus. Cute, Rebecca thought. She remembered the testimonials from Joy's website. It was funny to think of this little orange minibus bringing couples together.

Joy got out and walked up the path as two thirtysomething

women came out with travel bags, which Joy took. She loaded them into the back, then the women got into the bus and sat in the front row.

"Victoria and Maggie, this is Rebecca," Joy said as she put on her seat belt.

They said hi in unison and Rebecca quickly learned they were members of the Wiscasset Divorced Ladies Club, which was an official club started by the town recreation center. Members came and went depending on their mood and current romance situation. Right now, Maggie and Victoria and Ellie, who they were picking up next, were it.

Victoria, the louder of the two, was thirty-four and divorced two years, the mother of a five- and a seven-year-old, who were with their "cheating louse of a father" this weekend. She was tall and stocky and plain, yet had the most gorgeous hair Rebecca had ever seen, even prettier than Joy's. It was long and tousled, a true red, and highlighted naturally. She was dressed for a singles weekend in black slinky pants of undeterminable material and a slinky V-neck teal-colored blouse with cap sleeves and ruffles down the front. She wore black high-heeled sandals and had sparkly pink toes.

Maggie was thirty-seven, a Realtor, and divorced for only six months. She had the voice of a heavy smoker, but she didn't smell like cigarettes; in fact, she smelled lovely, like cookies. Rebecca discovered why when Maggie opened up a box from her tote bag.

"Fresh-baked chocolate and almond," Maggie said, holding up the box. "We always bring goodies for our trips." She took a bite of one. "Yum. Rachael Ray recipe. Delish," she added.

Rebecca smiled and took one. It was delish.

Maggie was prone to tears; her ex-husband was getting married this weekend, which prompted the Divorced Ladies Club to take her on the Portland tour. Tiny and dainty, Maggie was also on the plain side, but dolled up. Her swingy brown bob was highlighted, her sparkling hazel eyes smokily made up. She too wore Friday night clothes: white pants and a feminine, also ruffly blouse, in a swirl of colors. Pale pink strappy sandals with three-inch heels. She didn't have children, but considered her bichon to be her kid. Her mother was babysitting for the weekend.

Five minutes later they picked up Ellie. She was in her late twenties and petite like Maggie, with very dark pin-straight hair to her shoulders and true green eyes. She wore frayed jeans, a tight long-sleeved T-shirt, and red Crocs. She offered Rebecca a smile and a hello, then climbed in next to Maggie.

"This is what you're wearing?" Victoria asked her, but then a man came down a set of wooden steps from an upper landing, tucking his shirt into his pants. He gave a fast wave at Ellie, hopped in his car, and then drove off.

"Ellie!" Victoria chided. "Don't tell me you slept with that dickhead—again!"

Ellie's smile was sheepish as she pulled out a compact and freshened her red lipstick. With her dark straight hair and green eyes, the red lips were dramatic and suited her strong features. "I can't help it. He calls and says how much he misses me, and then a half hour later we're in bed. We would still be in bed if I hadn't heard the bus pull up. I didn't have time to get dressed in anything else. But I brought some girlie stuff— that red wrap dress that—"

"You left him for a reason, Ellie," Victoria said, throwing her long red hair behind her back. "He's a cheat!"

Ellie reached into Maggie's box of cookies. "I just need to meet someone, someone nice, to make me stronger," she said. "If I could just meet someone who gets to me the way Tim does."

"Maybe this trip," Joy said.

"Did you handpick someone for me?" Ellie asked.

"Well, no," Joy said. "But you never know. We're picking up the men next."

"Someone tall, dark, and handsome? But nice? And with an edge? You know, like that hot Irish actor?"

Maggie laughed. "That doesn't describe your soon-to-be-ex-husband at all. Or the two men you were involved with before him."

"I'm trying to avoid the blond lobsterman type," Ellie said. "My older and wiser sister told me that when I'm attracted to a man, I should instantly run."

"That sounds difficult," Rebecca said, turning to face the women.

"So are you divorced as well, Rebecca?" Maggie asked, sinking her pinky-red mouth into another cookie.

"No, I've never been married. I live with someone, though."

"My advice—don't get married," Ellie said. "Then when your boyfriend cheats on you, you can rationalize it as okay, 'cause you're not married yet." Her face crumpled and she started to cry. "God, you must think I'm a moron," she said to Rebecca as Maggie handed her a tissue. "Here I am, on a singles tour, when I'm still married. But I'm not really cheating because Tim and I are separated. I think he's even living with one of his girlfriends." She burst into tears. Rebecca rummaged in her big bag for her packet of tissues and handed it to Ellie. She wiped at her eyes and blew her nose. "Thanks," she said. "I thought once you made the decision to separate that the hard part was over. You know? I mean, I thought the leaving was the hard part. But it's not. It's like the hard part is just starting."

Victoria and Maggie each took one of Ellie's hands. "It's all hard," Maggie said. "But staying with someone who can't stop cheating with other women is even harder. Trust me, I know. My ex is marrying his skank tomorrow night. I give their marriage a month before he's sleeping with one of the secretaries in his office."

Ellie took a deep breath and nodded. "I know, I know. I just still *love* him. Why do I still love him?" She shook her head. "No, I am not doing this again. I'm here on this trip to meet someone. Not to get all emotionally involved or anything. Just someone to make me forget Tim. To make me realize there are other guys out there. I just need a little help moving on."

"How about no more sleeping with him, either," Maggie said with a wink as she fussed with her bangs and smoothed her shiny bob. "Joy, can't you help us out here? Separation is your territory."

Joy stiffened. "I wish I had something brilliant to say, but I don't. I don't want to be separated from Harry any more than Ellie wants to be separated from Tim. But if I understood how to make a marriage work or how to get back together, Harry wouldn't be living in the unfinished basement. If it weren't for Rex, Harry would have moved *out.*"

"At least Harry isn't a cheater," Ellie said. "He loves you, Joy. You'll get back together. You always do."

Joy raised an eyebrow. "Always? We separated once and got back together once. He moved downstairs again—that's a bad sign. Not a pattern."

"You need to start coming to our meetings," Maggie said. "You need to talk, Joy."

"I'm not *divorced,*" Joy pointed out.

"I'm not, either," Ellie said. "And I'm a member."

Victoria braided and then unbraided her long red hair. "Joy's not a joiner."

"But we're working on her," Maggie added. "You don't need to be divorced to join our little club. You just need a story." She turned to Rebecca. "So tell us yours. You live with someone but you're on a singles tour?"

"I'm not along for the singles part of the tour," Rebecca said. "I'm—"

"With me," Joy finished for her with a look at Rebecca. A look that said, *Shut the hell up about my private business.*

"Oh! Well, any friend of Joy's is a friend of ours," Victoria said.

"So, *are* you going to marry this live-in boyfriend?" Ellie asked. "I read in some magazine that half of couples who live together never marry. Not that you two won't! Or shouldn't. Forget my cynicism." She scrunched up her face. "There I go, sticking my foot in it again. Just because my marriage is a joke doesn't mean everyone's will be."

"I have no idea what's going to happen with me and Michael." She wondered if Joy were interested in her, in her answers, at all. Joy kept her eyes on the road and rarely chimed in. "We're having some problems."

Maggie squeezed her hand. "We know from problems." She sounded exactly like Rebecca's grandmother Mildred, her mother's mother, a native New Yorker, who died when Rebecca was eleven.

Everyone was gone. Everyone. She squeezed her eyes shut against a sharp stab in her chest. *Don't cry in front of Joy. Don't cry in front of Joy.*

"You okay there?" Maggie asked.

Rebecca took a breath, opened her eyes, turned back around, and nodded. "Are you a New Yorker?"

"Yes!" Maggie said. "We moved from Long Island eight years ago for my hus—my ex-husband's job. Then Mark suddenly turns into Mr. Nature, going on hikes. He went from a couch potato whose only interest in life was beer and the Yankees to a hiking vegan. Turns out some bimbo at his work was, too."

"Sorry," Rebecca said.

"On to better men," Ellie said. "Tall, dark, and handsome ones."

"So what line of work are you in, Rebecca?" Victoria asked.

"I'm a paralegal," Rebecca said. "At a divorce mediation firm. Fitting, huh?"

Victoria snorted. "I tried mediation. I jumped across the table and tried to strangle the breath out of my lying, cheating prick bastard ex-husband. Mediation is a crock."

"It can work," Rebecca said. "But it's definitely not for everyone."

Victoria snorted. "Yeah, I'm living proof. We didn't end up having a trial, though. He backed down just to get rid of me."

"I've heard of mediation, but I have no idea how it works," Maggie said.

"Well, instead of spending a fortune on lawyers and fighting back and forth and getting nowhere," Rebecca explained, "a divorcing couple will sit down with a mediator, someone who represents *both* their best interests. Which is to make decisions about child custody and visitation and splitting up assets in a way that is fair to both of them."

"So a divorcing couple who hate each other's guts will actually sit down and divide things up, just like that?" Ellie asked.

"Sometimes just like that, sometimes not," Rebecca said. "Sometimes one will sign anything just to be free of the spouse. Sometimes one will agree to nothing just to hang on to the marriage."

"Doesn't sound like a fun job," Ellie said.

It wasn't. "Well, *fun* might not be the right word. But it can be rewarding to help a divorcing couple reach agreement when agreeing is the farthest thing from their minds." That was true. And that was how Rebecca had felt about it in the beginning. "Making the path to divorce a little easier, especially when there are children involved." She sounded like Michael. And Marcie.

"That *is* important," Joy said, her voice tired and sad.

"How's the little guy doing with the separation, Joy?" Victoria asked.

"He's fine," Joy muttered. "Look, I don't want to talk about me, okay?"

"Hey, Rebecca, did you know Joy is planning a Rocky Relationships tour? For couples who could use a weekend away, but with other couples having problems, so you have someone to talk to, turn to. You should go and be the mediator!"

"I'm just a paralegal," Rebecca said automatically. "Not a mediator."

"Well, I'm sure you know your stuff," Maggie said, fluffing her shiny brown bangs. "Sounds like you do."

"Rebecca lives in New York," Joy said tightly. "She's going back after the weekend."

"Too bad," Ellie said. "We could use your expertise."

"*We?*" Maggie repeated. "Don't tell me you talked Tim into going, Ellie. He keeps making promises to you and then two days later he's screwing the Handy Mart checkout girl in the bathroom on her break."

Ellie shrugged and seemed close to tears again. "What am I supposed to do?"

"Maybe you really will meet someone on this trip," Victoria said, braiding her red hair and then freeing it again. "Someone good. Someone who will show you that a relationship is about respect."

Ellie nodded. "Maybe." She turned to Rebecca. "It sure would be great to have a professional along on the Rocky Relationships trip, though. Tim won't go for counseling. He says what he's doing is natural, that men can't be monogamous."

"What a crock!" Victoria said. "I know plenty of men who are monogamous. Not any of our husbands—Harry excluded,

Joy—but plenty of others. My friend Jackie's husband. My dad. My friend Richard—he'd never cheat. And my brother is still madly in love with his wife, who I can't stand, and they've been married for nine years already."

Rebecca was so curious about Joy, about why her marriage broke up. She waited for Joy to say something, but Joy kept her eyes on the road, her mouth shut.

"My brother, too," Maggie added, biting into another cookie. "And my dad. And my friend Sara's husband. Plus I know several men at my work who go straight home to their wives and children and come in happy and peppy every morning. Not all men are cheaters."

Michael included, Rebecca thought. He was true-blue in that regard. But then again, they weren't married. Maybe something happened when couples got married. The rings got too tight or something. The restriction to one partner. Rebecca had heard every reason in the book for why couples divorced. Why they cheated. This one refused to have sex. Or kinky sex. That one gained forty pounds. This one was a workaholic, that one became an alcoholic. People argued and argued and argued.

She wondered what it was that made her father cheat on her mother. Why Pia Jayhawk had been able to sway him from his wife, his vows.

"Rebecca, is cheating the main reason why couples divorce?" Ellie asked.

"Actually, no," Rebecca said. "It's high up there, but the main reason seems to be the ole irreconcilable differences. But really, I'm no expert about marriage or divorce or relationships. I don't know anything anymore. I don't even know if I still have a boyfriend."

"God, join the club," Ellie said. "Literally! You could join our group!"

"She's *leaving* after the weekend," Joy said again, her eyes on the road.

It was such a definitive statement that it led to some peace and quiet and contemplation for exactly one minute. Maggie then launched into a story about her sister, Frances, who lived in Massachusetts and was staying with her "loser fiancé" because she was fifty pounds overweight and didn't think anyone else would want her. That led to a discussion of weight and whether it was okay to not be attracted to someone if they gained fifty pounds, which was what happened to Victoria before she joined Weight Watchers. Apparently, losing forty-seven pounds did not bring her husband begging his way back.

The minibus was quiet for another few minutes until Joy pulled to a stop in front of a condo complex in Brunswick. "We've just arrived at gentleman number one's house," Joy said. "Prepare to meet the very attractive Clinton Witowski."

There was a flurry of compacts opening. Hair being smoothed and fluffed. Teeth being checked for cookie crumbs. And then a man appeared at the bus. He slid open the door with a "Hello, ladies" and a charming smile and sat in the row behind the women. Dead in the center.

Clinton Witowski appeared to be in his early forties. His thick dark hair was receding, but it was sexy man hair. And somehow the crow's-feet and grooves around his mouth added to his appeal. There was something Marlboro Man about him, though there was nothing cowboy in his appearance.

The women changed instantly when he boarded. They all sat up straighter. Victoria perked up considerably. "So we're members of the Wiscasset Divorced Ladies Club," she told him. "Have you ever been married?"

"Twice," he said, leaning forward. "But neither divorce was my fault. I took my vows very seriously. My first wife couldn't handle it when I was deployed, so that was that. So I made sure my second wife was also in the military, someone who'd understand, and she ended up falling for her commander." He went on for a bit too long about how he was a former military captain who now worked in a civilian capacity as an engineer for the Brunswick Naval Air Station.

The women swooned with their *sorrys*. Rebecca listened to the women's chatter—every now and then they'd let Clinton get a word in—and looked out the window. She supposed she and Joy couldn't very well talk in the bus; they'd have to wait until they arrived in Portland, where they could have some privacy.

A half hour later, Joy stopped to pick up Bachelor Number Two. Victoria, Maggie, and Ellie stared out the window. They were practically foaming at the mouth, until they got a glimpse of him. Also tall and very thin, he wasn't so much unattractive as he was awkward. He walked up to the bus and smiled so shyly that the trio's maternal instincts rose up.

"May I introduce Jed Harker," Joy said. "Jed, in the first row are Ellie Rasmussen, Maggie Herald, and Victoria Dale. Clinton Witowski is the gentleman behind them. And here in the passenger seat is Rebecca. Strand," she added after a moment.

The women said hello and shook Jed's hand. Jed was so shy he could barely look up. He sat next to Clinton, who slapped him on the back and almost knocked him off the seat.

The women were all over Jed, asking him questions, and he slowly opened up. He was single, never married, thirty years old. He'd only had a few relationships and had even been engaged for a few weeks. The fiancée had met someone else.

"Isn't that always the way?" Victoria said. "They meet someone else. What I don't understand is, why aren't they happy with what they have? Why is someone else's vagina so much more interesting than mine?"

Rebecca almost choked on the cookie she was nibbling. Joy glanced at her and smiled, then seemed to remember she didn't want to be friendly and refocused on the road.

Jed's eyes had bugged somewhat. Ellie patted his hand. "Get used to it."

"You know what?" Victoria said. "Last year I put a profile on Match.com, met someone, went on a few dates, and he told me it wasn't working out, that I wasn't what he was looking for. Well, I was everything on his 'Ideal Woman' list and in his stupid paragraph with its 'u' for 'you' and '2' for 'two' and juvenile 'b4.' I finally figured out that what's on a piece of paper and what's flesh and blood are very different things."

Clinton nodded. "You can't account for chemistry. You can want this or that in someone, but chemistry is chemistry."

And blood is blood, Rebecca thought out of nowhere. She glanced again at Joy, this total stranger who shared her DNA, who shared her father.

"I never seem to have chemistry with anyone," Jed piped up.

"That's because you're so shy," Ellie said, patting his shoulder. "We'll fix that."

Jed smiled. "That's why I signed up. I figured I'd do better in a group."

For the next ten minutes, Jed and Clinton talked about the Red Sox, while the women covered their former mothers-in-law. Rebecca realized she'd left Michael's mother's wedding gown on the hook behind the door to her office. That *had* to mean something.

"Okay, everyone," Joy said. "Last pickup."

Once again, the women were frothing in anticipation. Joy parked in front of what looked like a three-family house with a balcony on each story. She checked something in an overstuffed datebook, then rang one of the buzzers. A few minutes later, a husky man followed her to the orange bus, carrying an enormous duffel bag.

"Ellie, Maggie, Victoria, Rebecca, Clinton, Jed, meet Victor."

"Victor and Victoria," Clinton said. "Musical!"

Victor appeared to be trying to figure out which of the women *was* his musical match, then shoved his duffel bag in the back and climbed in next to Jed. Victor was pretty much the opposite of Jed. He never stopped talking. Or eating. He carried a baggie of what looked like gummy worms and held them above his mouth. Thirty-five, with something of a goatee, Victor had an attractive face and carried his extra fifty pounds or so pretty well. He wore the kind of patterned sweater and Dockers that Harold Goldberg favored for dress-down Fridays. He was a salesman of office chairs and knew everything about pneumatic seat heights and lumbar support.

"So tell us your story," Victoria asked him when he finally stopped going on about chairs and which sports teams he rooted for. She twirled a long red strand of hair around her finger. She's interested, Rebecca realized.

He turned to Victoria, his expression deadly. "My story? My story is that women are lying bitches."

Everyone stared.

"I kid!" he exclaimed, and then belly-laughed alone.

"Smooth," Clinton said.

"Real smooth," Jed added, then laughed his head off. And just like that, Jed had joined the party.

The bed-and-breakfast, in the Munjoy Hill section of the city of Portland, had a stunning view of Casco Bay and the Portland Observatory, but no room for Rebecca.

Joy frowned. "No, I called a few hours ago and booked an additional room at the single rate."

The proprietor shook her head. "I took no such call." She stopped. "Oh, goodness. You must have spoken to Lizzie, my daughter. She's fifteen and thinks it's hilarious to book nonexistent rooms. I'll make sure she's disciplined."

Joy sighed. "But we have an extra person."

The woman peered at her computer screen. "Well, we could bring a cot into your room. It'll be tight, but a cot will fit. No charge for the extra bed."

Joy let out a deep breath.

"I could sleep in the parlor," Rebecca offered. They'd passed a chintz-covered living room with a Victorian sofa and upholstered chairs.

"Okay," Joy said.

Rebecca's face fell.

"I kid," Joy said without a smile.

Everyone decided on Mexican for dinner. The restaurant the proprietor recommended was down a cobblestone alleyway of sorts that opened into the waterfront. The Old Port reminded Rebecca of a mini Greenwich Village, but with a crowded harbor and no Gap and no zigzagging yellow taxis. Only one-of-a-kind shops and charming restaurants and a condom shop called Condom Sense, which Clinton wanted to visit.

Ellie and Victoria had given handsome Clinton to Maggie, who needed him most this weekend. Ellie, who really only wanted her husband, took Jed under her platonic wing. Victoria, almost as tall as Victor, giggled as Victor pulled her in the condom shop's doorway with yet another "I kid!"

So far, so good.

Enchiladaville had a trio of serenading guitar players and a dance floor. Jed danced like Elaine on *Seinfeld*, his arms and legs jerking out at strange angles. But he seemed to be having his first blast. Ellie mostly did the twist. Victoria and Victor had progressed to slow dancing to fast music. And Maggie and Clinton, neither of whom could dance, were deep in conversation, each sipping a margarita.

Which left Rebecca and Joy alone at the table, with mostly empty plates and platters between them. They both faced the dance floor, which saved them from sitting awkwardly across from each other. Every now and then, Joy would wink or smile at one of her charges with genuine warmth and affection. It was clear she cared about people, cared about her work. And her work was romance. Rebecca wondered what Joy thought about Pia Jayhawk's affair with Daniel Strand. That her mother had fallen for a married man and had gotten burned bad? That her mother had fallen in love and should have won her man? *Had* her mother been in love with Daniel Strand? Rebecca had no idea of the circumstances.

Joy was grinning at Jed, who had dramatically dipped Ellie during a tangolike number and almost dropped her. Joy's smile faded when she realized Rebecca was watching her.

"I'm really glad you let me come," Rebecca said, taking a sip of her own margarita. "I didn't know what to expect, but even the ride down was fun."

"That's why I keep doing it. People just want to find love. And you never know who someone will connect with."

"How long have you been operating the Love Bus?"

"Just about a year. The Divorced Ladies Club of Wiscasset are my constant clients. I've had a few other strays, mostly their referrals. To attract male clientele, they drive an hour in each direction and put up my brochures on bulletin boards in health clubs, sports bars, everywhere they can think of."

"What did you do before?"

Joy reached for a tortilla chip and broke it in half but didn't eat it. "I worked on a farm, actually. Grooming bulls and taking care of the babies. I majored in math in college—that's where I met Harry—and got my teaching certificate to teach middle school and high school, but when it came time to apply to schools, I found myself applying to farms in the area. All of a sudden I wanted to work with bulls or alpacas. I really loved farmwork."

Rebecca didn't even know what an alpaca was.

"And then Rex came along, so I stayed home with him. I found I loved that most of all, actually. And last year, an eccentric old uncle of Harry's died and left him the orange minibus. He had a little tour company and drove people all over Maine, especially up north. And one day, just kidding, really, I mentioned to Harry that I could continue Uncle Jasper's life work and take the Divorced Ladies Club on singles tours to meet new loves, and Harry thought it was a wonderful idea, and all of a sudden, my new business was born. Just like that."

"Would you rather be grooming bulls?" Rebecca asked.

"I guess so. I just sort of fell out of that. And this came along, and it's fun and gives me my own money again. I like the idea of going back to farmwork when Rex starts kindergarten. That's in just two years. Maybe one day I'll have my own farm. But right now, the Love Bus is perfect. It's happy work. The tours aren't always successful—in fact, most aren't—but everyone usually has fun."

"Was your mother in love with our father?" Rebecca blurted out.

Joy glared at her. "Rebecca, first of all, please stop referring to your father as *our* father. He was not my father, except in the most base biological sense. And second, my mother's business is her own."

Rebecca felt her cheeks burn. "I—Okay, you're right. Sorry. I don't really know how to do this."

So your mother is still alive, Rebecca couldn't help thinking. She wondered if she'd get the opportunity to meet Pia Jayhawk.

"Me either," Joy said, offering a bit of a smile.

"He really did care, Joy. Your—Daniel Strand, I mean." She reached into her bag for the leather box. "He wrote you all these letters. He explains—"

Joy pushed the box back in front of Rebecca. "I don't care what his explanation was. And I'm not interested in reading the letters."

"Aren't you curious about your father at all?" Rebecca asked. She wondered what Pia Jayhawk had told her daughter.

"Nope," Joy said, dipping a tortilla chip into the little pot of salsa, her eyes on the dance floor.

"Really?"

She glanced back at Rebecca. "Really. He's nothing to me but biology and DNA. My mother married a very nice man when I was nine. *He* helped raised me. Why would I be interested in some stranger who couldn't even face up to the most basic of responsibilities?"

Rebecca stiffened. Joy was right, of course.

"He did all right by you, it seems," Joy said suddenly.

Rebecca nodded. "He was a good man. He really—"

Joy clunked her glass on the table. "A good man. Right. So good he disappeared off the face of the earth when he found out his mistress was knocked up. Don't come into *my* life and tell me what a good man my biological father was when it's clearly not true. You can't be a good person if you turn your back on your own baby. I know this is true more than ever now that I have my own child."

Again Rebecca's face burned. "I—" But what was she supposed to say?

Could you be a good person and still do something that was the opposite of good? What Daniel Strand had done couldn't simply be called a mistake. Or bad judgment. It was something else. Something Rebecca couldn't seem to understand. Her father *had* been a good person.

"Sometimes there are circum—"

Joy took a sip of her drink. "Like not wanting to mess up his perfect little life?"

"It's not that simple, though. Nothing is that black or white."

"Except a *child*," Joy said. "Your father got a woman pregnant, and when he was informed of that, he disappeared. What's gray about that?"

"I just think if you read his letters to you, you would—"

"Rebecca, look. I understand why you tracked me down. I get that. And again, I'm sorry you lost your father. But he's not my father. You're not my sister. There's no family connection here. I'm sorry."

But you're my father's daughter. You are.

"If you'd just read the letters, Joy—"

Joy stood and reached into her handbag for some bills, which she put under her drink. "I'd like you to leave in the morning, Rebecca. And I mean head back to New York City." She walked over to the dance floor and whispered something in Victoria's ear. Victoria nodded, kissed Joy on the cheek, and resumed dancing. And Joy walked right out of the restaurant.

No, no, no! How had this happened? One minute they were

talking math and bulls and alpacas, whatever alpacas were; they were talking *life* and paths, and the next, Joy and the closed door were back.

Her heart squeezing, Rebecca supposed that meant she should sleep on the chintz-covered sofa in the parlor, after all.

six

Two hours later, Rebecca was driving back north in a rental car courtesy of Joy Jayhawk's Weekend Singles Tours, Jed biting at cuticles in the passenger seat. His mother, with whom he still lived, had called him complaining of both chest pain and foot pain, and so Jed had asked Joy if he could apply his unused tour to a future date. Joy had said of course, then added that "Rebecca will be happy to drive you home."

So that was that. Joy had managed to get rid of her even sooner than she'd intended. At the car rental agency, Joy had handed her a printout of a Google map and driving directions, a twenty-dollar bill for gas, and not even a forced smile.

"I don't know what to do here," Rebecca had said. "I feel like this is it. You gave me a chance and I blew it and now this is it. I'm gone." *Your eyes are just like our dad's. And your chin, too.*

"We're not family," she'd said in such a low voice that Rebecca had to lean in, which made Joy step back. "Words, labels, whatever, don't mean anything in and of themselves."

But—Rebecca stood there, not knowing what to plead, how

to fix this. "I totally agree. But we can at least talk, can't we? Just talk?"

Joy sighed and glanced away, then back. "Rebecca, I am all talked out. I'm sorry, but I've been talking and talking and talking for a while now. I don't want to talk anymore. I'm sorry if that sounds cold."

Jed had walked over, his cell phone in hand. "That was my mom again. Her right big toe is tingling really bad. Anyone know what that's a symptom of?"

During the ride back home, he chatted nonstop about his mother and her ailments and his need to break free, move out, that Ellie was great and all, but that he had a little crush on Maggie, and did Rebecca think Maggie might go out with him, or did a guy like him have no chance with a guy like Clinton around? Rebecca dropped him off at his place with the assurance that the best thing to do in life, under any circumstance, was to ask for what you wanted.

"That is really good advice," Jed said. "Really good." Then he gave her hand a squeeze and headed up the path to his home, suitcase bumping his thigh.

Joy had instructed Rebecca to return the car to an agency in Brunswick, right off the highway. Apparently, someone would be happy to drive Rebecca to Joy's house to pick up her own car.

Someone was. Someone even chattier than Jed had been: "You're from New York? I just came back from there—family vacation. Have you ever been to the top of the Empire State Building? What about the Statue of Liberty? I climbed up to the chin when I was a kid. Someone behind me got vertigo.

Ever heard of that? I saw that movie, you know, the old one, but I didn't think people still suffered from that, you know?" He talked and talked and talked, so much that Rebecca didn't have to respond, for which she was grateful. She stared out the window at the passing scenery, at life speeding by—meandering by, really—and realized that as long as she was in this car, with this chatty middle-aged man, she was *somewhere*.

"And here you are," he said, pulling up at 52 Maple Lane in Wiscasset.

It was very strange to stand in front of the house knowing that Joy wasn't there, wasn't inside, that she was miles away, and Rebecca had been banished, basically, from there. From Joy's life.

As she got into her own rental car, she took one last look at Joy's sweet blue Cape Cod and then drove back to the center of town with the idea of finding a motel or a cute bed-and-breakfast, anywhere she could throw herself into a bath and think. Was she supposed to go home? Home to Michael and the firm and Marcie's smug face? Home to a life that felt off size, off-key, off everything? There was no family anymore, just Michael, and the more Rebecca got to know him, really know him, understand him, how his mind worked, the less like family he seemed.

She had nowhere to go, she realized as she arrived in the center of town. Mama's Pizza was aglow with lights and Rebecca could hear music, strange music, like a polka, maybe. Arlene would know where Rebecca *could* go, at least for the night. A few nights, maybe.

Inside, the restaurant was crowded with a party—helium

balloons imprinted with HAPPY 60TH TRUDY! were everywhere. The polka music was loud, and a makeshift dance floor was crowded with mostly the senior citizen set. She'd crashed a party. Just as she turned to go, Arlene sashayed over.

"Rebecca! Nice to see you again," Arlene shouted. She wore a dark fuchsia fuzzy sweater dress with a big flower pinned at the chest. "Come have the last slice of cake."

"I didn't mean to intrude on a private party," Rebecca told her. "I'll head out."

"Don't be silly. And I baked this cake myself. Trust me, you want some."

Rebecca smiled and accepted a plate of chocolate cake with pink icing, the edge of the letter Y adorning it. She took a bite and it melted in her mouth. Her mother had made cake this good, a skill Rebecca hadn't inherited.

"Told you," Arlene said.

The music changed from polka to square dance, and the crowd curtsied and do-si-doed. Arlene explained that Trudy was her sister and taught "Dance Styles Through the Ages" through the Wiscasset Recreation Department.

Rebecca had to shout to be heard over the music. "Arlene, could you recommend a hotel or an inn nearby? For a night or two?"

Arlene nodded. "Finch's just down Water Street is closed for the season, but the owner is an old friend. I'll call if you'd like. Why don't you go on out to the deck till I get a hold of her. There's a path leading down to the beach, but I'd better warn you that the water will be too cold for toe dipping."

Rebecca hadn't met many people like Arlene in her life,

kind for no reason. The woman's warmth and motherly spirit were so comforting at the moment that Rebecca didn't want to leave her presence, but Arlene was already heading to the counter and the telephone. She was spun around a few times along the way.

Rebecca headed outside to the deck with her cake. A man sat alone at a far table, a bottle of Sam Adams beside him and his feet up on the railing. She'd know that hair anywhere. Thick, dirty-blond, sexy. Underneath, the tanned neck, the broad shoulders in a dark green T-shirt.

"Theo, right?" she asked.

He turned around and smiled at her, his dark brown eyes sharp and intense. "Rebecca, was it?"

She nodded. "Nice view." Not that she could see much of anything. The deck lights barely lit up the grass below, and about a hundred feet away she could make out a rocky path. But she could hear the lapping of the ocean.

He turned the chair next to him in invitation, and she sat down. "So what brings you to Wiscasset in September?" he asked, reaching for his beer. "We're pretty much a summer town."

For a moment, she considered just spitting it out, the whole story, but again she had that nudging feeling that she shouldn't, that this was Joy's territory, that this was equally Joy's story, and she shouldn't be telling everyone Joy's personal business.

"Hypothetically?" Rebecca asked, taking another bite of her cake.

He glanced at her and smiled. "Sure."

But instead of saying anything, she burst into tears, the image of her father, frail in the hospital bed, his lined face, the strange expression in his eyes, suddenly overtaking her. What was the expression? Not guilt, not really. "Let's say someone's father dies," she rushed to say, "and right before, he confesses something, that he had another child and that this child is now an adult, just a couple years younger than, say, you are."

He reached over to the napkin dispenser on the table behind them and handed her a few napkins. She dabbed under her eyes and clutched the white scratchy paper.

"And let's say," she continued, "that your own life is just sort of—I don't know the right word exactly. Just sort of *not*. And something in this news, this startling piece of news, that you have a sister out there somewhere, means something to you, really means something. And you go in search of this sister and you actually find her and she wants nothing to do with you."

"Ah," he said, staring out at the darkness. "I would think she needed some time."

"Really?" she asked, turning to face him. "Even if she said we're not family, that there's no *there* there, basically?"

He nodded. "Yup, time is the answer."

Rebecca let out a deep breath and took another bite of cake, which sat in her stomach.

"My own father checked in and out pretty much my entire childhood," Theo said. "If a kid of his came knocking on my door and said, 'Hey, I'm your brother,' I wouldn't feel much of a connection. Not at first."

Rebecca nodded. "I can understand that. I guess I feel the connection because I did grow up with my father. His other daughter is part of him. But she doesn't have that. She doesn't have anything to go on. I'm a stranger."

"Hypothetically a stranger," he said, tipping his beer bottle at her.

She smiled.

"Theo, dear, I'm ready to leave."

Rebecca turned around to see one of the elderly square dancers smiling at them from the doorway. She wore a long, quilted down coat even though the temperature was in the low 60s.

"My grandmother," he whispered. "Roommate of the birthday girl." He closed his hand on Rebecca's for a second and added, "Time works. Sometimes even a half hour is enough."

And with a last smile, he was gone. In one fifteen-minute conversation, he'd managed to make her feel better than she had in a week.

Finch's Seaside Inn turned out to be quite fancy, a huge Victorian on the water, but since it was closed for the season, the restaurant and the spa and housekeeping were shut down. Marianne Finch, the friendly faced proprietor, said she would drop off linens in the morning, but Rebecca had to change her own sheets. Oh, and she had to put up with some construction noise from the new deck and back porch she was having built. For this, her room rate was less than fifty bucks, and what a room it was. Spacious, with a dark wood four-poster bed and white, fluffy down comforter and a marble bathroom and a balcony that overlooked the beach.

It was close to midnight, but Rebecca pulled on a sweater and her L.L.Bean wool socks and headed out onto the balcony with the leather box of letters and the liter bottle of Diet Coke that Arlene had given her as she left Mama's. For a few minutes, she listened to the lap of waves, let the calm, the peace surround her. Surprisingly, Theo came to mind—those gorgeous dark eyes—and then Michael's face, with the disapproval etched in his handsome features, overtook it.

He hadn't called once since she'd left. How could that be? How did you go from waking up next to someone every morning, sharing a bathroom, a bed, and then not call to even check in, to hear their voice, when they were going through something so . . . so what? Painful. Strange. Unmooring. If she didn't do what he said, what he suggested, he would fire her as a girlfriend? Seemed so.

She leaned her head back against the chaise and pulled the leather box tight against her. Not that the contents were a comfort. They contained someone else's secrets and were meant for someone else. Not for her. Charlotte had said she'd get to know her father through the letters, but did that mean she hadn't known him? That the man she had known as her dad was someone else, someone with a lie in his past, a secret emotional life?

Time works.

Rebecca closed her eyes and reached into the box and pulled out a letter at random.

Dear Joy,

You are thirteen, and I know what that means. I've been through it with Rebecca. TROUBLE. Not that Rebecca's trouble. She's a good girl. Well, most of the time. She has a boyfriend named Dalton. Dalton—what a name. He's her first boyfriend and, oh, is she crazy about this boy. Of course, Dalton broke her heart tonight, crushed her right before a school dance by just not showing up, so of course she and her friend Charlotte went to the dance anyway, and there he was, slow dancing with another girl. She called and asked me to come get her, and cried and cried, and asked why boys pick other girls, and what's wrong with her.

I'm the last person to have any answers about that, but it got me thinking about your mother, how I suppose I "picked her" when I had a perfectly wonderful woman, a wife, the mother of my little girl. I wanted to explain to Rebecca that you can love someone and get pulled away anyway by things that trigger other things in you, but how could I explain that? I ended up offering some platitudes.

You choose who ends up making the most sense for your life in that moment, not necessarily who you love most. Not that I loved your mother more than Rebecca's mother. Oh, Lord, I don't even know what I'm saying. I just know you make a choice in a moment, sometimes without conscious thought, and you figure that must be the right one, so you don't rehash the one you let get away too much. Until later, I guess.

Rebecca remembered that conversation with her dad about Dalton and her first broken heart: *"You'll be fine, honey. There will be other boys. He doesn't deserve you. By homeroom in two days, you'll have a new boyfriend."*

There wasn't a new boyfriend for a while, a very long while. Would she have preferred if her father had said, *"You want the truth, Becs? The truth is, you can really like a girl so much, think about her all the time, and then turn around and like a new girl just as much, and actually want both girls in your life, but of course you can't have both girls, so you choose the one that makes the most sense."* And Carrie Futterman had obviously made the most sense for Dalton, since she had enormous breasts at age fifteen, a.k.a. a C cup.

Rebecca picked up her cell phone and called the hotel that Joy and the group were in. She asked for Joy's room, then almost hung up when she realized it was midnight. But she knew Joy would be awake, with much more than Rebecca on her mind.

"Hello?" came the voice, as wide awake as Rebecca expected.

"Joy, it's Rebecca. I just want you to know that I get it, that I understand. I just read one of his letters to you and I don't think he gets it at all. He's explaining himself, but the explanation sucks."

"Of course it does," she said.

Rebecca closed her eyes and held her breath. "Can I come back tomorrow morning? Not to talk about him, not to try and explain anything. Just because we are sort of sisters—lousy, weak connection, and all. I just . . . want to understand something, but I don't know what."

Joy named a restaurant on Commercial Street and a time, then hung up.

So Theo was right. Time works. Sometimes in hours.

Her shoulders relaxed with the *in* Joy had given her, with the somewhere-to-go, and she headed inside with the idea to take a bubble bath before crawling into that inviting bed. Her cell phone rang. Joy rescinding already?

No. It was Michael. Her heart flip-flopped at his name appearing on the tiny screen.

"Hey," he said.

"Hi." She imagined him lying barefoot on the black leather sofa, three case files on the coffee table.

"So? Does she have two heads? Eight dirty children? A criminal record?"

Rebecca smiled despite herself. Despite him. "I'm sure you already vetted her, Michael."

"Of course I did. If there had been something even slightly off in her background, I would have come after you."

He would have, of that Rebecca was sure.

"She's . . . nice," she said. "A little prickly. Understandable given the circumstances. I was a total surprise."

"When are you coming home?" he asked.

She was due back at the office on Monday. But she couldn't imagine leaving on Sunday. "A few more days, I think. I just need some more time here."

Silence. "So you're just not coming to work?" he said. "Rebecca, you do have responsibilities."

"Responsibilities I suck at."

"You'll take the refresher course—"

No, I won't. "Michael, I've been a paralegal for six years." Were they really talking about this right now?

"Becs, honey, listen—forget that right now. I shouldn't have even brought it up. You've been through a lot this past week. I understand that you want to stay up there in this other universe. But you have a life here and you're needed here."

I don't want to go home. The thought inched up. She *didn't* want to go home. Not yet. Not until something with Joy was . . . what? Settled? Figured out?

"I'm not ready to leave here, Michael. Please understand, okay?"

There was a sigh. Then nothing. Then: "Rebecca, I shouldn't tell you this, not now, but I feel like I have to. That maybe drastic times call for drastic measures, you know?"

She waited, the silence scaring her.

"Things have been kind of off between us for a while now," he said. "And we've both coasted with it."

That was true. "I know," she said softly. "I don't really know what to do about it."

"I'm not sure, either," he said. "But I need you to know that I do have a new friend—just a friend, someone I met at the gym last month, and there's a real connection there."

Her stomach churned and she got up, tears pricking the backs of her eyes. "And?"

"And, you could swing it either way, Becs. You could come home and we could work on things between us. Try and figure out what's there. Or . . . not," he added.

She closed her eyes and said, "I don't know what to say to all that right now, Michael," then hung up like Joy had.

She imagined Joy sitting on her bed with a brick in her chest like Rebecca had right now. Overwhelmed with everything and nothing.

seven

Ellie was flirting with the waiter when Rebecca arrived at Wharf's Diner at 9:00 a.m. Her poker-straight dark hair was in a low ponytail, and her intense green eyes were made up in a smoky, nighttime way. Victoria and Victor were deep in conversation, their chairs turned toward each other. Victor kept twirling his hand through the ends of Victoria's pretty long red waves, seemingly unable to take his eyes off her face. And Maggie, also a bit heavily made up, her delicate features in too much mascara and pinky-brown lipstick, appeared to be stewing, holding her coffee mug tightly. She and Clinton the Marlboro Man were *not* sitting next to each other—and they'd been dancing pelvis to pelvis the last time Rebecca had seen them. Clinton, in a cowboy hat, was absorbed in the menu. And Joy, her blond hair off her face with a red suede head-band, not a shred of makeup on her pretty face, was looking over a map of the Old Port.

Rebecca felt her heart surge in her chest at the sight of Joy, at the new familiarity of her.

She'd read somewhere that twins separated at birth were later found to have much in common, from, say, choosing the same brand of shampoo to both not liking lobster. Rebecca wondered if Joy used Pantene and loved tuna fish sandwiches with cucumber slices, if red were her favorite color, if she cried at corny scenes in movies. If she was the only other person besides Rebecca who loved the movie *Hope Floats*.

If she would have told Michael something different on the phone.

But Rebecca and Joy weren't twins and they were *half* sisters at that. And Rebecca took after her mother.

"Look who's back!" Victoria announced at the sight of Rebecca. There was actually a round of applause, and Rebecca felt her slumped shoulders perk up a bit. Apparently, Joy had told everyone that Rebecca had volunteered to drive the nervous Jed home last night instead of making him drive alone.

Victor jumped up and slid over a chair from the next table, squeezing Rebecca in between the upset Maggie and Joy.

Maggie whispered, "Jerk in the fake Stetson told me, with my dress bunched up around my waist, that he wasn't looking for anything serious, that he liked me enough to tell me that. Asshat."

Ah. "I'm sorry," Rebecca whispered.

Maggie leaned even closer. "Though part of me wanted to knock on his door last night and tell him, 'You know what, jerk, I'm not, either. My ex-husband is getting married in twelve hours and I'm a wreck and just want some good hard sex.'"

Rebecca squeezed her hand.

"But I would have felt worse, right?" she asked, tears in her eyes.

Rebecca nodded and whispered, "Very likely. It's not him so much as it is the *meaning* you're looking for right now, assurances and comfort. You're not looking for someone else to tell you his heart isn't in it."

"That's exactly it!" she said, brightening some. "I couldn't figure out why I was so upset over a slick dick like Clinton." She slid her gaze across to the far end of table, where Clinton was asking the waiter for details on hollandaise sauce. "I mean, I know his type. Everyone does. But I was crying my eyes out last night."

"It wasn't him," Rebecca said. The waiter appeared between her and Maggie, and Rebecca ordered a Swiss cheese omelet. "And coffee, *two* cups, please." As Maggie ordered, Rebecca whispered to Joy, "Thanks for having me back."

Joy nodded and mentioned that another single had opened up in the bed-and-breakfast, so she'd booked it for Rebecca, and then she launched into the morning's itinerary, which included wandering around the Old Port and visiting Portland's other neighborhoods, such as Munjoy Hill and the West End.

So much for talking late into the night in their shared single room. Rebecca had envisioned them sitting cross-legged on their twin beds, facing each other, going back and forth about what they liked, what they didn't. There would be a constant refrain of "Me too!" And then Joy would ask a question about the father they shared.

Time, she reminded herself, Theo Granger's face, those deep brown eyes, that one dimple coming to mind.

As they headed outside, Rebecca breathed in the fresh, fresh air, marveling at the size of the seagulls swooping over the bobbing boats that lined the harbor.

"Wish I could push that asshat in the water," Maggie whispered to Rebecca as Clinton's gaze followed a shapely woman down Commercial Street.

"He'll probably fall in all on his own," Rebecca said as Clinton got perilously close to the edge while staring at another woman's large breasts.

Joy handed out brochures for the Portland Observatory and maps of the various neighborhoods. Clinton asked Victor if he wanted to see about getting tickets to a Sea Dogs game, but Victor tightened his arm around Victoria's and said he was booked for the day, then added, "Maybe for the rest of my life." Victoria practically purred next to him as they headed down the pier.

"Meet back in the lobby of the hotel at 1:00 p.m. if you want to join us for lunch," Joy called after the lovebirds.

Clinton then turned to Ellie and tried to wrap his arm around hers with a "Shall we, milady," but Ellie slugged him, and Clinton countered with a whispered, "Your loss, babe."

"You're overconfident, Clinton," Ellie shot back.

"Can we just get *going*?" Maggie muttered.

"Clinton, we'll meet back in the lobby of the hotel at one, okay?" Joy said. Meaning *Beat it, jerk.*

Clinton raised an eyebrow. "You're not going off to devise ways to murder me, are you?" he asked, then laughed.

"Someone got hurt here," Joy whispered to Clinton.

He eyed Maggie for a moment, then took off his hat and

held it in his hand. "Maggie, listen, I was just trying to be honest. Before anything happened, before we went too far. You know?"

Maggie bit her lip and stared at the cobblestones.

"Should I have made love to you and then left in the middle of the night? Told you in the morning that it wasn't like the sex meant anything?"

"We didn't *have* sex," she muttered. "Oh, just forget it."

"I don't get why you're so mad at me," he said. "Why am I the bad guy for being honest? I told you at just the *right* moment that you shouldn't have expectations."

"The right moment would have been while we were still in the bar," Maggie explained, her voice rising. "When you were telling me how beautiful I was. How you couldn't understand why my husband let me get away." She jabbed a finger at him. "Or better yet, when you told me you could look into my eyes forever. Maybe that would have been the *right* time."

"Honey, I had three margaritas," Clinton said, doing a ministagger.

Tears welled up in Maggie's eyes and she turned away, crossing her arms over her chest. Rebecca put an arm around her shoulder. For the past two years, Rebecca had not missed dating. She'd forgotten what it could be like: this.

Joy walked over to Clinton and pulled him aside to talk. After a few moments, they both walked back to the rest of the group.

"Joy's right," he said to Maggie. "Someone did get hurt, and that's what matters. I *am* sorry your feelings got hurt, Maggie. I don't know. Maybe you're just not my type or you just come off as too desperate or something."

Maggie took off her shoe and flung it at Clinton.

"What are you, crazy?" he said, jumping back. "Did you see that?" he said to Joy. "Jesus, I think I've earned a ten percent discount."

Joy retrieved Maggie's shoe and handed it back to her. "Okay, no shoe throwing. No name-calling. There was a moment between you two, and it didn't work out. Let's just leave it there, okay?"

"I already left it," Maggie snapped, her gaze narrowed on Clinton.

Clinton rolled his eyes and said, "Women," then ambled off.

"Does this happen a lot?" Ellie asked. "This is my first Love Bus tour," she added to Rebecca.

Joy pulled off her headband and ran her hands through her blond hair. "Sometimes. Dating might be even harder than marriage."

"Maybe I should have dated Tim longer than three months before getting married," Ellie said.

And just like that, there were actual guffaws and belly laughs and comparisons of how long everyone's courtship and engagement had been, which led to a discussion of worst wedding gift. Maggie won. Her new in-laws had given her a handwritten list of how to be a good wife to their dear boy, including how to cook his steak and with what side dishes—he liked a green vegetable *and* a root vegetable with his evening meal *and* those dorky dinner rolls—and he preferred the classic tightie-whities, not those boxer briefs you saw on the billboards these days. Maggie should take care not to starch them.

Maggie snorted. "My ex wore those with his beer gut hanging out. Sex-y."

Ellie was laughing so hard she tripped and fell on her butt. "And did you cook his steak just so?" she asked as Rebecca helped her up.

Maggie beamed. "I burned it, usually. And shrunk his tightie-whities on purpose, too."

Maggie entertaining them from the list, and Joy looking very relieved, the women headed to Exchange Street, which was lined with boutiques and other interesting shops. After the reading of her father's will, Rebecca knew she had—or would soon have—a bank account full of money and ridiculous investments whose interest alone would cover her monthly expenses and then some. But she'd done so much shopping in Freeport that she ended up just buying two sticks of jasmine-scented incense and a little ceramic holder.

In a pricey boutique, Maggie tried on a slinky sleeveless black wrap dress and high-heeled peep-toe pumps and brought both up to the counter to pay. "I can't afford either, but I just want to show that fake cowboy what he's not getting," Maggie said, taking out her wallet. "Jerk. Asshole. Stupid asshole!"

"You okay?" Joy asked, rubbing Maggie's shoulder.

"I guess," Maggie said. "But why is it all so hard? You like someone, they like you, then it . . ." She let out a breath. "I know he was honest. I know he could have totally used me and then been a bigger jerk in the morning. But why does it hurt so much?" She dissolved into tears and told the saleswoman that she didn't even like the "stupid dress," and the three women led her out of the store.

With her arm around Maggie, Joy told them about a place nearby called Soakology, where you could have a fancy foot massage and a thousand different kinds of tea and tiny pastries.

"God, I need a foot massage. And a lot of pastry," Maggie said.

In ten minutes the four women sat side by side in plush pedicure chairs, their feet luxuriating in hot, soapy water that smelled like lavender. Rebecca leaned her head back and settled in, selecting Deep Vibrate for the chair, which began gently squeezing into her back.

"This is heaven," Rebecca said. "Everything that was pressing on me feels like it's now floating high above my head."

"I'm beginning to feel better, too," Maggie said. "It just seems like everyone else is pairing off or connecting except for me. It's always like that. Always been like that. In high school, college, at stupid speed dating. I just always feel like the one who isn't picked." She leaned her head back. "Great, and now I sound like a whiny baby, too."

"If it's any consolation," Rebecca said, "Jed told me he has a crush on you."

Maggie smiled. "Really? That's nice, I guess." She burst into tears. "But see, if someone *does* pick me, it's always the Jeds of the world. I know that's mean. But it's always the damned case. Sometimes it seems like everyone leads a charmed life but me."

Rebecca squeezed her hand. "My dad died last week, and my boyfriend told me last night on the phone that there might be someone else unless I basically shape up as a girlfriend."

The other three women leaned forward to stare at her.

"Really?" Maggie's mouth hung open. "Now *that's* a jerk."

Ellie kicked up some bubbly water. "My husband told me that maybe the reason he 'has' to see other women is because I won't let him do anal."

Rebecca spit out her tea, and Maggie and Ellie laughed so hard that Ellie actually tipped halfway out of her chair.

"I don't know," Maggie said. "If Joy and Harry can be having trouble, maybe there's just no hope for any couple. You guys were so rock solid."

"Could you give us a teeny bit about what happened between you two?" Ellie asked.

Joy stared up at the ceiling. "We're just . . ."

"I didn't mean to pry, Joy," Ellie said. "Forget I said anything. It just makes me feel less crazy, less at fault to know that other marriages have problems, too, you know?"

Joy picked up her tea and took a long sip, wrapping her hands around the dainty cup. "I—" She put down her tea. "Why is this so hard for me? I hate that Harry's right."

"About what?" Ellie asked gently.

Rebecca thought, *If I lean as far back as possible in my seat, so that Joy forgets I'm here, she might answer the question.* She even held her breath.

"Well," Joy said. "Um . . . He . . . Oh, shit," she said, kicking at the water. "He told me I'm emotionally frigid. His exact words. And that he was sick and tired of it. It's pretty much why he moved downstairs."

"Is *he* a jerk?" Rebecca asked before she could stop herself.

Joy shook her head. "Well, sometimes. But he's mostly right. Not when it comes to Rex, though. Which is Harry's big complaint. He wants me to be with him the way I am with Rex."

"He wants you to treat him like a three-year-old?" Maggie asked with a devilish smile.

That her own husband had trouble breaking through Joy's shell made Rebecca feel a lot better. It wasn't *her*. Well, it was. But Joy was one tough customer, period. She had given Rebecca a real opening, though. And Rebecca was taking it.

That night for dinner, Joy, Rebecca, Ellie, and Maggie went to the famous Lobster Shack in nearby Cape Elizabeth. Victor and Victoria (the novelty of saying that hadn't worn off) had excused themselves for lunch (they were having sex in Victor's room) and dinner. Clinton called Joy and reported that he'd met someone and wouldn't be joining the group for lunch or dinner, but he would need a ride back Sunday, and he wouldn't mind getting half his fee back, since things "got a little ugly, especially with shoe violence." Joy had assured him she'd write him a check. Maggie thought he should pay an extra 10 percent for being an ass.

After dinner, after the best lobster Rebecca had ever had, they'd toured the stunning lighthouse on the rocky cliffs, and Rebecca understood why everyone she'd passed wore fleece. The wind whipped around her, yet she didn't feel cold; she felt invigorated, the expanse of dark blue endless ocean and the complete absence of noise as soothing as the lavender foot rub. She hadn't heard so much as a honk since she'd arrived in Maine. No wonder the sign proclaimed it the way life should be.

"I miss Rex," Joy said, staring out at the ocean, her arms wrapped around her slight figure.

"Does Harry take good care of him?" Rebecca asked, trying to keep her hair from whipping into her eyes.

Joy nodded. "I know he's in good hands and I'm used to going away some weekends for the singles tours, but it's different now that Harry and I sort of separated. We haven't done anything as a family in a while. I take Rex or Harry takes Rex, but we don't do anything together. Not since Harry moved downstairs. It kills me. I want Rex to grow up with happily married parents."

"You're like me," Maggie said. "I grew up without my dad. He moved across the country when my parents divorced—and the only dream I really ever had was to keep my own family intact when I married and had children. To make sure my own kids never had to go through all that crap and heartache. Well, that dream got blown to bits. It still kills me." She turned to Joy. "Oh, God, I'm sorry. I didn't mean to make you feel bad."

"It's okay," Joy said. "He's only downstairs. That gives me hope about us."

They were all quiet for a moment, then Ellie said to Rebecca, "Are your parents still married? Oh, wait, I'm so sorry. You said your father recently passed away. Foot in mouth, Ellie."

Rebecca squeezed her hand. "They were happily married until my mother died when I was nineteen."

Happily married. Rebecca realized how automatically she'd said that, how ingrained it was. Who knew how happily married her parents had been? How happily married, how *happy*, anyone was? *Seems* and *are* were very different.

"Oh my God," Maggie said. "You're an orphan!"

Rebecca stared up at the thousands of twinkling stars. "I guess I am."

"Which do you think is worse?" Joy asked, her gaze on the ocean. "Never knowing your father—never even meeting him—*or* loving him your whole life and then losing him?"

Rebecca stared at Joy, unsure where she was going with this, what her point was. It wasn't a competition.

"Joy, a little insensitive," Maggie whispered, darting her eyes at Rebecca.

"Our father is one and the same," Joy said.

Because Maine was so quiet, the collective gasps echoed in Rebecca's ears.

"Really?" Ellie asked, turning to Rebecca. "The dad you just lost is the same dad that Joy never knew?" She looked from Rebecca back to Joy.

That was something—Joy had clearly told Ellie and Maggie about her father. Which meant she did think about it. And that these women were more than just clients. They were *friends*.

Rebecca nodded. "My father told me the day before he died." She sucked in a deep breath. "I was wearing that stupid beautiful wedding gown and he just came out and said it: 'There was a baby.' I'll have that image, those words in my head forever."

"Wow," Ellie said. "And why were you wearing a wedding gown? Are you and your boyfriend engaged? Did I miss that?"

"Michael's mother likes me," Rebecca explained. "She thinks it's time we got engaged, and she gave me her dress right before I went to the hospital to see my dad. He asked me to try it on since he'd never get to see me in a wedding gown otherwise."

"That is so sad!" Ellie said.

Rebecca bit her lip. "And then a breath later, he told me I had a half sister who lives in Maine."

"Joy," Ellie finished. "Wow. Wow-wow."

"Your father must have really not liked your boyfriend," Maggie said.

Rebecca turned to face her. "What do you mean?"

"Well, there you are, in a *wedding gown*," Maggie said, "and a second later he tells you you have a half sister you never knew about? It's like he felt the need to tell you, in that moment, that he wasn't leaving you all alone in the world, after all, that you didn't have to marry your boyfriend just to have someone."

Huh.

Maybe.

Or maybe it was just coincidence. Her father had known he was dying. Every word was becoming a struggle. He had to tell her then if he was going to tell her at all. It meant something that he didn't want her to find out when she inherited the contents of his safety-deposit box. He'd told her himself. That meant something.

"*Did* he like your boyfriend?" Ellie asked.

An image of her father rolling his eyes at Michael two weeks ago at his birthday dinner floated through Rebecca's mind. Her father had made a very funny political joke against Republicans, and Michael, who liked to say that he was socially liberal (which wasn't really true) and fiscally conservative, had been offended and wouldn't let it go. There'd been lots of that.

"*Your dad needs to take X, Y, or Z more seriously,*" Michael would say.

"*My dad is a successful attorney with his own firm,*" Rebecca would counter. "*He understands serious just fine.*"

"*It's a wonder his firm is still afloat with that mind-set.*"

"*Can we not diss my father, Michael?*"

"*Sometimes, Rebecca, the truth is the truth.*"

The last time her father heard the words "*It is what it is*" come out of Michael's mouth, he made a stabbing motion to his heart. Her father hated that phrase and had banned it from his office. "*It isn't always what it is,*" he'd exclaim. "*It is multi-faceted. And if you manipulate just one layer, it can change, be something else.*"

Like a pregnancy. Like a baby. Like a little person growing up. Rebecca glanced at Joy. Twenty-six years ago, her father had undone "It is what it is" to suit himself. She squeezed her eyes closed. She hated when she'd be mentally defending her father long after Michael stopped arguing his point (because he'd either gone to bed or huffed off with "You are so stubborn") only to find out that Michael wasn't entirely wrong. Or wrong at all.

Rebecca kicked at the dusty pebbles lining the edge of the wooden railing. "My father *did* like Michael—well, he appreciated how earnest and responsible he is. He thought Michael was a little uptight, maybe. That he could have used a sense of humor."

"I think Maggie's theory is right," Ellie said. "Your dad

wanted you to know you don't have to settle for Michael, that you're not all alone in the world. That is *so* touching."

"Not from my perspective," Joy said quietly.

It was as though they'd forgotten her in the equation.

"But now you have a sister," Ellie said. "You went from being an only child to having a sister."

"Same here," Rebecca said.

"God, I would kill for a sister," Maggie added. "I wouldn't be such a lunatic if I had a sister to tell everything to."

"We're not *really* sisters," Joy said. "We have the same biological father, a man I never met and who's now dead. That doesn't make me and Rebecca sisters. It makes us related by DNA."

"It makes you sisters," Ellie whispered in Rebecca's ear.

Joy had said no to coffee, a drink, tea in the parlor at the bed-and-breakfast, and Scrabble. Ellie and Maggie had given up and whispered in Rebecca's ear, "She'll come around."

And so they'd gone back to the hotel and said their good nights (Rebecca and Joy with an awkward smile). Rebecca's friend Charlotte called, dying to hear the news about Joy and how things had gone, and Rebecca filled her in on everything.

"So you two are developing a relationship," Charlotte said excitedly. "That's great, Rebecca. I can totally understand why you want to stay up there a little longer. Don't listen to Michael. Do what you need to. Okay?"

"Okay," she said. "And thanks, Charlotte."

After they hung up, Rebecca changed into yoga pants and

a long-sleeved T-shirt, pulled her hair into a ponytail, and then slid beneath the heavy quilts, her eyes on the sliver of moon through the filmy white curtains on the window. She couldn't sleep, and so started counting sheep, but all the fuzzy little white cartoon sheep in her mind, the ones from the old bed commercial, had Joy's face. Last she knew, she'd counted six hundred thirty-two brown-eyed sheep with long blond hair.

At brunch, Joy announced that her personal life was off-limits as a topic for discussion, that she intended to revert to her usual professional self and would appreciate it if they'd all respect that. Rebecca had caught Maggie's *Yeah, right, professional—you mean emotionally frigid* raised eyebrow and smiled to herself. Joy ate her omelet in record time, then announced the day's activities. There was a choice of yoga, religious worship, if so inclined, and the Edward Hopper exhibit at the Portland Museum of Art. Then free time until the group met back at the lobby for checkout and the return home.

Victor and Victoria chose their room for more nookie. Clinton hadn't made an appearance. Joy said she was going to church. "Hopper or yoga?" Ellie asked Rebecca and Maggie.

"Yoga stresses me out," Maggie said.

Rebecca smiled. "Me too."

While buying a poster of a Hopper she loved, she realized she'd chosen it without considering—as she usually did—whether or not it would go with Michael's black leather and chrome.

• • •

Since Rebecca had driven her rental car to Portland, she would have to say her good-byes to the group at the hotel. With Styrofoam coffee cups in one hand and travel bags in the other, everyone stood outside, the spectacular September sunshine and warm breeze too good to miss out on. Victor and Victoria, unable to remove their hands from each other, hugged Rebecca in unison. Clinton poked his head out from behind the *Portland Press Herald* for a quick "Oh. Bye." And Maggie and Ellie each wrapped Rebecca in a fierce hug.

"Well," Rebecca said to Joy.

"Well," Joy said.

"So . . ." Rebecca began, but had no idea what to say. *What happens from here?*

"Okay, we're off," Joy announced with a final glance at Rebecca, then led the group to the parking garage. Rebecca had parked in a different one around the corner, and so that was that.

Ellie turned around and waved, then Maggie did, and Rebecca almost burst into tears. She wanted to run after them, stay with them, stay in their big, messy circle. Rebecca watched Joy's blond ponytail swing as she walked away.

Rebecca stood alone on Commercial Street, a big white seagull swooping at her feet for some spilled popcorn. When the last of the popcorn was gone, she had to face facts that there was no reason to stand there and stare at the ground.

Now what?

To have something sturdy to do, she retrieved her car, paid the ridiculously low parking fee, and followed the attendant's directions to I-295. It was Sunday at 3:00 p.m. If she drove straight home right now, she could make it to New York around ten, depending on traffic. She could "swing things" back her way with Michael. She could get a good night's sleep and arrive at nine sharp at Whitman, Goldberg & Whitman. She could do all that for the rest of her life. She could just float along instead of creating the current. She couldn't imagine going back to her job. Back to the noise and traffic and eight million people. Back to the lack of her father.

"Your dad wanted you to know you don't have to settle for Michael, that you're not all alone in the world. . . ."

At the traffic light, she could take 295 South to head to New York.

Or 295 North to Wiscasset.

The light turned green, but she didn't move. She glanced in her rearview mirror and realized there was a car behind her, waiting—patiently—for her to go. No honk. In New York, everyone in line would be pressing on their horns. Maine was a place where you could think, take your time.

It was where her half sister was.

Rebecca turned on her left blinker, the clickety-clicking and the tiny green blinking a comfort. She went North.

eight

The delicious smell of something baking—pumpkin pie?—and the on-again-off-again whir of a power saw greeted Rebecca when she came through the front door of Finch's Seaside Inn. After a weekend away, the old yellow Victorian felt familiar, felt like home. Rebecca knew which winding hallways, with their faded pink and orange runners, led to the reading parlor, the "media" parlor, the big country kitchen without a hint of granite or stainless steel, and the glorious backyard with its hammocks and wildflowers and birdhouses.

She followed the scent of pumpkin and, Rebecca could now hear, the strains of a Beyoncé song. The narrow hallway to the kitchen was lined—floor to ceiling—with photographs of people, landscapes, and animals, in frames of all shapes and sizes. There were framed children's paintings and drawings as well. The stairway wall in the house Rebecca had grown up in was similarly covered with photographs and several Rebecca Strand originals.

Marianne, in jeans and a hot-pink apron with a tiny cartoon

moose, her shiny gray hair in a low bun at her nape, stood at the stove, stirring a huge pot with a long wooden spoon. She was swaying her hips to the music. On the tiled counter were two trays of Marianne's famed whoopie pies, those little round cream-filled sandwich cakes. Rebecca remembered seeing Marianne's whoopie pies for sale on the counter at Mama's, the cellophane wrapping with its Finch's Famed Whoopie Pies sticker and tied with a red and white polka-dotted ribbon.

The idea of starting her own kitchen-based business in a small town in Maine suddenly seemed not only enchanting but entirely possible. Not that Rebecca knew how to bake. She once sliced refrigerated premade cookie dough and baked the cookies for exactly the time on the label, but they came out both undercooked and burned at the same time.

"Ooh, Rebecca, I didn't even hear you come in. Be my taster, will you? I'm working on a new filling." Marianne dipped a spoon into one of the many pots on the stove. She held it out to Rebecca. "What do you think?"

"I knew I smelled pumpkin," Rebecca said. "Mmmm, wonderful. Just delicious."

She felt her smile fade. Thanksgiving was coming. She'd never gotten used to celebrating the holiday without her mother. The sight of a roast turkey ready for carving on a pretty platter used to make her cry. A bite of stuffing, even when it wasn't the bacon-and-sausage-enhanced perfection of her mother's, would bring forth Norah Strand's face. And a glance around the table would remind her that her mother wasn't there, would never be there. Now her father would never be there, either.

The day that Michael's mother had come down to visit, the day she'd given her the wedding gown, she'd told Rebecca she'd be happy to whip up Thanksgiving dinner in Rebecca and Michael's apartment and then pack it all up and serve it in her father's hospital room. They could bring in a large folding table, a beautiful tablecloth, and Glenda Whitman's good china, and set up a cozy dining room around her father's bed.

That was kindness.

Rebecca hadn't mentioned Glenda Whitman's offer to Michael; in the wake of her father's confession about the affair, about the baby, she'd forgotten all about it. And then he was gone.

Michael wouldn't have come right out and said, *"That would be depressing, no? To have Thanksgiving dinner in a hospital room? Why don't we bring him a plate—two helpings, even—after we've eaten."* But she knew he'd think it. Michael would have his meal in room 8–401 of New York-Presbyterian Hospital, smile through it, clink cider cups with her dad, and maybe even give a heartfelt toast. But what was unspoken— *That antiseptic smell is overpowering . . . all the IVs are ruining my appetite . . .* would shout in Rebecca's ear.

"I did mention the price cut of the room included construction noise, right?" Marianne called over the whir of the power saw, shooting Rebecca a smile. "Putting up with the saws and hammering will be worth the back porch and deck for next spring and summer, though." Marianne filled a thermos with coffee and added milk and sugar. "Do me a favor, Rebecca? Will you bring one of these whoopie pies and this thermos of coffee to Theo? He's been working for hours, poor dear. If you go out the front door and around back, you'll find him. When you come back, the pumpkin mixture should be ready. I'll make you up a special one."

Theo was here? Rebecca could use a bit of his wisdom.

"More than worth the noise," Rebecca said, taking the whoopie pie and the thermos and heading out the kitchen's back door. Once again, the evergreens and the oaks—were they oaks? Rebecca didn't know much about trees—stopped her in her tracks. She breathed in the clean scent of nature, of trees and grass and birds and butterflies.

Theo, in a black T-shirt and faded army green cargo pants, kneeled on the foundation of the deck, hammering. The sun lit his sandy blond hair. She watched him until she realized he would catch her staring.

"Hey," she said.

He turned and his warm, genuine smile sent little goose bumps popping up along her arms. "Noise too much?" he asked. "I'd think a woman from New York City would be used to noise worse than this, but I guess you stop hearing it there."

"About an hour ago I was daydreaming at a red light," Rebecca said, "and when it turned green, the person behind me didn't honk. That would never happen in New York."

"They don't put 'Vacationland' on our license plates for nothing."

She smiled and held up what was in her hands. "Marianne asked me to bring you coffee and a whoopie pie."

He jumped down from the platform. "Time for a break, then." He sat, then patted the place next to him. "Give you half." He held up the whoopie pie.

"I'll take you up on that." She sat down beside him. She was so aware of him, of his nearness, of his thigh so close to hers. "I just tasted her pumpkin pie filling. Hope I don't get too hooked."

"Vacationland, remember?" he said, splitting the little round cake as best he could. He licked a bit of white cream from his thumb.

Rebecca took a nibble. "I don't even know if I'm on vacation. I don't know what to call this. A leave of absence from my life, maybe."

"Most people should take those every now and then," he said, those deep brown eyes on her for a moment. "So, how's that hypothetical situation going?"

Rebecca stared up at the trees, where the pines met the sky. "Well, unhypothetically speaking, I just don't know where to go from here. This person—who I didn't know existed a week ago—is my half sister. My *sister*. That word has to mean something."

"In and of itself?"

She glanced at him. Those had been Joy's words, too. "Well, shouldn't it? The word *does* mean something. I know my *father* wasn't a father to her, though. So that word has a very different meaning to her than to me. I suppose the word *sister* is no different."

"Except you're here. That's a big difference between you and your father—to her, I mean. Words in and of themselves don't have weight. It's how they're backed up and supported."

"I just wish she'd let me near her," Rebecca said. She watched the smallest bird she'd ever seen teeter at the entrance to one of the many birdhouses dotting the backyard. "She's opened the door a teeny, tiny crack."

"That's all you need."

"I wish I knew what to do, how to proceed with her."

"You could suggest a walk around the park path at Hazy Beach. You can even sneak down through these trees," he said, pointing straight ahead. "Bring one of Marianne's killer whoopie pies and a thermos of coffee and two cups, and you're set."

"I can't see Joy agreeing to a picnic."

"Ah, Joy Jayhawk. I don't know her very well, but I've worked jobs with her husband. He's an architect. He designed this addition, in fact."

"What's he like?"

"Good guy. Strong-and-silent type. Seems to love his kid like crazy."

"Do you have kids?"

He laughed. "Me, no. I don't even have a wife."

"Girlfriend?" she asked, then turned red and slapped her hand over her mouth.

He laughed again. "I will say there are a couple of women I see now and again, but no one's set my heart on fire."

"The last time someone set my heart on fire I was seventeen," she said.

"So no boyfriend? I'm surprised."

She couldn't help the smile at the compliment. "I actually do have a boyfriend. A live-in one named Michael back in New York. But he might be dating someone else." She let out a deep breath. Why in the world had she said that? "This will be a nice place to sit outside. I can see sitting here with tea and a book, nothing but trees and birdhouses and nature."

Theo was about to say something, but Rebecca's cell phone rang, the silly chimes more shrill to her ears than the power saw had been.

What timing. Michael. The universe worked like that. She wondered if it were telling her something, making a point.

"I'll let you take that," Theo said. "I'd better get back to work."

Don't go, she thought. He was so easy to talk to.

But he was already back where he was when she'd first come out, his attention on the smooth, unfinished wood. The sudden absence of him was like the sun moving behind a cloud.

"Thanks for sharing your whoopie pie," she said.

He flashed a smile. "Anytime."

Her phone rang its chimes over and over. Once she was around the side of the house, she answered, heading through the front door to her room.

"I'll assume you're on I-95 somewhere in Connecticut, due back in about two hours," came Michael's voice.

"I'm in Wiscasset."

Silence. Then a sigh. Then: "So you won't be at the office tomorrow."

"Michael, I told you, I need a little more time with Joy. Can't you understand that?"

"Actually, no. I honestly don't get what you're staying up there for. You've spent some time with Joy. You can make plans to visit again. You can email and call. But you have a life here. You have a job and a boyfriend and an apartment."

"A boyfriend who likes someone else," she reminded him.

"She's just a friend, Rebecca. I haven't crossed any lines."

She sat down in the rocking chair by the window and glanced out at the trees. "I'm just not ready to come home, not until I . . . establish something with Joy, I guess. That's all I know. I want to get to know Joy up here, on her turf."

"Or maybe you're just running away," he said. "Things got tough at work, things aren't so hot between us, so off you go. I'd think if you'd learned anything with your work in mediation it's that running isn't the answer."

She hated when he pulled that. The condescension. The *I know better.* And she didn't like the lingering threat: *Come home or it'll be your fault that I sleep with another woman.*

"Becs, I know you're grieving. I know you miss your dad. But his illegitimate daughter isn't a connection to him. They never knew each other."

"They will through me," she said.

"Please, Rebecca. That's not why you're staying."

No, it wasn't. She was staying because everything inside her—heart, mind, and soul—was telling her to.

In the morning, after a bracing walk around the village, Rebecca called Joy.

"You're still here?"

"Oh. You're not going home yet?"

"Sorry, I'm really busy this week."

"No, I really can't slip away for even a cup of coffee. No, Rex is in preschool, so he couldn't join us, anyway."

And then: "Rebecca, look, you sprang yourself on me two days ago. I just spent the weekend with you. Give me some space. Maybe in time I'll want to talk. I don't know."

Click.

A moment later: "I'm sorry I hung up on you. Okay?"

Click.

Okay. And yes, time. Time, time, time. *Time* was the answer. The word, so vague, so indefinite yet so sturdy, gave her something to hang on to. There was a lot she could do to fill the time between, too. She could crack open one of the many guidebooks to exploring Maine that filled the bookcases of the common room. Or a novel. She could take up knitting. Italian cooking. Italian.

Rebecca flopped down on her bed and stared at the pretty pattern of wallpaper, the most delicate, faded of cabbage roses.

Why *was* she staying? Because Joy was her *sister.* Because that word *did* mean something in and of itself. Because it did and didn't, didn't and did. Because Joy was this walking, talking, living and breathing tangible connection to her. A fuzzy connection, maybe, like when an ice storm messes with the cable wires.

She was giving herself a headache. She needed to get out of this room, away from these four walls, however soothing the pale apricot cabbage roses, and somehow internalize this strange new something, this strange new nothing.

I Am Here and Here Is Where? was a game she used to play on long road trips with her parents. "*I am here and here is where?*" she'd ask while peering out the window of their blue car, her parents turning around to smile at seven-, eight-, nine-year-old Rebecca taking an interest in geography by reading the huge, green highway signs. Mystic, Connecticut. Woodstock, New York. Entering here. Exiting there.

Here, at the moment, was her room at the inn. *Go ask Marianne if she needs help with dusting or whipping up a batch of some exotic new flavor for whoopie pie filling,* she told herself.

"Hello?" came a muted voice as Rebecca put a dark green sweater over her tank top and slipped into her Danskos. "Hello?"

She opened her door and peeked down the hall. Ellie, in red Crocs and a tan trench coat, stood in the foyer, her face crumpling. Were those mascara tracks down her cheeks?

Rebecca rushed toward her. "Ellie, what's wrong?"

"Nothing, I just thought I'd come say hi. I remembered you mentioning you were staying here," she said, then burst into tears.

Rebecca led Ellie inside her room and sat her down on the rocking chair. She grabbed the box of tissues from the bathroom and handed them to Ellie, then sat down across from her on the edge of her bed.

"Tim?" Rebecca asked.

Ellie dabbed under her red-rimmed eyes with a tissue. "Why aren't I enough? That's what I want to know?" She dissolved in tears and slumped down in the chair.

Rebecca's heart squeezed. Oh, Ellie.

"I don't understand what I'm supposed to do to be what he wants," she said, sniffling, her eyes pooling with tears.

"You can only be you, honey," Rebecca said. "And you're great."

"Tim doesn't think so."

"He married you," Rebecca pointed out.

"So why aren't I enough?"

Rebecca wished she had the magic answer for that. And she hated giving Ellie the standard but true answer.

"It's not about you, Ellie. You know that, right?"

"Of course it's about me. If I were more something, *something,* we wouldn't have all these stupid problems. He wouldn't cheat."

"Ellie, you know that's not true, really, right?"

"Then what am I supposed to do to save my marriage? If it's not me, I can't fix it, can't change it. If it *is* me, I can. I can stop nagging so much. I can get my boobs done. I can go blond. I can stop getting into stupid arguments with his moronic mother. Whatever. But if it's not me, I can't do anything about it. It's out of my hands. I need it to be about me so I can change things."

"But you can't change *him.* Only he can do that."

She let out a deep breath and stared at the ceiling. "He came over last night. At around midnight. Pathetic, I know. I called him and told him I didn't want to talk, I just wanted us to be together. So he said okay and came over. And so I changed into something sexy and turned off the lights and lit the candles and put on Kid Rock, who he loves, and we had the most amazing night. It was like when we first started dating. So romantic. And then in the morning—"

She burst into tears again.

"And then in the morning what?" Rebecca asked gently.

"Well, I made us breakfast—a real breakfast, eggs, bacon,

the works. I even slipped out to the store for orange juice because I know he loves it. And he wakes up to the smell of bacon frying, his favorite smell, and he says he can't stay, he's going fishing with his friends. So I say fine, eat fast, and then come over after, and he says he doesn't know with this big pause. So I tell him I want us to work on this marriage, that we have to work on it. And he said it shouldn't be such hard work. And when I told him that marriage *is* hard work, he said it shouldn't be, that his parents have been married for thirty-two years and get along just fine. Which is a total fucking joke, by the way. His parents hate each other's guts. Anyone with a brain can see that."

Rebecca smiled, and Ellie's face brightened for just a moment.

"So I asked him if he would do one thing for me, just this one thing, and come on Joy's Rocky Relationships Tour this weekend. Tim really likes Joy and Harry, he respects them, so I figured he'd at least consider it, and he said there's no way he's doing something all New Agey like that."

"Is it New Agey?" From the little Rebecca had heard about the Rocky Relationship Tour it was a camping tour of sorts, but the group would stay in a private lodge with several bedrooms. They would laze around the big room with its wood-burning stove and fireplaces, talk as a group at three designated times—after breakfast, after lunch, and after dinner—then hike the trails, or do absolutely nothing. The *nothing* was supposed to put the focus back on the individual, the couple, without the distractions of friends or buttinsky relatives. The lodge was isolated enough so that leaving on foot wasn't an option.

"Not at all. There's no Enya or meditating involved. It's just about getting away from everyday life, everyday problems. I told him it would be almost like marriage counseling, but without the therapists, which he totally isn't into. And he still said no."

"That doesn't mean he won't go, just that you need to *work* on him a little. Like you and Maggie told me about Joy: She'll come around. Tim will, too."

"You think?" Ellie asked, glancing up.

"I hope," Rebecca said. "How long have you been separated?"

"Almost two months. But he comes over a few times a week. We have sex, and I think we're going to work things out, and then it's back to the same old disappointments, same old problems. No, he's not going to some marriage counselor. No, he's not reading any self-help books. No, he's not agreeing to not going out with his asshole friends for one week."

"What's Tim like? When he's not being a jerk?"

Ellie's face brightened again. "He's wonderful. He can be so sweet and tender and funny. And just when I'm thinking I can overlook what I hate, someone will whisper in my ear, 'I saw your husband out with some bleached blond last night.'"

"Maybe you can't overlook what you hate," Rebecca said. "Maybe you shouldn't."

"I know. That's why I went on the singles tour. To force my-self to accept that he's cheating. That *he* walked away from this marriage. I know I should move on. I know being with Tim means nothing but heartache. I know, I know, I know. But knowing doesn't seem to help."

"Is the heartache mostly to do with the cheating or were there big problems before that?"

"Well, I didn't know he was cheating for a while. Before I caught on, we argued about everything—what to spend money on, how much to save, if he should go out practically every night after work with his stupid friends and get rip-roaring trashed. Do you know that the last time he went out with those morons one got so drunk that he misaimed a metal dart and it hit someone in the back of the neck?"

"Maybe it's time for an ultimatum," Rebecca said, handing Ellie another tissue.

"I've tried those. A million times. He gets all scared and comes rushing back, promising me things will be different, and they are for a week. Then it's back to his old ways. Maybe I just have to accept him the way he is. If I love him. That's what my mother-in-law says. 'Men are men,'" she added in a singsong voice. "'Like the famous saying goes, it's the wife's job to be a cook in the kitchen, a hostess in the living room, and a whore in the bedroom, all while not nagging about nonsense like socks on the floor and keeping her figure nice and slim.'"

"Your mother-in-law actually said that? She sounds worse than Maggie's!"

Ellie nodded, then laughed. "The only good point about my marriage ending is that she goes with the marriage." Ellie sobered up fast. "I don't want a divorce, though. I want my husband. But I want him different. I want him to be like the guy he was when—"

"What?"

"I was gonna say like when I married him, but he wasn't

so different. I just thought marriage would change him. That he'd settle down. God, I'm such a stupid cliché."

"No, you're just a woman in love with her husband. A woman who wants her marriage to work."

Ellie let out a deep breath. "I think he might do Joy's tour. If I tell him this is it, this is our last chance to try and fix this marriage or I'm filing for divorce. He doesn't want a divorce. He doesn't even want to be separated. He just wants to do what he wants and have me, too. Please, please, please tell me you'll come, Rebecca. Joy is great at getting conversations started and opening dialogues, as she calls it. But you're the expert. You have to come. You can really guide us."

Rebecca would love to go. To see if she could really think about a career in counseling, if going to graduate school wouldn't be a waste of her paralegal certificate. And to spend the weekend with Joy again, in a setting of sharing and opening up, could do wonders for their stalled relationship. But Rebecca couldn't imagine Joy suddenly saying, *"Sure, stick around even longer, listen to my most innermost problems and the details of my marriage."*

"Ellie, I would love to, really, but I don't think Joy wants me sticking around until the weekend."

"I'll bet she wants you to come. She might not be able to handle one-on-one with you yet, but she seems comfortable with group stuff. She asked you to come this past weekend, didn't she?"

She did. That was something. Something big. It wasn't just an impersonal cup of coffee at Starbucks. It was a weekend away with her *friends.* The Wiscasset Divorced Ladies Club wasn't made up of random singles who Joy barely knew. These women had known about Joy's father. They knew about her marriage. And however grudgingly, Joy had invited Rebecca to come on their weekend away.

"I'll ask her," Rebecca said. "But I can't promise anything."

Ellie nodded. "If she says okay, will you go? We really need you. Not just me and Tim, but Joy and Harry, too. You're a divorce mediator from New York City. That'll mean something to Tim and Harry. They'll respect what you have to say."

Whoa. Joy and Harry were *both* going? Rebecca hadn't known that.

But still. "Ellie, I'm not a mediator. I'm not a therapist. I'm a *paralegal*. And given that I didn't show up at work this morning after a week of bereavement leave, I'm very likely going to be an unemployed paralegal."

Ellie shook her head. "Experience is experience," she said. "Right?"

After Ellie left, with two of Marianne's whoopie pies in her hands and an assurance to knock on Rebecca's door anytime, day or night, Rebecca called Joy.

"I'm not calling to ask you to coffee for the hundredth time, I promise," Rebecca said. She explained about Ellie, about the Rocky Relationships Tour. "I'd like to come, if it's okay with you. Maybe I really can help."

Silence.

And I think it could help me, help me figure out what I'm supposed to be doing with my life when everything waiting for me in New York feels so wrong.

"Ah, I just realized you must think I'm a total idiot for thinking I can help when we haven't even talked about what you envision. I heard a bit about what you're planning, and Ellie filled me in, but—"

"No, it's not that."

Rebecca waited for what it was, but Joy didn't say anything. "I think the tour would help me, too," she rushed to say. "I know what I *don't* want to do with my life is help couples divorce—even nicely. And that's been my job for the past two years. I want to help couples *not* divorce. I want to help them work toward reconciliation, toward what made them fall in love in the first place, toward how to honor that every day while dealing with everyday crap. If that's what you envision for the Rocky Relationships Tour, then I do think I can bring something to the table."

Silence. Perhaps Joy didn't go for corporate speak.

Rebecca let out a silent sigh of frustration. *You are emotionally frigid,* she wanted to scream. *Respond! Say something! Get all pissed off the way you did in Portland. Tell me to go away.*

But don't really tell me that.

"Well, why don't you think about it and let me know," Rebecca said, liking the idea of Joy having to call Rebecca one way or another.

"Actually, I do think you'd be a big help on the tour. You're more than welcome to come."

Rebecca's heart leaped. She closed her eyes and sat down on the edge of her bed, relief flooding through her. She now had a purpose, a defined reason to stay through the coming weekend.

And she would get to know Joy on a whole new level.

"And I have no idea if what I do envision is even going to work," Joy added. "This is the first time I'm leading this type of tour. And I'm one of the participants. So this is new territory for me, too. Weird territory. If I envision anything, it's three couples—well, three if Tim agrees to go—being away from the distractions of their everyday life, with a little shop talk, a little relaxing, a little enforced time together. But considering I am one of the participants, I think having someone impartial, someone with experience with warring couples, would be great."

"So I'm hired?" Rebecca asked.

"You're hired. Not that I can pay you."

Rebecca laughed. "I know."

"Your room at the lodge will be covered, of course, since you'll be working, really."

"That's okay, Joy. I'll pay my own way."

Joy let out a deep breath. "I was hoping you'd say that. Ever since Harry moved downstairs, I've been using only my own mon—" Dead silence. "Ugh, see, you *are* good at getting people to say things they don't mean to or don't want to. I have to go. The group is meeting at my house on Friday at six thirty."

"You won't be sorry," Rebecca said as though Joy had just hired her for the job of her dreams. "I know this isn't . . . easy for you. Having me drop on your head at all, let alone when you're going through a separation of sorts, and—"

"So there'll be three couples on the tour," Joy interrupted, the sharp edge in her tone saying, *Back off, chickie. We're not on the bus yet.*

"Three couples sounds manageable. So you and Harry, Ellie and Tim, and another couple?"

"The Cutlasses. Aimee and Charles. I don't know them—well, I know Aimee from the library, she's one of the librarians. I don't know if you've been over there—she's the tall, slender redhead? Anyway, I don't know her very well. She saw one of my flyers posted. I've never met her husband. We'll all meet at my house on Friday for a brief hello and then take the minibus to the lodge."

"I'm looking forward to it," Rebecca said. "I really think I can do some good."

"See you Friday." Click.

Purpose! Rebecca leaped up and looked in her closet for a weekend's worth of outfits befitting a . . . what should she call herself exactly? She didn't think throwing the words *divorce mediation paralegal* would ease the anxiety of the men on the trip. *Divorce* was a big ugly scary word, but then again, perhaps that word would scare everyone into paying attention to their marriages since the alternative was so bleak. And mediation was a word that required definition. No one ever seemed to know what a paralegal did, so that was helpful.

I help couples reach agreements. That was what she did, what she liked to do, what eased something in her own heart.

As Rebecca was wondering if a tweed skirt was too therapisty and too much for a Maine camping lodge, the phone rang.

Please don't be Joy rescinding, Rebecca thought.

It *was* Joy. Rebecca held her breath.

Joy cleared her throat three times before the rush of words finally came out. "My mother and stepfather are coming this weekend to babysit Rex while Harry and I are gone on the tour. If you happen to see her on Friday at my house when the group gathers, I would appreciate it if you didn't let her know who you are. I'll tell her about you when I'm ready."

Pia Jayhawk. Rebecca wondered how she'd feel when she saw her, if she'd feel anything. If she'd understand something then she couldn't now.

"Okay," Rebecca said. She wasn't so sure she'd be able to even speak to the woman, let alone introduce herself. *"Hi, I'm Rebecca Strand. You had an affair with my father twenty-six years ago. Remember?"*

"I have your word?"

Does my word mean something to you? she wanted to ask. "You have my word."

"Thanks," she said, and hung up.

A chill seemed to seep through Rebecca's room, moving inside her sweater, into her skin, into her bones. She wasn't even so sure she wanted to meet Pia Jayhawk, look upon her, this woman who'd had an affair with her father, a married man, a married man with a child.

Pia was the "other woman" in this scenario. Yet she'd somehow become the "victim," the scorned woman, the woman left alone and pregnant.

Because Rebecca's mother had been none the wiser till the day she died? Because more than twenty-five years had passed? Because circumstance was circumstance?

Because things were . . . relative. Nothing minimized Pia Jayhawk's experience as a woman who'd faced pregnancy alone. Who'd raised a child alone.

Suddenly, Rebecca was consumed with the idea of knowing everything there was to know about Pia Jayhawk. She glanced at the leather box of letters on her bedside table, the box she hadn't opened in days. Perhaps there was something in there about Pia. How the affair had started. Why her father had fallen for Pia. What was so special about her that it trumped his feelings for her mother.

And how that worked.

Maybe it would unlock the mystery of why people cheated in the first place.

Rebecca was pretty sure she knew the answer to that one, though: because. A shrug of the shoulders.

There was no real answer. It wasn't about having a hotter body or an interest in parasailing. Why people didn't cheat was a lot easier to answer: because the couple was committed to each other, plain and simple.

If her father had been committed to her mother, to their relationship, their marriage, their vows, he might have enjoyed a boosting conversation with Pia Jayhawk, but he wouldn't have touched her, wouldn't have kissed her that first time. There would have been no first time. His strongest impulse would have been to his marriage, to his wife.

Instead, at a particular moment, there was a stronger impulse, and he gave in to it.

You didn't have to, though.

Rebecca just wasn't sure what it meant for those who did. And how many divorces had Rebecca worked on in which adulterous spouses had been forgiven? What broke up the marriages 98 percent of the time was that one spouse wanted out.

Rebecca bit her lip. She knew nothing about marriage. She'd never been married herself, so who did she think she was, claiming to be able to help couples in trouble?

Maybe there were answers in her father's letters, something that would help her make some sense of all this . . . mishmash. Wrong, right, right, wrong.

There was an outside temperature gauge on the tree outside Rebecca's window. Sixty-one degrees. Hammock weather. She made a cup of tea, shoved the leather box in her tote bag, and put on a chunky Shetland sweater to ward off the chill that wouldn't leave, then headed outside to the hammock on the far left side of the backyard.

It was blessedly quiet. No sawing. No hammering. No Theo. Just the ever-present chirping of birds and the occasional sound of a passing car. Someone had ingeniously hung a little shelf onto the tree bark over the hammock so that Rebecca had somewhere to rest her tea. She settled herself in the hammock, the box beside her. She skimmed through the letters, looking for more than a casual mention of "your mother."

And then Rebecca found what she was looking for.

Dear Joy,

You're eighteen years old. My God. You're an adult. How did that happen? How did the years pass like this? On the one hand, I've been waiting anxiously for this day, wondering if this is the day you'll try to track me down, come look for me. I suppose you could have done that before, but something about being eighteen, a full-fledged adult, makes it seem more likely. Or something I could

imagine a teenager saying: "When I turn eighteen, I'm
gonna look for my father."

Of course, I don't know if you ever said that, if you
even want to find me. And if you did come knocking at
my door, I wonder how I'd react. If I'd do like I did to your
mother when she told me you were born. If I'd close the
door as though you weren't standing there. I suppose I'd
still be scared, of the weight of you, of how Rebecca would
feel.

You two could be sisters. Are sisters. And yet you don't
even know of each other's existence. Well, you might know
of her existence. I've always wondered what your mother
shared with you about me. If you know you have a sister,
two years older.

Rebecca let the letter flutter down to her stomach. She
stared up at the cotton-candy-white clouds, at their slow drift
across the blue sky.

Had Joy known that Rebecca existed? Had her mother told
her that her father had a wife and another daughter?

Had Joy grown up knowing she had a sister, a half sister, out
there somewhere?

Why hadn't she asked Joy that question?

Because something told Rebecca that Joy *had* known, had
grown up knowing. And she couldn't imagine what that felt
like, the awareness of something so solid, a *sister*, somewhere
on Earth. The knowledge of it these past weeks had given Rebecca a certain strength: I have a sister.

She wondered if Joy had felt that her entire life, when she

was sad or troubled, that she had this guardian angel looking out for her.

Or maybe Joy had just felt the emptiness of it all. The nothingness. The unsisterness.

A breeze fluttered the letter off her stomach, and Rebecca grabbed it before it was carried away. She took a deep breath and read.

I've held back from talking much about your mother and our relationship because I didn't think it would be fair to you, but now that you are eighteen, I think it's okay. I can't imagine you've heard much about me from Pia, but then again, I didn't know her that long or necessarily very well. I felt like I knew her, though.

And something tells me she didn't share much about me with you. Likely because she felt she made a very big mistake in falling for me, and who wants their father to have been a mistake? No, I can't see that she'd tell you what a jerk and an idiot I was. She saw something in me, something about me captivated her, her—this beautiful free spirit. Apparently, I made her laugh. Me, a short Jewish lawyer from Noo Yawk.

I know you're probably thinking, "Yeah, right," like there's anything funny about what I did. On both counts. Having an affair with Pia and then just turning my back on her. If it helps, which I'm sure it won't, I knew Pia would be all right. Your grandparents are gold. I met them once, just once, and of course they didn't know about me and Pia, but they were such warm, friendly people. I had

no doubt they'd help her, see her through. That eased things in me, somewhat.

The first time I saw her was on the beach in Wiscasset, way down by the old pier where no one much goes. I'd gotten into a big argument with my wife, and Rebecca was throwing some kind of wild tantrum, and I'd slammed out of the cottage and gone for a walk, ending up on the desolate stretch down by the old pier, where it's all seaweed. I was throwing shells into the water, pissed off that they were so light and wouldn't go very far.

And all of a sudden, a woman said, "Try this," and I turned around, and there was a Madonna look-alike, you know, with the crazy cut-up black clothes and wild hair and hundreds of silver bangles. She handed me a rock that she said she'd found up along the path. She said she was planning to paint it, its jagged perfection, but she thought the heft of it would be of more use to me.

So she put it in my hand, and she had this crazy black nail polish on her fingers—I remember that so vividly—and I was about to throw it, but it felt so good, just to hold, and I gave it back to her. And she said something like "Rough day in the office?" I guess making fun of my khaki pants or whatever, and we just walked and walked and talked and talked. We talked about everything, and the chemistry between us surprised us both.

How I made her laugh that day! She was laughing when I kissed her for the first time. She was laughing that big, crazy laugh of hers and I just turned and stopped and kissed her, and there was no hesitation, not a moment's.

And she kissed me back. We stood there and kissed for like an hour by that rotting old pier. We didn't talk much after that, we just held hands and walked and kissed, then we stopped and sat and watched the ocean and each other. Have you ever had a relationship that didn't require any talking at all? Like you could answer all your problems, all your questions by just looking into someone's eyes? That's how it was that day.

We made plans to meet that night, same spot, and it's there that we . . . were together for the first time. We met every day for the rest of the two weeks I was there. And when it was time to go home, I imagined keeping the relationship going on vacations, a "this time next year" type of thing.

We spoke a few times on the phone once I was back home. But whatever strain there'd been between me and Norah—that's Rebecca's mother—had been mended somewhat, almost like that affair gave me myself back. I don't know if this makes any sense. I told Pia I cared for her but that I wanted to save my marriage and that I didn't think we should talk anymore. She was gracious, not that I gave her much time to say anything. Six weeks later, I heard her voice again, alerting me to the pregnancy. I just went numb and dumb and didn't say a word. And finally she hung up. And then, eight months later, she called to tell me you were born and that her parents helped her buy a little blue Cape in town on Maple Drive and that's where she would be. I thanked her for informing me and that was that. I closed my mind to

it, and it's amazing how the mind can shut down, close itself off to what it can't handle. What it doesn't want to handle, I should say.

I'm sorry, Joy. I didn't do the right thing. And now that you're eighteen, now that you'll be finding your own man to marry one of these days, I hope my actions don't bear any weight, that you don't make choices based on what I did or didn't do. I hope you choose a good guy, someone who'll love you like crazy and stand by you through thick and thin.

Happy eighteenth birthday, Joy.

—Daniel Strand

Rebecca shoved the letter back in its envelope and stuck it in between the others. All she could think was, if she hadn't had a tantrum that day, her father might not have stormed out of the house and therefore been on the beach at the very moment that Pia Jayhawk had been out looking for the perfect rock to paint.

And as love stories went, it wasn't so great. So they had chemistry. So they talked and talked. So they kissed. BFD.

She watched a drifting cloud, sure she could lie there for the rest of her life and watch it. She didn't get it, didn't get how her father had fallen for a total stranger dressed like Madonna. She still couldn't understand how it happened. So they'd met on the beach, so they'd been oddly attracted to their polar opposite. Suddenly, they're making out with seaweed wrapped around their ankles? No need for words? Just staring into each other's eyes like they were fourteen?

She couldn't see it, couldn't imagine it.

What she could see, what she could imagine, was Pia in her ripped tank tops and giant, silver cross medallions, her belly getting bigger and bigger. She could see Pia, with frosted wild hair, with toe rings, standing all alone on the beach, the seaweed under her feet.

She wanted to see this place, this spot of beach where her father and Pia had met. But she had no idea where it was. That was what long walks were for.

nine

Rebecca slipped into her clogs and headed down the path Theo had told her about. She stuck to the wooden trail, not wanting to step on the sand where her father and another woman had fallen in love—if that was what happened. Was what her father described in his letter *love*? Was it something else?

She stared at the sand, the ordinary, everyday sand, and a stabbing pain of grief overtook her. She would never see her father again. And she was stuck with all of these letters, the truth of him, in these secret bits that had nothing to do with her, nothing to do with their family, their lives. The letters, Joy, Pia Jayhawk—they were all so outside of Rebecca. Outside of everything she knew and understood.

And yet they were what was left, they were what *was*. Perhaps that was why she wasn't ready to go home. Because the secret bits were here, here on this beach, here in this town in Maine. In New York, she would be among the familiar, her father's truth creeping into her heart and stomach as she

walked down the street, as she tried to work, as she tried to
sleep.

She needed to understand, to settle something inside her.
And then she'd be able to go home.

Way up ahead, a man threw a stick and his little brown dog
raced after it, his wagging brown tail making Rebecca smile.
She squinted against the sunlight as she watched the dog jump
high in the air to catch the stick, then scamper to return it to
the man. As she walked farther along the path, she realized it
was Theo. Wiscasset *was* a small town. She liked this, seeing
the same people everywhere she went. Especially when they
were very cute men who were so easy to talk to. When she'd
left Finch's this morning, she'd run into Arlene from Mama's,
then Maggie, who was leading her elderly grandmother into
a doctor's office. Twice, a car horn honked a hello—one was
Marianne, delivering her whoopie pies, and the other was
the antiques shop owner who lived next door to Finch's. This
was new to Rebecca, this community of hellos and honks and
waves. In New York, she never ran into anyone she knew, even
on her own block.

Theo's dog brought the stick to her, the tail wagging. He
was a scrappy medium-sized mutt with happy, black eyes. She
kneeled down to pet him, his comical face managing to remind her of sad-faced Bingo.

She threw the stick and the little dog went running.

"Do you have a steak in your pocket?" Theo asked as he
came over, his smile rendering her speechless for a moment.
Rebecca found herself staring at his bare feet. "Spock isn't
usually so friendly."

Rebecca laughed as the dog came trotting back over, stick in mouth. His pointy ears did give him a slightly Vulcan quality. "My dad wanted to name our dog Captain Kirk. But I was six so Bingo won." She scratched Spock under the chin and the dog rolled over, exposing his belly. Rebecca kneeled down in the sand and rubbed his pink tummy. "I forgot how much I miss having a dog."

He sat down beside her and hurled the stick, sending Spock running. "Spock doesn't take to everyone, you know. I always think a dog *knows*."

Rebecca smiled. "My dad used to say that when Bingo growled at someone he couldn't stand."

Theo leaned his face up to the sun and closed his eyes for a moment. She took the opportunity to study him, the strong lines of his nose, of his chin. The golden hair on his tanned arms, at his biceps and triceps just below the sleeves of his white T-shirt. "I've been feeding a stray for the past few days," he said as Spock returned the stick. "Scruffy little black and white mutt I've been calling Charlie. I've called the local shelters to see if anyone's reported him missing and put a few posters up, but no one's come to claim him. I'd keep him, but I can't get him to come inside. I think Spock's ears scare him. He's yours for the taking."

A little black and white dog to love sounded wonderful. But Rebecca had no idea where she'd be after Sunday. Here? New York?

So what if she'd be in New York? Dogs were allowed in her building, and permission wasn't even required if they were under twenty-five pounds. She *could* come home with a little black and white dog. Not that Michael particularly liked dogs. Or cats. Or animals in general.

"Think he's hanging around now?" she asked.

"Likely. I live about a quarter mile from here. Take a walk with me," he added, getting up. He extended his hand.

Her stomach flipped like she was sixteen and the cute boy had just asked her to the junior prom. She took his hand and he helped her to her feet. She was so conscious of him, of the way his hand had felt on hers, that she brushed sand off her butt to have something to do.

"I'm going away for the weekend, though," she told him as they headed back in the direction she'd come. "So I wouldn't be able to take him till I got back."

"Well, if you decide to take him, I'll entice him to stick around with special treats until you can pick him up."

"So you live right on the beach?" she asked. "Must be nice."

"It is. I go for very long walks with Spock without needing shoes." He wiggled his toes in the sand.

"So you know this beach pretty well, then?"

He nodded. "Had my first kiss on this beach. With a girl named Samantha. I was twelve. A few years later, I had my heart broken for the first time on this beach by a girl named Jessie. There were a lot of firsts for me here."

She squinted up in the sun at him. "So, if two people were having a clandestine affair on this beach, where would they go?"

"No one usually goes this far up over here. They call this part Seaweed Beach. There are lots of hidden spots. Sometimes I find teenagers here, doing things they shouldn't." He eyed her. "Planning to have a secret affair?"

She smiled. "Just digging into the past. My mother and father and I came up here for vacation when I was two. That's when my father met Joy's mother. He saw her for the first time on this beach. He wrote about it in a letter. I thought if I came here, maybe I'd understand something, but I don't."

"About why he strayed?"

She nodded. "It's just so . . . common. I guess I thought my parents had a fairy-tale marriage until my mother died. But if someone was able to tempt him away like that, even for a week . . . Maybe true love really is just a fairy tale."

"I know some people who've been married for forty, fifty years," he said. "They get dressed up to go to the greasy spoon diner on Sunday mornings. They're still in love. But love is hard work, period."

"I guess what short-circuits my mind is how something so temporary, like their affair, created something so permanent, like a child. I mean, a life came out of that chance meeting on the beach. A relationship that lasted two weeks had very serious repercussions." She picked up a shell and threw it. "I must sound like a naïve twelve-year-old."

"Not at all. You sound like someone who's trying to find answers. I prefer that to the head-in-the-sand trick."

"So you don't think ignorance is bliss?"

"Not remotely."

"I went on Joy's singles tour this past weekend—not as a single," she rushed to add, "but because Joy told me I could come, and I thought I'd be able to get to know her a little. And two of the singles got together, but the man told the woman, right before they were about to . . . have sex, that she shouldn't have expectations. She got all upset, and though he was basically a jerk, I guess he did do the right thing. She said she might have preferred him to say nothing, to give her that night, and let the pain come in the morning. That at least she would have gotten that perfect night."

"Doesn't sound so perfect, though. She likely dodged a bullet."

"Tell me something, Theo. Why do you think men stray? If they love their wives, I mean."

"I can't possibly answer that. I've never been married. And I've never cheated on a woman I've loved."

"Do you think you could? I mean, could you imagine it?"

"Not really."

"Me either," she said. "But it happens."

He nodded but didn't say anything else.

She wanted him to say more, to tell her about his family, his parents. That first girlfriend and the second. She wanted to know everything about him. How he liked his eggs. If he liked eggnog. Bruce Springsteen. Women who had no idea what they were doing or where they were going.

Women who had boyfriends whose mothers gave them a beautiful wedding gown.

She kicked at the sand. "Ugh. I don't know why I'm going on this weekend's tour. It's for couples in rocky relationships, and I'm supposed to be the impartial sort-of mediator, but I don't know anything! Because of my work in divorce mediation, even though I'm just a paralegal, I'm supposed to help, but what the hell do I know about marriage and how it works? Or even relationships?"

"You're in one, first of all. And you've had plenty, I assume. And anyone who's worked with divorcing couples must have plenty of experience. Plus, sounds like you and Joy will have a chance to really get to know each other."

"I hope so."

"Hey," he said, putting his fingers to his lips. "There he is. Charlie."

Rebecca glanced up at the beautiful, gray shingled cottage. Up on the deck was a small black and white dog, a cross between a Jack Russell terrier and a beagle. Its short tail wagged at the sight of Theo, yet his ears lay flat as Spock scampered along behind them.

"Why don't you go sit on the steps and let him get to know you," Theo said. "I'll put Spock inside."

Rebecca sat on the second step. The little dog watched her for a moment, then slowly approached her and sat down in front of her. She let him sniff her hand. He sat there, not moving.

"I think that's a good sign," Theo said.

"He's adorable," she said, her heart melting at his sweet face. She reached out to pet him, and he let her, then rested his chin on her hand.

Theo went inside and came back a moment later with a bowl of dog kibble, handing it to her. She put a few pieces in her palm and held it out to Charlie. The dog glanced at her with his little head tilted, then ate out of her hand and sat down beside her, resting his head on her leg.

"Do you want to play?" she asked him. "Do you like fetch?" She picked up a twig and tossed it, and Charlie went racing after it and returned it, his tail wagging.

"Oh, little cutie. You are so mine," she told him, throwing the stick again.

Theo laughed. "I'll take good care of him till you get back Sunday. But feel free to stop by and feed him or walk him until you leave. That'll give you a chance to get to know each other."

She rubbed the dog's belly. "I will. Charlie," she said. "That's his name. It just suits him."

"He does look like a Charlie. I have no idea why."

Rebecca laughed. She had a dog. She was sort of nowhere at the moment, but she had a dog. And she had somewhere to be this weekend.

She and Theo sat there on the weathered steps, trading stories about pets, and suddenly Rebecca wanted to kiss him. She wanted to kiss him so badly that her toes tingled.

And this was how it happened, she thought. You're sitting somewhere, talking to someone about the guinea pig you had when you were nine, and he's telling you about the time his pet rats disappeared for two days, and suddenly you have a stray dog in common, and even though you have a boyfriend, a serious boyfriend, a live-in boyfriend whose mother gave you her wedding gown, you have an overpowering "I must" urge to kiss another person.

But you cannot.

And so Rebecca got up and gave Charlie one last hug, told Theo she'd be by to see the dog tomorrow, and then started to walk away, but Charlie came running after her. "No, Charlie, you need to stay here."

But the dog followed her.

"Maybe Marianne will let you keep him at her place," Theo said, smiling. "I'll come by Saturday and Sunday and walk him and feed him."

"Really?" she asked. "Thanks."

And that was how Rebecca found herself walking back to her hotel with a little black and white dog named Charlie, who stopped to sniff every tree, flower, and leaf. A dog who stopped to smell the flowers was her kind of dog.

When she returned to her room at Finch's, there was a note on her door.

> Hi, Rebecca! Missed you—I realized I don't have your cell number. Can you come for dinner Wednesday? I'm just having a few people over—including Tim! Bring someone if you'd like . . . 45 Marigold Lane (white house, third on left) —Ellie (555-8259)

A dog, weekend plans, a crush, and now a dinner party invitation. Rebecca's heart leaped again, and she went in search of Marianne, who immediately said yes to letting Charlie stay and even gave Rebecca two ceramic bowls for his food and water.

The next morning, there was a blue plastic bag hanging on Rebecca's doorknob.

"What's this, Charlie?" she asked her little dog, who waited patiently at her feet after their morning walk. Inside the bag was a red collar with a silver medallion in the shape of a bone. CHARLIE was engraved on one side. Her name, REBECCA STRAND, on the other.

A note inside the bag said:

> *Rebecca, least I could do to thank you for taking the little guy. I would have had them engrave your number below his name, but I don't have your number. (I'd like it, though.) If you bring the tag into the Dog Den on Route 1, next to the flower shop, they'll engrave it at no charge. —Theo*

Rebecca's hand flew to her heart at the kindness, the thoughtfulness of the gift, of the gesture. She kneeled down to unhook the old collar and leash that Marianne had pulled out of the inn's Lost and Found for her, and attached the red collar. It looked so perfect against his short black fur with its white spots. "How about I get you a snazzy leash to match when I put my phone number on your little bone tag?" she asked Charlie, giving him a pat under his chin, his favorite area.

Unable to stop smiling, she took Charlie inside her room and he immediately curled up in his makeshift bed, an old chair cushion that Marianne had in the garage.

She called Ellie. "Ellie, I'm wondering something. Your note said I could bring someone to dinner on Wednesday. Do you know Theo Granger? He did something so nice for me," she said, explaining about Charlie and the collar, "and I thought I could thank him with an invitation to your dinner party."

It was a way of acknowledging how touched she was without repaying his thoughtfulness with something solo, like making him dinner, not that she had her own kitchen. Or taking him out to dinner.

"I know Theo. Everyone does. He's wonderful. Of course bring him. He's very single, you know."

"I'm not," Rebecca reminded her. "Well, not really."

She wasn't asking him on a date, she reminded herself. It was just a thank-you. This was a small town, and people were friendly and did this sort of thing.

She got Theo's number from Marianne. He probably wouldn't want to go. Then her problem would be solved. He did something exceptionally nice, she'd extend a dinner party invitation as a gesture of thanks, he'd decline, and they could go back to being *friends*.

"Sure, I'd love to," was his response.

This is not a date, she told herself with her face in the closet. *So stop fussing about what to wear*. Rebecca's hand kept stopping on her red wrap dress. But that was definitely a date dress. Passing it by, she grabbed her camel-colored corduroys and the cream cashmere sweater her father had given her for her birthday last year. She pulled on her brown suede boots and added the gold bangles she'd inherited from her mother. Then just a little bit of makeup.

"How do I look?" she asked Charlie, who was half napping, half eyeing her from his little cushion next to the bed. "Not trying too hard, right? I *am* going to a dinner party at someone's house. I can't show up in my yoga pants."

"Admit you like him," she could have sworn she heard Charlie say.

"I do like him." Which was why she drew the line at the spritz of Chanel N° 19. This was *not* a date. Not a date.

Yet as she left, practically skipping down the street, she also had to admit she felt like doing the Snoopy dance of happiness. She did feel happy. Because she did have the smallest of crushes on Theo or because Joy had invited her on the tour this weekend or because she had a little black and white dog to love or because she had plans tonight, with friends she had not had a week ago? All of the above, perhaps.

She stopped at Mama's, which was crowded with diners, to buy a basketful of Marianne's whoopie pies to bring to Ellie's. She would have gotten them right from Marianne, but she knew Marianne wouldn't have accepted money, and she wanted to bring at least fifteen, since she had no idea how many people were coming (she assumed eightish).

"You've cleaned me out," Arlene said. "Marianne will be thrilled. I won't tell her you bought them, though," she added with a wink. On the house, she threw in a bottle of cider she'd made herself, a new recipe she was trying out. Rebecca assured her she'd tell her everyone's honest opinion.

As Rebecca was leaving, Matteo came stomping in, slamming doors. As he rushed past Rebecca and Arlene, he slammed his fist down on the counter; the pastry platters jumped. The little restaurant went quiet.

"Matteo, honey, protect your hands," Arlene whispered.

"I don't care about my stupid hands!" the boy shouted, tears in his eyes. "I don't care if I ever play the stupid cello again!"

He went through the swinging doors into the kitchen, and Rebecca heard him thudding on the stairs.

"Uh-oh," Arlene said. "Sounds like girlfriend trouble. Times like this I really wish his father were still around."

"Where is he?" Rebecca asked. For some reason, she'd thought Arlene was a widow.

"California. He calls Matteo pretty often—a few times a week—but it's not the same as being here. Theo's talked to him before, in times of boy crisis. Maybe he can help."

"I'm seeing Theo tonight," Rebecca said, then blushed. "I mean, we're going to be at the same dinner party."

Arlene grinned. "Is that why you look so pretty? Well, then, maybe you can ask Theo to stop by tomorrow and check in on Matteo. I'll go do my best now."

"It's a promise." And with the basket of whoopie pies and a hand-labeled green bottle of cider, Rebecca continued down Ocean Avenue until she got to Theo's cottage. She'd never seen the house from the front. It was a great house, a craftsman-style bungalow, small, yet somehow majestic all the same.

She knocked, and Theo opened the door, and she almost fell off the porch. God, he was handsome. He wore a long-sleeved button-down white shirt and dark gray cargo pants. A watch with a brown leather band. And he smelled like soap, clean and fresh. In his hands were two boxes with Mama's label. Rebecca laughed and held up the basket and cider.

"Well, no shortage of dessert tonight," he said. "I got cheesecake and mud pie. You look nice," he added as they headed up the quiet, dark street. His compliment lingered in the gathering dark, the surf and the seagulls like background music in this "he's gonna kiss her" movie moment.

"Thanks. You, too," she said, and they held each other's gaze just long enough for Rebecca to know this was a date.

ten

As they walked the half mile to Ellie's, Rebecca told Theo about Matteo and his tears.

"Poor guy," Theo said. "I've been talking to him about girls for years now. Well, since he was twelve. He's had his heart broken three times and he's only seventeen. He'll be okay. He forgets how much his music means to him. It's everything, really. He's very lucky to have it."

Rebecca smiled. "He's lucky to have you, too."

"He'd prefer his father to me. We've talked a lot about that, too. My father wasn't around much at all, so I get it. And I didn't tell my mother much of anything, like Matteo. I kept things to myself."

"So how'd you get to be so good at talking about this stuff?" Rebecca asked.

"Good question. No idea. I was kind of a loner as a kid and a teenager. Made me introspective, I guess." He stopped in front of Ellie's beautiful white Greek Revival house with an impressive entry porch adorned by four white pillars. Narrow black-shuttered windows framed the red-painted door. "Here we are."

Rebecca stared up at the gorgeous home. "I can't believe Ellie has this huge house all to herself."

"Not the whole house. It's broken into four apartments. Many of the huge houses you see around are actually apartment buildings, or have an 'in-law' apartment attached to the main house."

"Ah," Rebecca said, recalling her first day in Wiscasset, when the Love Bus had picked up Ellie and she'd watched Tim come down wooden steps from a second-story landing. Theo led the way to the side entrance and rang the bell.

Ellie, decked out in a slinky red dress with black heels, opened the door and glanced past Rebecca and Theo down the steps. "I was hoping you were Tim. Not that I'm not thrilled to see you both," she added with a smile. "Rebecca and Theo are here, everyone!" she called over her shoulder as she carried in their desserts and the cider.

No, wait a minute. We are not here. I'm here. And Theo's here. But we're not a couple. I do have a boyfriend back in New York. And an apartment. And a job being held for me.

Suddenly, she felt like a fraud. Like she was living one life here while she had another far away, with people waiting for her to come back. Not that anyone was necessarily waiting. Michael was likely out to dinner with his "friend" right now, perhaps talking about how his girlfriend had gone crazy and had moved to Maine. And Charlotte had her husband.

She could work things out with Michael. Maybe if she finally owned up to hating her job, to liking the relationship aspect of her work but not the legal aspect, she would get somewhere. If she went home, if she stayed with Michael, she could have Glenda Whitman.

That didn't seem a good enough reason.

"I smell something Mexican and delicious," Rebecca said. "I hope whoopie pies go with it."

Ellie smiled. "Whoopie pies go with everything." She peered around Rebecca and Theo out the window. No sign of Tim.

Ellie's apartment was a tiny one-bedroom, but cozy—except for the Tim-inspired décor. The living room was a blend of his and hers. There was a tattered black leather sofa that had been attacked by a cat (his), but a red velvet love seat strewn with colorful pillows (hers). For every folksy touch there was dive-bar-inspired art. "Tim was here" was spelled out in beer caps above the bathroom door.

In the small dining alcove, a built-in china cabinet housed a collection of their wedding photos. The Rasmussens looked so young and so happy: Ellie, beautiful in a strapless gown, and Tim, a good-looking guy who reminded Rebecca of bouncers she'd seen in front of popular nightclubs in New York. He was at least six feet four and very muscular. In a photo of the wedding party, Rebecca counted twelve bridesmaids and twelve groomsmen. Ha! Rebecca had thought Charlotte, with her seven bridesmaids, had had a big bridal party.

In the living room were three couples Rebecca hadn't met before. Ellie introduced the Mayfairs, a twentysomething couple married three years who looked remarkably alike, from their curly blond hair to their matching silver rimless eyeglasses. The O'Connors, married eleven years, seemed mismatched yet held hands constantly. Julie O'Connor was tall and slender and never stopped talking; Otto O'Connor was shorter, with a visible potbelly, and said three words. Next were the Ludenowskys, married twenty-two years, both of whom were accountants and shared a practice. Once everyone had been introduced and shaken hands, the men zoomed around Theo and then drifted over to the corner table where the cheese cubes and crackers and beer were.

The women turned out to be members of Ellie's knitting circle, which met in a Brunswick yarn shop.

"I'm hoping to inspire Tim by showing him examples of happily married couples at various stages of life," Ellie explained. "This weekend, he'll get the opposite, so I thought I would show him what it *can* be like. Long-term, too." Ellie seemed on the verge of tears. A half hour had passed and there was no sign of Tim. "I was going to ask my neighbors—they've been married, like, fortysomething years, but I thought that would scare him." She let out a deep breath. "He's not coming, is he?"

"Give him a chance," Rebecca said. "It's still early."

By eight o'clock, Tim still hadn't shown up. "If I hold the meat any longer it'll be too tough," Ellie said as she and Rebecca headed into the kitchen. Rebecca laid strips of sizzling steak and chicken on the colorful Fiestaware. Ellie had gone all out with plates of cut-up vegetables, refried beans, guacamole, olives, salsa and tortillas. When they set everything on the dining-room table, Tim still hadn't arrived.

"Do you think I went overboard?" Ellie whispered to

Rebecca as they headed back into the kitchen. "Maybe this is just too much, this dinner and then the tour this weekend. He promised to come tonight, though. Well, promised he'd try to come. But what else could he possibly be doing? Poker? Watching *CSI*? Why doesn't he want to be here? I just don't get it. I'm his *wife*. He married me to be with me for the rest of his life. I mean, that part was made very clear during the vows. He could have run at any time during the ceremony before the important part."

"I'll make you a margarita," Theo said as he came into the kitchen. "They're my specialty."

Ellie ladled sour cream into a pretty bowl and stuck a spoon in it, tears in her eyes. "Glasses are in the cabinet above the toaster. Make mine *extra* strong."

"Mine, too," Rebecca whispered to Theo.

And finally, as Ellie called everyone to the dining room, she said, "Tim was held up at the office." But considering he had his own landscaping company and cut the lawns of almost everyone at the table, she added, "Well, held up by stubborn weeds." Then she ran out of the room.

The marrieds glanced at each other, their forks in the air.

Theo whispered, "I'll take over as host. You can go talk to Ellie." He smiled at the little crowd. "Bon appétit," he said, filling a tortilla. And within seconds, the group was talking and laughing and building their fajitas and raving over the guacamole, which Ellie had made from scratch.

She went in search of Ellie, who was easy to find. Ellie sat on the top step of her little deck, her arms wrapped around her knees, her dark hair curtaining her face.

Rebecca put her arm around her friend. "Sorry, honey."

"Me, too," Ellie said, and lay her head on Rebecca's shoulder.

"So this was an intervention of sorts?" Theo said as they walked back along the dark road. They carried doggie bags of leftovers that Ellie insisted they take, if not for themselves then for Spock and Charlie.

"Good word for it. Ellie wants to save the marriage. I don't know Tim at all, but based on what Ellie's told me, I'm worried for her."

"And based on what I've seen of him around town, me too," he said.

Tim never did show up that night. Ellie had dried her tears, freshened her lipstick, and returned to the table. She even managed to eat. And laugh. "I have to remember that these couples represent the possibilities. The best of marriage," she'd said. "They're an inspiration. Even if Tim isn't here to meet them."

Rebecca was truly beginning to adore Ellie and her optimism.

"We can cut to the beach here." Theo led her down a long, winding path. They walked in silence for a bit, the late September night air so fresh, so perfectly balanced between still warm and cool. Rebecca stopped and just breathed, and Theo smiled. "I do that a lot. Ellie will be needing to do a lot of that, too."

"You said you knew happily married couples, right? It is

possible. Like the couples Ellie invited. Happily married. Finishing each other's sentences."

"It's more than possible," he said, kicking at the leaves under their feet. "My parents had a crappy marriage, but my grandparents seemed loving till they died, within a few days of each other. The doctor said my grandfather died of a broken heart without his beloved."

Rebecca smiled, her dear tiny paternal grandparents coming to mind. Murray and Mildred Strand—who'd dressed up for dinner every night, even in their own Brooklyn apartment—had died within days of each other of natural causes. "My father's parents, too. Oh, what a sweet, sweet couple they were."

He squeezed her hand for a moment. "See, it is possible."

Her hand tingled and she wanted to slip it into his, but she didn't. "What's so amazing is that my grandparents were set up on a blind date, by their families, and they were expected to like each other, *expected* being an order, really, and they fell in love on the first date and were married within two weeks. And it was happily ever after for the next sixty years."

"Maybe not happily ever after on a daily basis, though. I'm sure they went through their share of hard times and tragedies like my grandparents."

"That's the thing. They did. But nothing was able to tear them apart. Was it the time? What?"

Theo shrugged. "I think people overlooked a lot in the past. Social mores, customs, signs of the time, whatever you want to call it, had a lot to do with staying power. What was considered 'acceptable' thirty or forty years ago, a certain acceptance of your fate, isn't now. And what wasn't acceptable then, like leaving a bad marriage, is. Not much is swept under the rug these days—and that's a good thing. People are always saying they wished life could be simple like it was in the fifties, but that's bullshit, really. Just because you didn't talk about some very big problems or acknowledge them didn't mean life was simple or easy. It must have been very difficult for some."

"Agreed," she said, letting his words of wisdom hang in the air. "But now that so much *is* acceptable socially, like never getting married, why would someone like Tim get married when he doesn't want to be in a committed, monogamous relationship with his wife? Is it that he wants some of what marriage offers? Maybe he really did love Ellie, but then—I don't know."

How was she possibly going to help on the Rocky Relationships Tour when she couldn't answer these questions? Perhaps the questions just had to be posed. That gave her some comfort, something to hang on to. Maybe it was more about asking the questions than answering them.

"And then there's the flip side," Theo said. "Someone like Ellie who wants to be married so bad that she ignores even the flashing neon warning signs. Maybe she invested so much in the relationship that she couldn't imagine breaking up with him. Even though it meant starting out marriage on a rocky path."

"Maybe a couple just has to be madly in love."

"But that 'in love' feeling doesn't necessarily last. The relationship has to be backed up by other stuff. Like maturity."

As they neared Theo's house, Rebecca could hear Spock barking. "He must know you're coming."

"He knows my footsteps," Theo said. "And I'm sure he smells his fajitas. Come on in. Give me a second to find his leash and we'll walk you back to Finch's."

Rebecca's heart leaped at the thought of going inside, of seeing where he lived, where he sat, ate, slept. Took showers. She walked in behind him and smiled. Not a black leather piece to be found. Spock had a plush bed near the stone fireplace. The house was so nice that Rebecca wondered if he'd lived here with a woman.

She sat down on the sofa, a wood base covered with cushions in a subtle leaf design. It looked like nature. The entire downstairs did, with its sisal rug and bark curtain rods that held muslin drapes. "Your house is beautiful," she said as he attached Spock's leash. "Did you build most of the furniture yourself?"

"Actually, yes. That's where I make most of my money." He stood by the door with Spock at the ready, but she wanted to stay. She was starting to really like this guy. Which was why she got up.

And within five minutes, they were at Finch's.

"I built that swing for Marianne two years ago," he said, gesturing at the beautiful swing for two on the side porch.

So of course she sat down on it and he sat next to her and kicked off the porch to sway it. Above them were twinkling white stars in the black sky, a crescent moon. She stared up at them, forcing herself not to make a wish. Forcing herself not to fall for this gorgeous, insightful, intelligent, wonderful guy.

They sat so close she would barely have to move an inch to kiss him.

"You still wish on stars?" he asked.

"I see that mind reading is among your many talents. Though actually, if I were honest, I'd tell you I was making myself *not* wish on a star."

"Complicated?"

"Very," she said, one perfect twinkling star beckoning her. "Last night I came out here and wished that this would all make sense, my being here. That I'm supposed to be here, that I'm doing the right thing."

"Worried you're not?"

"Joy doesn't want me here," she said. "And then there's *this*."

"This?"

She hesitated, then just blurted out, "I'm sitting on a porch swing with a man I want to kiss, when I have a live-in boy-friend who's waiting for me to come home."

He smiled. "Do you want to go home?"

She glanced at the moon, at the perfect sliver of it. "I don't know. This doesn't feel like home. I'm not in my own life. I'm trying to foist myself in someone else's life. I've done that kind of thing before. You know when you're hanging on too long to a relationship, and the person has made it clear you're not wanted, but you can't leave. That's kind of how I feel—how I think Joy feels."

He nodded. "And what about this guy you want to kiss. Is he adding more weirdness to the equation?"

"He's more helping me figure things out, without his even knowing it."

"Interesting how people do that. I'll bet he'd let you test out that kiss, if you need to. Just saying."

All she had to do was tilt up her face and in seconds she *could* test it out. The gentlest of breezes beckoned her closer, but she hesitated. If she was going to kiss this guy, this beautiful man, shouldn't she be free to do so?

You're not married, she reminded herself. *That's different.*

But it shouldn't be so different. She and Michael were committed, they were living together. Though not exactly at the moment.

Why do I feel so comfortable with you? she wanted to ask. *Why does this feel so comfortable? I'm in the middle of nowhere, somewhere else, wanting to kiss a guy I barely know. But a guy who makes me feel like I belong exactly where I am.*

I am here and here is where?

"This is probably where you should offer to see me to my door," she said. "To keep me safe from coyotes and wild rabbits."

"And me?"

"And you."

With that, he got up and so did she, and he walked her to the front door. She used her key to go inside and he plucked a little purple flower from the ones that lined the bushes.

He tucked the flower behind her ear. "I'll come get Charlie tomorrow around five. Sound good?"

"Perfect. How do I look?" she asked, turning to model her flower-adorned ear.

"Beautiful. Like always. Night," he said, then walked off into the inky darkness under the stars.

● ● ●

The first thing Rebecca saw when she opened her eyes the next morning was the little purple flower. She'd put it in a tea-cup filled with water.

"You're going to be in good hands this weekend," she told Charlie.

And when Theo came to pick up the dog as promised, right on time at 5:00 p.m., with just a squeeze of the hand, no mention of their almost kiss, nothing except "I'll be home after three on Sunday, so come pick him up anytime," Rebecca knew that she was in good hands with him, too.

eleven

As Rebecca pulled up to Joy's house, a stylish fifty-something woman came out and walked over to a car parked in the driveway. She rooted around in the backseat, then the trunk. The breath caught in Rebecca's throat.

Pia Jayhawk. Rebecca was sure of it.

Her blond hair was cut in an A-line chin-length bob with heavy Louise Brooks bangs. She was dressed all in black, like a New Yorker, and had something resembling a belly dancer's scarf with beads around her hips. Long metallic earrings dangled from her ears. Each arm sported several bracelets and bangles. She carried what looked like an easel into the house.

Everyone said Rebecca looked like her father, that aside from the chestnut brown wavy hair and the light brown eyes and the slightly long nose and the slightly wide mouth, there was something in her expression that reminded everyone of Daniel Strand. She wondered if Pia would recognize her. If she'd look at her and *know*.

Doubtful.

It took Rebecca a few minutes to leave the comfort zone of her car. But finally she collected her travel bag and her purse and rang the bell.

Joy opened the door a crack. "Remember our deal."

Rebecca nodded, and Joy opened the door wider and gestured her through. She stepped into a small mudroom with tiny shoes and rubber rain boots and preschool paintings hung adorably on a clothesline across the narrow room. As Joy led the way into the living room, Rebecca immediately noticed that she and Joy did have similar taste in home décor. Folksy meets modern meets thrift store. The plush, comfortable cream-colored sofa with its interesting texture and colorful throw pillows, the big muted rug and interesting lamps with elephants as bases. Rebecca had a few lucky elephants among her possessions at Michael's.

Michael's. Interesting that Rebecca didn't think of her home in New York as her apartment. It was and had always been Michael's apartment.

"You know Ellie, of course," Joy said.

Ellie was biting her lip and glancing out the window for Tim. She popped a cheese cube into her mouth. "Not here yet." Rebecca watched Ellie's expression alternate between hope and despair in the same second. She hoped Tim showed up this time.

"And this is Aimee and Charles Cutlass," Joy said, leading her over to a thirtysomething couple who sat very close together on the love seat. "Aimee is a librarian and Charles is the manager of the Honda dealership in Brunswick." They were both tall, thin redheads, but Aimee's frizzy curls were almost orange, and Charles's hair was more auburn. They both wore white turtlenecks, khaki pants, and had matching navy blue windbreakers. Joy smiled at the couple. "Rebecca is the mediation specialist I mentioned would be joining us." After a few minutes of small talk, Ellie pulled Rebecca away to the little table of refreshments by the window.

"I wonder what their story is," Ellie whispered. "They seem to be very happily married. Right down to the matchy-matchy clothes."

"*Seems* is always the key word," Rebecca pointed out.

The doorbell rang, and Rebecca could feel Ellie stiffen. *Please be him*, she said silently for Ellie's sake.

And it was. Rebecca breathed a sigh of relief at the sight of Tim Rasmussen. At least six feet three and with a football player's neck, he filled the doorway and smiled awkwardly at Joy, then glanced around. His gaze rested on the now beaming Ellie and he gave a little wave. She ran over to him and whispered something in his ear. Rebecca heard him say, "I'll try."

Good enough for now.

Rebecca looked around, hoping for another glimpse of Pia Jayhawk. She heard a child's voice, then the cutest giggle-laughter, and followed the sound, pretending to be in deep study of the small paintings along the living-room wall where it narrowed into a hallway. Through the French doors of what appeared to be a playroom, she saw Pia sitting on a big round rug, building a fort of blocks with Rex. Joy walked in, scooped up Rex, and hugged him tight, twirling around with him. Rebecca heard murmurings of "See you in two little days" and "You're going to have so much fun with Grandma." There was another hug, and then Joy slipped back through the doors again. Rex settled himself in Pia's lap on the rug and played with the long chain of her glasses.

Rebecca stared at Rex, her nephew, her father's grandchild. She wanted to run into the playroom and get down on the floor and build a tower of blocks and make a Play-Doh cat. But now certainly wasn't the time. Perhaps when they returned from the tour, Joy would agree to letting her join her and Rex at the playground or at the library for Story Time.

She watched as Harry Jones came in and did much the same as Joy had. Harry was very good-looking in an easygoing way, like a model in an L.L.Bean catalog, with his brown windswept hair and hazel eyes. Harry and Joy looked like a couple, looked like they belonged together. They had on the same low-slung jeans and J.Crew-ish sweaters and Merrells. They both had the same friendly kindness in their attractive faces. You could imagine going up to Joy in the produce section of a supermarket and asking her if she knew how to tell if the mangoes were fresh. And car-greenhorn Rebecca could easily see herself calling over to Harry at the gas station pump to ask if there was any point in using the premium gasoline.

Pia, on the other hand, had that intimidating quality that most New Yorkers had.

Of course, since Rebecca was staring, Pia Jayhawk glanced up and smiled. In that moment, Rebecca saw Pia in her Madonna tatters and bangles, seaweed twisted around her ankles as she searched for the perfect rock to paint.

Rebecca dashed away. Yet as she headed down the short hallway to the living room, another painting stopped her cold.

Her father.

She was sure it was him. It was a small painting, on an unframed eight-by-ten canvas. A young Daniel Strand sat on a stretch of beach, his arms wrapped around his legs, looking neither happy nor at peace. He seemed to be searching for answers in the blue water ahead of him. There was something in his hand, and when Rebecca leaned closer she could see it was a rock, likely the one Pia had given him to throw when they'd met. Rebecca stared at her father's face. There was the slightest hint of heartbreak in his expression, as though he were trying to hide it. Pia had captured the essence of her father in the painting; it was so visceral Rebecca almost wanted to reach out and touch the paint.

Pia had loved Daniel Strand, of this Rebecca was sure.

And though Rebecca recalled from one of her father's letters that this house had been Pia's, it was now Joy's home, and the painting was still there, on the wall. Did Joy know that the man on the beach holding the rock was her father? Perhaps she did and liked having the painting in her house, albeit along a short stretch of hallway that didn't beckon one to linger and look at the art. Perhaps it was enough for Joy to know it was there. Every now and then, she likely stood where Rebecca was now and studied it, looking, wondering.

"Who's that?"

A child's voice.

Rebecca jumped, until she realized that Rex Jayhawk-Jones was talking about *her*. He stood a few feet down the hall in front of the French doors and stared at her with those huge hazel eyes, glancing from her to Pia.

"I'm sure that's a friend of Mommy's," Pia said. She glanced at the painting that Rebecca stood in front of, then looked at Rebecca, her gaze so sharp that Rebecca bit her lip.

She knew. She knew. She knew.

"That's right!" Rebecca said to Rex in that overly cheery voice people used with kids, then hurried back into the living room. She stood at the table of cheese and crackers and focused on the painting above the upright piano, this one of Pia and a man jumping off a cliff.

"We weren't too sure," a voice said from behind her. "Boy, we were wrong." Rebecca turned around. Pia stood there, her gaze on the painting. "My husband and I married seventeen years ago. We're renewing our vows in November."

She could hardly believe she was standing here talking to Pia Jayhawk. In front of this painting, no less. "Is seventeen significant for you?"

"Not particularly. But Jack had a cancer scare last year, and so it's something we've been wanting to do."

"My father just died of cancer," Rebecca said, then shut her mouth fast.

There was no reason Pia Jayhawk would know of Daniel Strand's death. Or necessarily care. Though Rebecca imagined you'd always care.

Pia held her gaze for a moment. "I'm so sorry. Are you here for Joy's tour?"

Rebecca was speechless for a moment. *You had an affair with my father. You slept with him on a beach. You had his child.*

Did you love him? Do you think about him? Did you keep tabs? Do you know that he's gone?

Pia was staring at her, so Rebecca finally nodded.

"Good luck, then."

"I—" But it's not as if she could explain she wasn't a participant on the Rocky Relationships Tour. And besides, she did need luck.

She glanced down the hall. There was Harry, with Rex on his shoulders. And Joy was going over something on a piece of paper with a man she presumed to be Jack, her stepfather. Rex's schedule perhaps.

Joy's gaze locked with Rebecca's. There was the slightest narrowing of her eyes. "Mom, could you come take Rex. We're going to be leaving in five minutes."

Pia smiled and headed back down the hall. Pia and Joy hugged, then Joy took Rex from Harry and hugged him tight and covered him with kisses before handing him over to Pia. Joy didn't introduce Rebecca to Harry, presumably because she couldn't very well say in front of her mother, *"Oh, and, Harry, this is the half sister I was telling you about, the one whose father had an affair with my mother and then pretended it and the resulting pregnancy never happened."*

Rebecca's heart squeezed. She was in Joy's house, among Joy's family. *She* was the odd one out here, the one who didn't belong. When Rebecca's father told her about the baby he'd turned his back on, *Joy* was the one not connected to the *Strands*. But here, Joy had her whole world, her whole life, family, friends, a husband, and a child. Rebecca was the outsider.

• • •

During the thirty-minute drive from Wiscasset to South Freeport, Rebecca learned from Aimee Cutlass that she and Charles had been trying to have a baby since their honeymoon five years ago. Aimee was ready to adopt. Charles was ready to adopt a dog. Maybe even two. Aimee believed she couldn't get pregnant because Charles really didn't want a child; she'd heard on *Oprah* about a book called *The Secret*, and apparently the secret was that you had to think positively. Apparently, Charles was thinking that babies cost money, that babies were life-changing, wailing, helpless, dependent, demanding little creatures, and therefore sperm was not making its way to egg.

Aimee told Rebecca, Ellie, and Joy this from her seat next to Ellie in the first row. If Charles was listening, it wasn't obvious. He sat in the middle row, but was facing sideways, talking to Harry and Tim in the back row. Joy had suggested this seating arrangement so that the trip started out easier for Tim, with him talking guy talk instead of sitting next to his complaining wife and listening to a list of his infractions as a husband.

"Rebecca, maybe you could lead a discussion about what we all want in a marriage," Ellie whispered.

"Actually, I think we should let things be," Rebecca whispered back. "Look, Tim's having a great time back there, talking about the Red Sox and whether they're gonna make the playoffs. That good mood will carry over to dinner."

"I agree," Joy said as the orange minibus turned onto a dirt road with a sign for Harborview Lodge.

A half mile down, the beautiful old stone house came into view. It looked more like a small castle than the ski lodge

Rebecca was expecting—not that Freeport was skiing country. The house was surrounded by evergreens and paths meandering up through the woods in every direction. Inside, Rebecca was surprised to see the lodge was actually charming and cozy but rustic. In the huge living room were overstuffed sofas and floor pillows, soft, faded rugs, and a massive stone fireplace that Harry lit in less than a minute. Well-cared-for plants were everywhere, and each doorway was lit by twinkling white Christmas lights. There was a large kitchen, two full bathrooms, and a screened room that led out to a back deck with its view of the ocean. Upstairs were five large bedrooms and three bathrooms.

Rebecca's room had a tiny balcony facing the woods. She unpacked, then stood out there, taking in the red and orange leaves of the trees, until she saw Aimee and Charles come out onto their little balcony. They still wore their matching white turtlenecks and khaki pants. They embraced, and from the way they looked at each other, the way they hugged, Rebecca knew immediately that they loved each other in a way that would transcend their problems. They were here to talk something through, but their marriage was safe.

She didn't get that sense with Ellie and Tim.

Or with Joy and Harry. Mostly because Joy was so unreadable.

Joy had announced that everyone was due in the kitchen to help with dinner, her famous four-cheese ravioli, salad, and fresh garlic bread. Rebecca headed downstairs and into the large country kitchen. The Jayhawk-Joneses were on pasta. The Rasmussens, salad. The Cutlasses were all about the garlic bread. Rebecca was in charge of choosing a wine and setting the dining-room table.

So far, so good. Until Tim asked Harry and Charles if they wanted to find a dart bar after dinner.

"Tim . . ." Ellie said with an embarrassed smile. "I'm sure Joy has something planned for all of us after dinner."

He popped a cheese cube into his mouth and glanced at Joy. "Do you?"

Joy dropped the ravioli into the large pot of boiling water on the stove. "Well, I know it's not Thanksgiving yet, and it might sound a little hokey, but I thought we'd all sit around the fireplace with a glass of wine and talk about what we're grateful for. Something to start us off on a positive note—what we're thankful for, what we're happy about."

Tim stared at her as though she'd grown another head. "Uh, that's not really my thing. When Ellie asked me to come, she said it would be like a few couples going away together for a weekend. You know, a good time. Not a bunch of sad sacks sitting around."

Ellie's cheeks flushed. "We're here to try to save our marriage, Tim."

"*I'm* here to get away." At her expression, which Rebecca would describe between close to tears and embarrassment, he added, "God, nothing's ever enough with you. I'm here, aren't I?"

Actually, you're not. Tim. Rebecca glanced at Ellie, who clearly knew it, too. Had known it long before now, but had held on. Ellie threw up her hands and walked over to the sink with a head of lettuce. She turned on the water full blast, which Rebecca figured meant she was crying.

Shoot.

Before they'd boarded the Love Bus, Rebecca had asked Ellie if she wanted Rebecca to really probe Tim, to ask him some hard questions. Ellie had said yes, that it was time to take her head out of the sand. Rebecca wasn't sure if now was the time or not, if she'd send Tim running for the hills within thirty minutes of arriving or if she'd say something that would get *in there*, in where Tim loved Ellie, where he'd proposed, where he'd said, "I do."

Rebecca poured seven glasses of a white wine she really had no idea about (she chose by prettiest label) and handed one to Tim. Tim was so tall—and so much taller than Rebecca's five feet two—that she had to crane her neck to look up at him. "Tim, do you want to be married to Ellie?"

He downed the wine in two gulps. "What do you mean? I am married to her."

"Do you *want* to be married to her?"

He glanced at Ellie, who'd frozen at the sink, then handed the glass back to Rebecca for a refill. "Yeah." Pause. Then: "I just—"

Ellie turned around, her green eyes intense. "Just what?"

He shrugged. "I just find it hard not to . . . try to score."

Ellie let out a breath, set the wet head of lettuce on a cutting board on the table, and dropped down in one of the kitchen chairs. She'd clearly had this discussion before. And it was a discussion that seemed to make the other two men nervous. Harry and Charles were deeply focused on their jobs, Harry stirring the steaming large pot of ravioli at the stove, Charles laying garlic remarkably evenly across the long loaves of Italian bread. Every now and then, they'd glance up from what they were doing, looking curious or embarrassed or like they wished they could bolt.

"Why do you want to score with other women?" Rebecca asked.

Tim laughed and butchered the cucumber he was slicing. "*Why?* I mean, come on."

Harry stopped stirring. "Well, you do have a beautiful wife. So it's a reasonable question."

Everyone turned to Harry with "good point" expressions, relieved for the reprieve.

Tim glanced at Ellie, who was ripping apart the lettuce in slow motion. "Yeah, I know."

Keep going, Rebecca told herself. *But carefully.* Tim's expression had softened somewhat. Tied for first place with a hundred other rules in divorce mediation was to never make either party feel attacked.

"So . . . scoring isn't about just sex, then?" Rebecca asked.

Foot in mouth, Rebecca. Why had she asked that? That wasn't the right question. She didn't want to lead him to *yes*, that he was looking for more than a casual romp.

She rushed to add, "I mean, because you do have this beautiful wife at home, this woman who loves you, this woman you did marry, what makes you want to hook up with other women?"

She wasn't sure that was better. But at least it wasn't such a yes-or-no question.

"Jesus, this is all a little *personal*," Tim muttered. "Why does any guy want to screw other women? Why do you?" he said to Harry. "Why do you?" he added to Charles.

Rebecca glanced at Joy, who was now working on the sauce at the center island. Joy's shoulders stiffened for just a moment. It was clear she was waiting—holding her breath, perhaps—for the answer.

"I don't," Harry said.

Tim rolled his eyes. "Right."

Harry gave the ravioli a stir. "It's the truth. Whatever problems Joy and I are having, it's not about me straying. Would never and have never."

Tim raised his eyebrow. "Please. You've been married, what? Like, four years. Talk to me when you're married ten."

"Tim, we've been married for *two* years," Ellie said. "So what's your point?"

Tim gulped his wine. "I'm just sayin'."

"And they have a three-year-old child," Charles put in. "If a child doesn't add stress to a marriage, I don't know what will."

Aimee's shoulders slumped.

"Well, that's an entirely different area of discussion," Rebecca quickly added. "Tim and Ellie don't have children. So then, what's your deal, Tim? Why are you acting like you're still single?"

Tim hacked another cucumber. "I'm not acting like I'm single. I just like to party. What, I can't go out and have fun because I'm married?"

Ellie shook her head. "It's the kind of fun you're having that's the problem."

"The scoring part, I presume?" Rebecca asked. "You never really did answer the question. Why do you mess around with other women when you have Ellie at home?"

Tim slid the mess of cucumber slices into the salad bowl and then slammed the bowl down so that the cucumbers flopped right back out. "Jesus Christ, what do you people want from me? I don't know, okay? No, I do know—for the fun of it. Satisfied?"

"Tim, no one's ganging up on you," Harry said. "It's just a conversation. We're all just trying to figure out what's going on with us, and right now, you're up."

"Lucky me. Can I at least have a beer?" Tim asked. "I'm not really into wine."

Harry got a Sam Adams from the refrigerator and uncapped it. "Not cold yet, but here."

Tim gulped half of it.

"Let me just ask you this," Ellie said, her eyes red-rimmed. "Is it fun because there's no emotional component? Nothing tied to it? Or is it fun because there's the possibility of that, too—that you might actually fall for someone you hook up with?"

He barely looked at Ellie, preferring the floor or the rainbow-colored tile backsplash along the stove wall. "It's not like I'm looking for another *relationship*. I know I'm married. Sometimes it's about the thrill of the chase, sometimes it's just about the fun of how it is when you first meet someone and you're flirting."

Ellie's face crumpled. "So you're saying you don't really know? You could see meeting someone and falling in love?"

Tim glanced around at everyone. "Oh, come on, who can't?"

"I can't," Harry said.

"I can't," Charles seconded.

"Me either," Ellie said, and burst into sobs.

Rebecca ran into the bathroom off the kitchen for the box of tissues. She handed it to Ellie, who clutched it like a lifeline.

"Can I ask you something, Tim?" Rebecca said as she helped Charles slide four loaves of garlic bread into the oven while Aimee cleaned up the garlic and put away the butter. "Why did you propose to Ellie? I mean, she's a lovely young woman, but why did you want to get married in the first place?"

Tim let out a deep breath. He glanced at Ellie, who was trying to stop crying. "I didn't, really. You kept pressuring me, though, right? Hinting about a ring . . . And then, I don't know, my father died and I was really low about that, and Ellie was really great—you were really there for me—and I guess I just got her a ring one day and proposed, but then a while later, I started feeling like I always did, like I wanted to go out and party and meet women and have fun."

"But now is now," Ellie said, dry-eyed. "Now is now and I need to know. Will you stop running around? I need to know now."

"You've been saying that since we hooked up two and a half years ago, Ellie."

"And if she's now saying your affairs are a deal breaker?" Rebecca prompted.

Tim glanced from Rebecca to Ellie, who stared at him. "She can say it, but I don't think she means it because she never means it. She always lets me come home eventually."

Ellie stood, her hands braced on the chair. "What if I told you right now that this is it. That there's no coming back. That if you can't tell me right now you choose me, you choose our marriage, that I'm filing for divorce on Monday?"

He shrugged. "I don't believe you, I guess. I don't think you'll do it."

Rebecca noticed that he didn't even seem to flinch at the word *divorce*.

"So you won't tell me right now, pledge in front of all these people to be faithful, to be my husband?" Ellie asked Tim.

"Jesus, Ellie, come on. I do love you. Doesn't that count for something? It's not like I want to break up."

Everyone stared from Tim to Rebecca.

Rebecca turned on the light switch to peer at the garlic bread. "Break up? Tim, when you're married, it's called divorce. That's very serious. And very painful."

"Yeah, man," Charles said. "You're not in high school, for Pete's sake."

"I'm who I am," Tim said, then gulped the rest of his beer. "Take me or leave me. Whatever."

Whatever. What an ass. Ellie deserved so much more than this.

"Timothy Rasmussen," Ellie said, staring at him. "Do you want to be married to me? In all that that means."

"If *that* means being fucking miserable for the rest of my life, then no, I don't." He slammed down the beer bottle on the counter.

Ellie ran out of the kitchen. Rebecca heard her heels on the stairs. "I'm filing for divorce on Monday," she called from the landing. "So just go, Tim. Get out of here. There's nothing left to say."

All eyes turned to Tim, who was pulling open the refrigerator in search of another Sam Adams.

"*Is* there anything left to say?" Rebecca asked Tim. "Are you going to walk out of here? Walk out on your marriage? Let her divorce you?"

He stiffened, but resumed his search of the beer. He took out a bottle and uncapped it, then sighed and set it down on the counter and walked into the living room.

Rebecca glanced at four people holding their breath. They all crowded into the doorway so as not to look like they were spying, which of course they were.

Tim stopped just before the landing. He stared up at Ellie. "For what it's worth, Ellie, I'm really sorry."

"It's worth shit," she called back, and ran inside their room, then reappeared a moment later with his brown leather jacket and his duffel bag, which she flung down at him. The jacket hit him in the face, and the duffel bag landed with a thud at his feet. He picked it up.

"I'm gonna walk down to the tavern we passed," he said to no one in particular. "I'll call a buddy to come get me."

And with that he was gone.

When dinner was ready and gentle knocks on Ellie's door hadn't brought her back down, Joy brought up a plate, but reported that Ellie waved the plate away and sobbed on her bed. Rebecca planned to try a little later with an Irish coffee and one of Marianne's pumpkin whoopie pies.

And so the heavy-hearted group sat at the beautiful old

farmer's table in the dining room and poked and picked at the food. Only Charles seemed to have an appetite.

"This is Tim," Harry said, taking his fork and using the back of it to smush a cherry tomato. But it was too firm and he gave up. "Fitting, since I guess he did win."

Joy speared a piece of ravioli, but then put her fork down. "He lost, really. Ellie's the best thing that's ever going to happen to an ass like Tim. It's hard to imagine another great person actually falling for him."

"He doesn't seem to want that, anyway," Charles said, taking a piece of garlic bread from the basket in the center of the table. "He doesn't seem to know what he wants."

There was no disagreeing or discussion to be had about that bit of truth, so they ate in silence until Ellie could be heard coming down the stairs in the high-heeled ankle boots she'd bought especially for the trip.

"I called Maggie," she said as she came into the dining room. "She's coming to pick me up." She carried a pack of tissues in her hand, but seemed to be out of sniffles or tears at the moment. She glanced around the table. Joy had taken away Tim's chair and everyone had moved over to make his absence less glaring. But perhaps the gesture had the opposite effect.

Joy stood. "I'm sorry, Ellie. I know you had very different hopes for this trip."

Ellie sat and took a piece of plain Italian bread from another basket, alternating between eating little pieces and ripping the chunk into shreds. "At least I know for sure. At least there's no more, 'What do you think that meant?' He made himself clear in front of witnesses."

"Are you going to file for divorce on Monday?" Aimee asked.

Ellie nodded. "Maggie said she had a really good lawyer." She burst into tears and Rebecca pulled her chair closer, sliding her arm over Ellie's slight shoulder.

"I'm so sorry, Ellie," Rebecca said.

Ellie sniffled and dabbed under her eyes with the wad of tissue. "I know you're probably feeling bad about the conversation not exactly turning out the way I wanted. But you did what no one's been able to do since we've been breaking up and getting back together for two years. You got him to the truth. And you got him to say it. I've just wanted him to say it, you know? Or maybe I haven't. I guess I haven't. I guess I was never ready for it. But I am now, as much as it hurts."

"We're all here for you, Ellie," Joy said. "No matter what you need, okay?"

Ellie sniffled and nodded and managed to eat a few bites of her pumpkin whoopie pie. Harry fixed her an Irish coffee in a thermos, and thirty minutes later, when the crunch of a car could be heard on the gravel drive, Ellie and her bags were gone.

Harry made Irish coffees for everyone (a virgin for Charles, who didn't drink) and the group gathered in front of the big stone fireplace in the living room. The two couples each shared a love seat, and Rebecca sat on the rocking chair facing them.

"Aren't you supposed to ask how the Ellie-and-Tim business made us feel?" Charles asked.

Rebecca smiled. "Told you I wasn't a therapist. But how *did* it make you all feel?"

"I'll tell you how it made me feel," Harry said. "Sick to my stomach." He looked at Joy and took her hand with both of his. "It made me realize that we've got our share of problems, but immaturity isn't among them. That we can work on what's been causing these stupid fights and cold wars."

Joy's face crumpled with emotion, relief, and happiness, and then she burst into tears. She could only nod. He took her by the hand and led her upstairs.

Watching a marriage implode in front of their eyes had done something to the two other married couples, and by breakfast on Saturday, there was a magic in the air. The fragility, what they stood to lose, had turned both the Jayhawk-Joneses and the Cutlasses into "whatever you want, honey" peacekeeping romantics.

"No, whatever *you* want," Charles said to his look-alike wife when Joy asked if anyone wanted the heat turned on. The temperature gauge attached to the bark of a tree outside the kitchen window read 51 degrees. Cold enough to Rebecca to turn on the heat, but perhaps not for true Mainers. Everyone except Rebecca wore a fleece pullover.

"My work here is done," Rebecca said with a smile as she set down the carafe of coffee on the dining-room table. Once again, the group had cooked together, Harry on western omelets, Charles on bacon, Aimee on bagels (Mainers did not eat untoasted bagels the way New Yorkers did), Joy on the fresh-squeezed orange juice, and Rebecca on coffee (she was on her third cup).

Charles Cutlass added a helping of bacon to his plate, ate a piece in two bites, and said, "They scared the shit out of me."

His wife's eyes widened and she laughed. "Did you just swear? He never curses."

Charles placed his hand over his wife's. "I don't want something to happen to us. I'm really not so sure if I'm ready to be a father right now. But if it'll make you happy, truly happy, I'll go ahead with looking into adoption. China, Guatemala, whatever you want."

Aimee squeezed his hand. "And I want you to be happy. But I really believe that you won't feel differently a year from now or two years. You'll always think you're not ready. And I'll just be sitting in wait. I think once you become a father, once you hold that baby in your arms, you will feel what I feel. I say that based on having known you for seven years, Charles. I love you enough not to force you into something I don't think would make you happy."

"Then let's do it," he said. "I mean it. Kids are great, right?" He directed this last at Harry.

Harry nodded. "Rex has made me want to be a better person."

"So what *are* the main issues between you two?" Aimee asked, looking between Harry and Joy.

Joy stared at her eggs. "It just feels like we've grown apart somehow. We're both only twenty-six. With a three-year-old child. And it's like we're this old married couple who eat in silence, who have nothing to say after 'So how was Rex today?'

After dinner, I go read or plan a tour, and Harry's in his office, working on a design or on the computer."

"What do you want to say?" Rebecca asked.

"Everything. I want there to be this rush of conversation, like in the beginning." She shook her head. "I sound like Tim."

"No you don't," Rebecca said. "You sound like you want your husband back. You sound like you feel as if you lost him inside your own house, inside your marriage."

"That is exactly how I feel," Joy said softly.

Harry picked up his mug of coffee. "She's been saying that. And I've been saying, 'I'm right here.' And she says, 'You don't understand,' and I say, 'You're right, I don't.' And then we go back to our silence, our separate rooms. I've been living in the half-finished basement for the past six weeks."

Joy stared at him, then down at her plate, then back at Harry. "You say I'm cold and emotionally frigid. How do you think that makes me feel? I am the way I am."

"Didn't Tim just say that?" Aimee asked gently, tucking her frizzy orange curls behind her ears.

"I'm not making excuses," Joy snapped. "Sorry," she added.

"Yes you are," Harry said. "You're saying you're just not warm and fuzzy. But you *are*. I've seen how you are with Rex. I've seen how you let that wall down when you're with him. I'm asking you to *keep* it down."

"Does anyone want more coffee?" Joy asked, jumping up.

"Tim ran off, too," Harry said loud and clear.

"I'm going into the *kitchen*," Joy snapped.

Harry rolled his eyes and walked over to the fireplace to add another log. The flames mesmerized Rebecca. She wished they'd offer some wisdom, the right thing to say.

When Joy came back with her mug full of steaming coffee, Rebecca said, "Can I ask you something?"

Joy shifted as though she were about to get up, but then resettled herself. She had been about to storm off and had stopped herself. That was good. "Okay."

Rebecca picked up her own coffee mug and took a bracing sip. "Your mother is renewing her vows. How does that make you feel?"

Joy leaned her head back and stared up at the ceiling. "Truth? Like a total failure."

"Does she know you and Harry have separated?"

Joy nodded. "She tells me we can talk about it, but I can't. I think she thinks renewing her vows will make me focus on *my* vows."

Ha! Like vows mattered to Pia Jayhawk, Rebecca thought. Her father had no doubt been wearing his wedding band on the beach that day. She knew when she'd kissed him, when she'd slept with him, that he was a married man, that he'd taken vows to love, honor, and cherish someone else.

"You know what I think?" Harry said quietly. "I think you've been thinking a lot about your father. And then all of a sudden, his other daughter comes looking for you. The universe is telling you it's time to deal with it."

"You were thinking about him?" Rebecca asked.

"Not *thinking* about him. I mean, there's nothing to think about. I never knew him. It's like he doesn't exist."

"But he does exist," Harry said. "He always has. There's a painting of him in our house, Joy."

So she did know.

Now it was Joy's turn to roll her eyes. "I *know*. And I also know that you throw his existence in my face whenever we're arguing about something. I didn't know my father. My father wasn't interested in knowing me. So what? It hasn't affected me. I never knew him, so there was no loss involved. It's like kids who are conceived through sperm donors."

"Well, not really," Aimee Cutlass said as she poured a glass of orange juice.

"No, not really at all," Harry said, his eyes on Joy. "That's how you've rationalized it, though. And that's okay. But maybe it's time you let yourself really grieve it or something."

Joy stared at him. "Grieve it? Grieve the loss of someone who turned his back on his own child? That person isn't worth my trouble."

"That person is your father, Joy," Harry said.

"God, this argument is boring," Joy snapped. She got up and stalked into the kitchen, then appeared in the doorway a moment later with another cup of coffee. She stayed there. "That person isn't my father. He's just DNA."

"She's right, really," Charles put in. "A father isn't a father because of biology alone. I mean, aside from technically."

"But Joy wasn't conceived via a sperm donor," Harry said. "Her mother had an affair with a married man, got pregnant, and when he heard the news, the man disappeared off the face of the earth."

"Oh," Aimee said, her expression softening.

"And that man had a daughter at the time. A two-year-old. In fact, she's right there," Joy said, pointing at Rebecca.

Aimee and Charles stared at Rebecca.

"My father died a few weeks ago," Rebecca said. "He told me about Joy. I thought I should find her."

"What was your plan?" Aimee asked. "I mean, once you found her?"

Rebecca shrugged. "I didn't have one. I just wanted to find her."

Joy's pale brown eyes were trained on Rebecca. "Why? And if you say because we're sisters, I'll throw this mug at you."

Because we're sisters, Rebecca said to herself instead. *We are, at the most base level.*

"Well, you *are* sisters," Harry said for her. "DNA says so. DNA says you're half sisters."

Joy raised her chin. "My biological father is not my *father.* And just because Rebecca and I have his blood in common doesn't make us sisters. It gives us something in common, that's all."

"Something big," Aimee said.

Joy let out a breath. "I'm so *tired* of this. Whenever Harry and I fight, it's because of my father. And how am I supposed to argue back about it when there is no father? I say, 'There is *no* father,' and he says, 'That's my point.' And suddenly this is what we're fighting about. Dead air. Nothingness. Emptiness."

Emptiness. It was a word Joy hadn't used before about her feelings about her father.

"I don't mean to 'throw it in your face,'" Harry said gently. "Or use it like a weapon. I just want you to acknowledge it instead of not talking about it. You never talk about it, Joy."

"Well, I hardly have a choice now," Joy said. "And considering Rebecca is here—I mean, I invited her—I'd say that shows . . . something."

Harry walked over to Joy and took her hand. "It does. A big something."

Joy's face crumpled and she turned away, but then wrapped her arms around Harry's neck and sank into him.

Rebecca gave her the moment, then said, "If you want to know the why of your father, Joy, it's all there in the letters he wrote you. Every year on each of your birthdays. Starting with your first. Ending with your last."

"I just can't. I can't bring myself to even think about it."

"Why?" Harry asked. "Aren't you curious?"

"Sometimes I am and sometimes I'm not. Every now and then I do look at my mother's painting of him, the little one in the house. But I look at it and there's nothing there."

"Maybe you're blocking that, Joy," Rebecca said. "Maybe you're afraid of what letting yourself feel something about him will unleash. A flood of frightening emotions you can't control from years of repressing them? Years of not knowing? Of wondering? Of not having your birthright? Your father in your life?"

Joy stared at her, her lower lip trembling. She caught herself, though, and the hardened expression was back. "Maybe."

"You *are* good," Harry said to Rebecca.

twelve

By Sunday morning, both couples were kissing in the kitchen, walking hand in hand upstairs, giving impromptu backrubs—well, the Cutlasses more than the Jayhawk-Joneses. For every Joy and Harry embrace Rebecca had spied (not that she was spying), she'd seen one of them huff off with a "You just don't listen" (Harry's favorite) or "That's not what I'm saying!" (Joy's usual).

Over bagels and cream cheese and more fresh-squeezed orange juice and strong coffee, Aimee and Charles asked if they might leave early, since the weekend was such a success for both couples, and just get back to their lives. Aimee was eager to start filling out the application she'd had in her desk drawer for months. Joy and Harry missed Rex and said they'd be glad to get home, too. Rebecca had a feeling that being back on their home turf, where their little guy was, might help them find their way back to each other more than this place would at the moment.

And so Rebecca found herself back on the Love Bus at

10:00 a.m. and home by 10:40. With no one to greet her, not even Charlie. Theo had said he'd be home after three o'clock, so she'd just have to wait to collect her little dog.

She called Ellie, who assured her she was fine, though not really, and that she and Maggie were starting the Bitter Ex-wives Club of Wiscasset, though exes of any kind were welcome, from ex-girlfriends to ex-husbands. She asked after the fate of the two other couples and was pleased to hear there was hope out there for the right matches, the right couples, that long-term love wasn't doomed. Two years of marriage might not be considered long-term to most, but two years was the longest Rebecca had been in a relationship. She wasn't so sure if relationships were supposed to go through these ups and downs, these "I don't even like you" ups and downs, or if the way she'd been feeling for the past year meant she should have gotten out long ago. Sometimes she did love Michael, in a way that moved something inside her heart, made her toes tingle, made her grateful to be alive. And then for long stretches she'd look at him every morning and want to pour the contents of his prissy water pitcher (that always had to be on his bedside table) on his face. Slowly.

He'd arranged her father's funeral.

He'd called Joy trashy.

That was how it was, though. He'd do one huge thing, something so vital to her ability to take a breath, and then in the next moment he'd do something that would suck that breath right out of her body.

Was this what marriage was? This push and pull, give and take? She'd once heard Charlotte say she hated Peter's guts, that he was the biggest asshole on the planet. Then the next day, they'd be arm in arm, nuzzling noses. And when Rebecca would ask Charlotte how they'd made up so fast, Charlotte would look puzzled and say, "Rebecca, we're *married*" as if Rebecca understood what that meant.

Well, Rebecca didn't get it. Did it mean you forgave everything? How *did* you know, really, what a deal breaker was—and when? It had taken quite a while for Ellie to reach the deal-breaking point.

She wondered what her mother would have done if she had known about her husband's affair with Pia Jayhawk that summer. If she'd known about the baby. Rebecca had first thought her mother would leave her father, that she wouldn't tolerate the betrayal, but Rebecca had no idea, really. She knew her mother, knew her father, but to a point. Their marriage, the real inside of it, was private. From what she did know of her mother, the deal breaker would not necessarily have been the affair. It would have been the back turning.

She heard Marianne come through the side door. Rebecca found her in the kitchen in her church clothes, little hat with veil and all, putting away groceries. Rebecca told her she'd put everything away, she needed to do some mindless work, and a grateful Marianne went off to change her clothes. When she came back in a fleece top and jeans, they set to work on five trays of whoopie pies with traditional cream filling.

"Marianne, why do you think husbands cheat on their wives?" Rebecca asked as she measured the flour and dumped it into a silver mixing bowl.

"Big question," Marianne said, working on mixing the

sugar, butter, and eggs. Rebecca handed her the half cup of oil and the vanilla extract, then added the cocoa powder in her own bowl. "I don't think anyone knows the answer, either. Not God or marriage therapists or Einstein. I'll bet there are as many reasons why men cheat as there are men."

Rebecca sighed. "I guess so."

It was interesting to Rebecca that her father had had an affair only three years into marriage with her mother, yet then hadn't "even committed adultery in my heart like Jimmy Carter" (per one of his letters to Joy) with another woman for the next fifteen years. Why? Rebecca could only assume it was a combination of fear and guilt and the utter gravitas of the situation. Even if the vasectomy had nixed the chance of another phone call interrupting his crossword puzzle, the "invisible" consequence of what his affair had resulted in had been like an albatross. *That* was what kept her father from so much as glancing at another woman. Rebecca was sure of it.

Marianne turned off the electric mixer. "You're not married, are you?"

"Me, no. Just curious." Rebecca measured the baking powder and baking soda and poured them in the bowl.

Marianne regarded her for a moment, then said, "My husband cheated on me twice. And to be honest, yeah, it hurt, but I didn't pay it much mind."

Rebecca raised an eyebrow. "Why not?"

"Well, the first time, an enemy I made at a P.T.A. meeting went for him whole hog. Just went after him to hurt me. She worked in the same office and started dressing all sexy, sidling up to him in her low-cut blouses and Miracle bras, and he finally couldn't resist. She made sure the gossip got back to me. And her work was done."

Rebecca paused with the salt in her hand. "So you weren't upset?"

Marianne wiped her hands on her apron and sighed. "At her more than anything. I wished he'd been strong enough to ignore her, but between the flattery and her huge breasts and all the hot-breath whispers in his ear about what she wanted to do with him, he went for it right there in the inventory room."

"And there was a second time?"

"A tramp at work again. But this time she really did like him, thought she could steal him away. What a mess that was. He was carrying on a sexual affair, and she thought she was having a love affair."

Rebecca handed the dry mixture to Marianne, who poured it into her bowl. She added some milk, then began beating again. "How did you find out about it?"

"Woman from his office called. She said she thought I should know my husband was canoodling with a coworker. She used that word, too. *Canoodling*. Made it sound less sleazy. Anyway, he told me he was trying to end it with her, but she wasn't taking no for an answer. I told him he'd just better up and quit before we had a *Fatal Attraction* scenario on our hands. He was out of work for three months before he found another good-paying manager's-level job."

"Any more phone calls?"

Marianne turned off the mixer. "No. But I have no doubt he had his dalliances."

"And . . . that was okay?"

"Yes or no. Oh, Rebecca, it's complicated, really. No, it's not okay. Of course it's not okay. But yeah, if it's just sex and a midlife crisis and a little fun in the humdrum every day of life, fine. I knew Aaron loved me, loved me in his heart and soul. I guess I made it okay for me, since he was going to cheat anyway."

Rebecca began spooning circles of batter onto the cookie trays. "And if you'd given him an ultimatum?"

"I think he would have said okay and then been very careful about his affairs."

"Do you think it's possible for some men not to cheat at all? To be monogamous till death do you part?"

"I most certainly do think so. I know some of them, too." She slung an arm around Rebecca. "I didn't turn you off to marriage for all time, did I?"

"No. Truth is always good, don't you think?" Rebecca finished her second tray and began scooping batter onto a third.

"Well, as long as you remember that there's rarely a truth to be found even in absolutes. Yes, there are facts and there are lies, but there are usually mitigating circumstances, even the smallest of ones, that can make sense out of anything. My mother called that 'being flexible.'"

My mother would call that rationalizing, Rebecca thought. But she wouldn't say that to Marianne. "But how do you know when you're being too flexible? How do you know when you should refuse to bend on something?"

Marianne slid the trays into the oven. "You just do. You wake up one morning and you just know. You wake up different. And I'll tell you—if you give in after that, after you've woken up different, after you've reached your *point,* it'll kill you. It'll take a while—a few months, maybe a year—but it'll break your spirit. Then you're done for."

That was sobering.

At Rebecca's expression, Marianne added, "Honey, you've heard the expression 'Follow your heart?' That's what it really means. You follow what you've been waking up with for days on end, for weeks on end, even if your head isn't too sure. That's how you don't regret things, even your mistakes. The heart isn't as stupid as some people think."

"I'm confused. On the one hand, I understand what you're saying, and on the other, I don't get it at all."

Marianne smiled. "That's not always a bad thing."

Rebecca glanced up at the moose clock on the wall. It was ten minutes to three. She took off her apron and hung it on a peg with the others. "If you don't need me anymore, I'm going to pick up Charlie from Theo's. I miss that little guy so much."

Marianne smiled. "You go ahead. You helped too much as it is for a paying customer."

Rebecca liked baking with Marianne. She wouldn't go so far as to say she loved baking; she found measuring ingredients boring, and she often forgot if she'd added the baking powder or the baking soda, which meant having to start over. But she liked baking with another person, talking through it. And she loved when the delicious smells began emanating from the oven into the entire house, smelling like Christmas morning, when her mom always made her cinnamon rolls. And, of course, Rebecca did love the finished product, the warm whoopie pie straight out of the oven. She liked to take just a half of a little round cake and top it with cream that would melt over the sides.

What she didn't like about baking was how arbitrary it was. You measured, you mixed, and set the timer on the oven. And what you got wasn't always the same. That was what Rebecca didn't get. Why some of her creations, when she did attempt to cook, came out fine and other times came out like crap. It was why she had a kitchen drawer full of delivery menus in her New York City apartment.

With some of her thoughts and some of Marianne's knocking around in her head, Rebecca walked to Theo's, taking the path by the beach and hoping the cool ocean air would clear her mind. It didn't. What did clear her head of all other thought was the sight of Theo Granger in his backyard. She watched him, mesmerized by the afternoon sunlight on his sandy blond hair, on his tanned forearms. On his delicious, tall, strong body in his long-sleeved T-shirt (dark green this time) and low-slung jeans. A *thing of beauty*, she thought absently, recalling a favorite line of her mother's, from a poem Norah Strand had loved. They'd be walking down the street and it would start to snow, and her mother would marvel over a snowflake and say, "A thing of beauty is a joy forever," even as the snowflake melted on her palm at first contact.

Charlie barked and began racing around in circles, and Theo looked over to see what had caught his attention. At the sight of her, Theo's smile lit up the rest of him.

Oh God. He liked her, too.

"No wonder you're so excited, Charlie," Theo said, opening the gate for her. "Welcome back."

She kneeled down and hugged Charlie, rubbing his belly when he rolled over onto his back. Theo threw a chew toy, and Charlie and Spock went running. The dogs were friends. Theo was clearly a good mediator himself.

She wanted nothing more at the moment than to flop into his arms the way Joy had into her husband's. To have those strong arms around her, supporting her, giving her strength. The way Michael's arms had made her feel the day she'd found out about Joy. Now she wondered if that comfort had been about him and his muscular arms in particular or if she'd been in desperate need of a hug and anyone's arms would have helped.

"You look exhausted," Theo said. "Beautiful, but exhausted. How'd the weekend go?"

"Ellie and Tim didn't work out. But the other couples seemed to be on surer footing."

"Too bad about Ellie," he said. "She okay?"

"She left early. Maggie's taking care of her."

He nodded. "Have you eaten? I just picked up a pizza from Mama's on my way home."

"I had a huge brunch, but thanks."

"Well, hang out, then," he said. "You can be my trusty assistant on this cello. Arlene commissioned it for Matteo." Behind him was a worktable and a block of beautiful wood that he'd begun carving into.

"Is he feeling better these days?"

"Nope. His girlfriend dumped him."

"Awww, poor guy." Everyone was having trouble in the love department. The big, sticky, difficult department of love.

She envisioned Theo storming off after an argument, disappearing into his workshop for hours to carve something. Theo canoodling. She was suddenly very tired, bone-tired. "I am exhausted and need to head home. But thanks again. And thanks for taking such good care of Charlie."

He turned to look at her. "So . . . *home* home or Finch's?"

"I don't know." Tears pricked at her eyes and she blinked them away. "I really don't know."

He stopped working for a moment. "A good reason to stay in Wiscasset, then. Since you're already here."

She stared out at the ocean, the great vast endless blue-brown of it. It was a good reason, actually. "Agreed. So it's Finch's for the moment. Something about that place makes me able to think."

"The secret ingredient is the air," she remembered Arlene saying. The woman had been right. There was something about this Maine air, this Wiscasset air, that did something calming to Rebecca's soul.

"Anyway, I could use a quiet walk with Charlie right now," she said.

He nodded. "See you soon, then."

It was as good as a hug.

She sat with Charlie in the little park with the gazebo, appreciating the plastic bag dispenser next to a sign that said: PLEASE PICK UP POOP! since she'd forgotten to bring her own bag. The park was a simple grassy field with a path along the wooded edge, and the lovely wooden gazebo topped with a wrought-iron weather vane. At the other end of the park, she saw a couple walking two golden retrievers. "What now, Charlie? I'm back to that same old question."

Charlie rested his sweet little face on her arm.

"You don't know either, huh?" she said, scratching behind his ears. "Where am I supposed to go? What am I supposed to do? And why don't I know?"

The chimes of her cell phone rang. Michael.

Rebecca bit her lip and answered. "Hi."

"It's Sunday, Rebecca. Sunday number two. Are you coming home now?"

Yeah, are you? she wondered.

"Michael, I wish this made sense. To me, too. But I'm just not ready to come home. I think I want to stay here for a while. I want to work on my relationship with Joy. Here."

He sighed in her ear. "I don't get this at all. You're just staying up there? What the hell for?"

"I just told you. To work on my relationship with Joy."

"Right. With Joy. With this stranger who you told me doesn't even want you there. Well, do you want to know why I think you're staying up there?"

Actually, she did want to know. Michael could be cold, but he could also be incredibly insightful.

"I think you're staying up there because you're really just running away, Rebecca. Your father died. You're screwing up at work. We're having problems. So you booked out of here. And as long as she's pushing you away, there's no pressure. You get to stalk her to your heart's content."

"I'm not stalking her, Michael. Jesus."

"Whatever. She's not coming to you, so you get to go to her, as it feels right to you. You say things are on her terms, but they're really on yours. You're the one making the decisions. You're the one deciding to stay."

"So I'm not running from anything, then, am I? I'm pursuing something. Why can't you understand that?"

"Because it's bullshit, that's why. There's nothing to pursue. You're going to make a relationship out of nothing? Out of thin air?"

God, he was like an old-school grandmother. You couldn't win.

"Something happened this weekend, Michael. I went on one of Joy's tours, this one for couples in troubled relationships—not as one of the participants, I mean. My background in mediation was really—"

"You're *not* a mediator, Rebecca. You're a paralegal. And one who's made a lot of mistakes lately. I hope Joy's having you sign a legal waiver limiting—"

Jerk! "Will you say *anything* to get your way?" Rebecca interrupted. "Is that what mediators do? Put things so that the person has no choice but to agree because you're not wrong? Well, there's something called shades of gray."

"Fine. Here's a black and white question. The firm needs to know if we need to hire a temp—or a replacement." He sighed again. "Rebecca, everyone knows you're going through a tough time. We'll hold your job. But I need to know what you're doing."

"I know," she said, and suddenly realized he was talking about more than just her job. She stared up at the evergreens across the park, then closed her eyes. "I think you should hire a replacement. I don't know when I'll be back. I'm hardly irreplaceable."

"You're not so fucking replaceable," he said, and hung up.

When she got back to Finch's, there was a small basket on the floor in front of her door. Rebecca picked it up. Something warm and delicious was underneath a white cloth napkin. A loaf of freshly baked bread and a jar of strawberry preserves with a label that said STRAWBERRY, SEPTEMBER in black ink.

There was also a little card: *Thanks.—Joy.*

Rebecca smiled and called Joy. "Did you bake the bread yourself?"

"It helps me think."

"What are you thinking?"

"That the weekend was a very big success, even for poor Ellie. She's ready to let go of Tim."

I'm not ready to let go of you, Rebecca thought. There was still barely a connection between them, despite two weekends away, despite everything that had been said. There was no . . . *something.*

"So, are you going back to New York?" Joy asked.

"Do you want me to?"

Silence. "I don't necessarily want you to go. And you're hardly a stranger anymore. You know more of my personal business than anyone."

Rebecca's heart leaped in her chest.

"The situation, our situation, is what it is," Joy added.

Rebecca smiled. Joy had definitely not grown up with Daniel Strand.

"I mean, you are who you are, Rebecca. My half sister. That's not going to change, regardless of whether you're here or hundreds of miles away in New York. I guess it might be even harder to deal with you in New York *because* of the wonderful 'out of sight, out of mind' thing. Because I can't push you out of mind. I've tried, trust me. If you're here, at least I can make some sense of you, try to figure out how I feel and what to do. I mean, we can't just blink and *become* sisters."

You're going to make a relationship out of nothing? Out of thin air? . . .

"I know. And I don't know what to do about it, either. Maybe it would be easier if we had some big life thing in common, like if we were both new mothers or mothers of preschoolers or single and unemployed and completely alone in the world."

"Is that how you feel?" Joy asked.

"That's how I felt. But there's something about this place, the people I've met. And, of course, you."

"I don't want to talk about our mutual father," she said. "Harry will think I've taken a giant step backward, but I really don't want to go there."

"I can understand that."

"What else is there for us to talk about, though?"

"I don't know," Rebecca said. "We could talk about your marriage, but that might come back to you know who."

"Right. So I guess we'll have to think of something else."

Relief flooded through her. This was so strange, this being

at the mercy of someone else. Someone who wasn't a boy-friend who wanted to dump her. *That* Rebecca had experience with. But this thing with Joy was something very different. Joy *did* get to call the shots here. She got to decide whether or not she wanted Rebecca in her life. Rebecca didn't feel like she had the reins here at all. Though she *was* beginning to remind herself of that hilarious and pathetic woman on *Seinfeld* who'd refused to allow George Costanza to break up with her. "No," she'd just kept saying.

"Joy, I was wondering—could I take Rex to the playground sometime? Or to Story Time? I'd really like to get to know him. If you're okay with that."

Silence. And then: "I'm taking him to Story Time at the library tomorrow morning at ten thirty. You're welcome to meet us there."

"Thanks, Joy. That means a lot to me. I'll see you there."

"Well, good-bye for now," Joy said.

"Good-bye for now," Rebecca repeated, something easing inside her heart.

Rebecca lay in her bed, staring at the ceiling. She couldn't sleep. She cut yet another slice of the bread, forgoing the jam this time, and made a cup of tea and sat with it by the window. It was just before midnight. Charlie was nosing around by the door, so she put on a sweater and socks and her clogs and went out, in a different direction than she normally took, Charlie scampering at her feet, sniffing the leaves that covered the sidewalks. The streets were deserted, yet Rebecca felt utterly safe. She was about to turn the corner when she saw the most beautiful old tree, its changing colors illuminated in the glow of moonlight—red, gold, yellow. She crossed the street to stand under it. Her mother had once told her that when something was bothering her, when she couldn't make a decision about something or figure something out, she would go to Central Park and stand under a berry-bearing tree, and for some reason, the answer always came to her. This old tree wasn't berry-bearing, but it seemed so old and all knowing.

Rebecca stood underneath its lowest branch, the still soft leaves just brushing against her temples. Perhaps if she stood here for days, her heart would tell her something, like Marianne said it would. She would know whether she did love Michael or not. If she should go home or not. *Did* people have to ask themselves if they loved somebody, though? she wondered. Didn't everyone always say you just knew?

Why was the one thing she knew, with certainty, that she wanted to be here, where Joy was? Because Michael was right? Because it gave her somewhere to be, somewhere to run and hide where not much was asked of her? Was Michael right? Or was where she'd been just so . . . wrong?

The answer would have to wait because Charlie had tangled up his leash around her legs. As she spun and darted to free herself, she saw the house.

The house.

The one in the painting at Mama's that she'd seen her first day in Wiscasset. The little yellow house with the white trim and the flower boxes and the cobblestone path. It was a cross between a craftsman bungalow, like Theo's, and a Cape. She stood there and stared at it, at the yellow sweetness of it, at the small porch with its rocking chair. The house wasn't the same one as in the painting, she realized. But it was so close.

She imagined the porch swing Theo would build for her. She imagined sitting there with him, holding hands. She imagined herself inside that house, coming and going.

Living here.

And there was a FOR SALE sign in the yard. She smiled at it. She imagined running up the three little stone steps to the porch with her tote bag full of textbooks from her grad school program in counseling. She glanced up at the second-floor window and envisioned herself sitting at a desk overlooking the tree in the front yard while typing a term paper and researching happily with a cup of tea and Charlie at her feet.

But it was just a fantasy. And reality was the fact that there was something to work out with Michael, something true, despite all their problems. He wasn't completely wrong when he accused her of running away from what bothered her in New York—from her job to their problems to the stress of the city itself. She *was* a New Yorker visiting someone else's life for a little while. She couldn't just up and buy the little yellow house of her dreams in a tiny town in Maine.

But she jotted down the name of the real-estate agency and the telephone number anyway.

thirteen

A little before ten thirty, Rebecca was waiting inside the Children's Room of the Wiscasset Public Library. Six or seven children were seated on colorful little cushions in a semicircle around a young woman with a big smile and great enunciation. Parents and caregivers sat on sofas and chairs along the back walls, reading or chatting or watching. Rebecca glanced at her watch. Perhaps Joy had changed her mind.

But there they were. Adorable Rex wore a red Superman cape and blue swimming goggles, which elicited happy laughter from the other kids. He squeezed between a boy and girl he seemed to know, and stared up at the young woman. He was so cute! The Story Time leader held up a book, *Caps for Sale*, which Rebecca remembered reading as a little kid. When the woman began reading, the children focused on her. Joy came over to Rebecca's love seat and sat down beside her.

As the kids giggled over the antics of the naughty monkeys in the story, Rebecca thought about how she and Michael used to lie in bed and talk about the children they'd have one day. Two boys and two girls. Michael liked classic names like Catherine and Henry. Rebecca liked Clementine and Milo. They'd finally agreed that he could name two kids and she could name two kids. But those conversations had stopped long ago. Now, she couldn't imagine having children with such a rigid person, a father who'd tell his three-year-old daughter she was operating under an "information deficit" when she wanted cake for breakfast.

"I love his cape," Rebecca whispered to Joy. "And his goggles. He's just adorable."

Joy smiled. "Harry has a picture of himself as a kid in a Superman cape, and you'd swear it was Rex."

Rex did look like Harry in terms of coloring—the same thick, shiny brown hair and hazel eyes. But the features were Joy's—the round shape of the eyes, the slightly aquiline nose, the strong chin. There was Strand in him.

After the story, the kids scrambled up and began choosing books from atop the low shelves. Rex came over with *Curious George Flies A Plane* and squeezed between Rebecca and the edge of the sofa, then put the book on her lap.

"Wow," Joy said. "He usually wants only me to read to him. He must like your face."

Rebecca laughed. "Do you like my face?" she asked Rex.

Rex didn't answer, but he did lean his head against her, the straps of his little blue goggles cool against her skin. He stared at the book, waiting, and so Rebecca opened it on her lap, and Rex pointed at George staring out a large airport window at a small airplane. "He fly the plane!" Rex said, giggling.

Rebecca laughed again and let Rex turn the pages and comment on the pictures, which he seemed more interested in than the story itself.

"You're good with kids," Joy whispered, and the compliment made Rebecca ridiculously happy.

This was her family, no matter how much Joy had tried to resist her—or might continue to resist her. This woman and this boy were her *family*. Immediate family, interrupted.

When Joy took Rex to the bathroom, Rebecca opened her purse and fished around for the receipt she'd used to scribble the name and number of the real-estate agency. The moment she got back to her room at Finch's, she was calling that number. Suddenly, having a place of her own here in Wiscasset didn't seem like a crazy fantasy. She *did* have family here. And Maine *was* Vacationland.

"Coastal Real Estate, Maggie Herald speaking."

Maggie? Ah—Rebecca had forgotten that Maggie was a Realtor. "Maggie, it's Rebecca Strand." She paced her small room at Finch's, excited, nervous energy coursing through her.

"Hi, hon! If you're calling about Ellie, she's doing much better. Last I spoke to her, which was in the middle of the night last night, she had five Hefty bags full of that jerk bastard's crap and had dumped them all in the backyard for him to pick up."

"That must be so hard, getting rid of his stuff."

"She's purging. Vomiting him out of her life like the rotten egg he is. She'll be okay. I have all my best divorce books in a pile for her. *Spiritual Divorce, The Good Divorce.* Like there's any kind of divorce but a shitty divorce. Oh, and, speaking of divorce, did Ellie tell you we started a new club? The *Bitter* Ex-wives Club of Wiscasset? We had to start a new club since Victoria is so sickeningly in love with Victor and can't stand to be around us bitter hags. You think the town recreation department will let us call it that in the catalog?"

Rebecca laughed. "It's catchy."

"We're going to have weekly meetings. Ellie and I were hoping you could come and lead the discussions, help keep us on track so we don't start sharpening knives or anything."

"I'm not sure there is a track with clubs," Rebecca said. "You really just need each other and maybe some good junk food."

"Oh, we'll have the junk food, definitely. But we think having an impartial person might really help. Will you at least come to the first meeting? If it's too boring, we'll totally understand. We'll pay you in booze and really good appetizers. Nachos with the works. Chocolate. None of that cucumber sandwich crap. First meeting is Thursday night at six at my house. Two other women will be joining us, and one man. We might have to change the name to just Bitter Exes Club to be inclusive."

Michael's voice rang in her ears. *"You're not a mediator . . ."* But she was a person with a brain and a heart, and she happened to be good at helping people make sense of their own lives, their own hearts, even if she couldn't seem to do it for herself. "I love pigs in a blanket. So it's a deal. Oh, and,

Maggie, I was out walking last night and I noticed this adorable yellow house, like a craftsman-style bungalow."

"Oh, yes—on Elm, right?"

"That's the one."

"Well, it's been on the market for over six months and the price has been dropped twice already. It's tiny is the problem. Only two bedrooms. One and a half baths. People like a full second bath. And a third bedroom, whether to turn it into an office or a guest room."

Tiny? It was a whole house! After a one-bedroom apartment in New York, shared by two people, a house was . . . huge. "I realize the sign said it was for sale, but, by any chance, is it available for a month-to-month lease? Till it sells?" She realized she was holding her breath.

"Absolutely. I've listed it in the local paper and on Craigslist every month and a few people have been out to see it as a rental, but no takers. A house without a garage in Maine scares people off, even renters."

Thank you, universe, Rebecca said, ceilingward.

As for the lack of garage and winter looming (not that she necessarily anticipated still being here when the blizzards began), Rebecca figured that was what Home Depot was for— snowblowers and ice scrapers. "I'd love to see it. Can you show it to me today by any chance?"

"Tell you what—I've got a few appointments over in Brunswick this morning, some properties I'm showing, so why don't you take a look inside the house yourself and let me know what you think. Oh—it's lightly furnished, but the owner will rent it unfurnished if you prefer. She lives over by Sebago Lake now and will just have the stuff put in storage. If you like the place, I'll come back with you and give you the details. You'll find the key in the little can in the flower box window on the side, just before the fence. Let yourself in and look around. Good thing I can vouch for you personally."

She smiled. "Thanks. I'll call you later." She was about to hang up when she remembered Charlie. "Maggie, are dogs allowed?"

"Dogs *and* cats. The owner is one of those animal rescue types, fostering three-legged everythings. I think she's fostering a one-eyed ferret right now."

Rebecca laughed. "Thanks. Call you later."

Rebecca put on Charlie's leash and practically ran over to the little yellow house. It had its own wonderful tree right in the front yard, shading the porch. The houses on either side weren't too close, either, and they were as adorable as this one, but they were both white.

She found the key, then walked up the three steps to the little porch and unlocked the door, which opened into a tiny foyer with a round braided rug and a wrought-iron coatrack. The hardwood floors were wide-planked and old, yet weren't scratched. The living-room walls were painted a pretty pale blue. There was a stone fireplace with a decorative mantel, above which was hung a particularly nice painting of five brightly colored rowboats docked in water. And the furniture was decent—a cranberry-colored denim sofa, another braided rug, and a coffee table made of what looked like sticks. Three tall windows were covered by filmy white curtains dotted with a tiny red filigree design. Down a short hallway was a small bathroom with a toilet and an antique round white wooden mirror above the sink.

Down another short hallway was the kitchen. It was small, but a good square shape with hardwood floors and a big window over the white-enameled sink, which reminded Rebecca of her late grandmother's old apartment in New York. The appliances looked sound; she liked the fact that there wasn't stainless-steel anything in this kitchen. And she loved the white wooden pedestal table with its matching chairs by a window covered with yellow curtains. Rebecca could absolutely imagine eating her Special K and the occasional bowl of Crunch Berries there.

Up a flight of ten or so stairs was a short landing and two decent-sized bedrooms, both with four windows each and double closets. One of the bedrooms, the one with the pale yellow walls, had a queen-sized bed and a dresser; the other had a twin bed. Between the bedrooms was a great bathroom with a claw-foot tub and a beautiful vanity that reminded Rebecca of a movie star's dressing table.

This was definitely a woman's house, Rebecca knew. A man had not lived here recently. It seemed a place where the owner had transitioned, perhaps, between lives.

This was Rebecca's house.

She stood in the small backyard (fenced—another plus) and called Maggie. "I love the house. I absolutely want to rent it."

"Great! You just earned me a commission. I'll come by

Marianne's tonight with a month-to-month agreement. I'll need the first month's rent and a month's rent as a security deposit, and you can move in immediately if you want. I'll prorate the rent."

"What *is* the rent?" Rebecca asked. She realized she had no idea what it cost to rent a whole house. The apartment she shared with Michael was thirty-one hundred dollars a month.

"It's eleven hundred plus utilities. I could probably talk Anna down to ten-fifty, though, since it's been empty for so long. She'll be thrilled to rent it. Then again, she might insist on the eleven hundred because of the fence she had installed this past summer. Did you see the backyard? Theo Granger did the fence. Ellie said you brought him to her bust of a dinner party last week. You two dating?"

Rebecca smiled and spun around in her yard, her gaze on her white picket fence that Theo built. "Nope. Just friends. And eleven hundred is just fine." Thanks to Michael's frugal ways, she had a fat savings account.

"So you're not interested?"

"In Theo? Maggie, you know I live with someone."

"But you're renting a house in Maine. Unless the boyfriend is planning to move up here, too?"

Good point.

"My life is a little complicated at the moment."

"All our lives are complicated at the moment," Maggie said. "You're lucky, though—Theo has his pick of single women in this town, and he hasn't been interested in anyone. Except you."

"He's not interested, Maggie. We're just friends."

" 'Just friends' don't go to dinner parties together. 'Just friends' don't take long walks together on beaches. 'Just friends' don't sit on Marianne's front porch and talk late at night."

Humph. Small-town life had its drawbacks. "I'll give you that he is cute. But like I said, I don't know what I'm doing. I just know that I want this house."

"Well, that *I* can give you. I'll meet you at Marianne's at five?"

"Five is perfect."

As Charlie scampered around his new yard and christened one of the trees, Rebecca made mental notes of what she'd need to buy: new mattresses, for starters. Bed linens. Towels. Cleaning supplies. Kitchen everything, from silverware to pots and pans. Her list was getting so long that she reached into her bag for her little notebook and pen. She was up to *shower curtain* when her phone rang—a New York City number she didn't recognize.

"Hello?"

"Rebecca, this is Martin Fischer." Her father's lawyer. He was a good friend of her father's, and after the funeral he'd let her know she'd hear from him when the estate was settled. "As you know, you're the sole beneficiary of your father's estate. I have several documents that require your signature, and then I'll have a check for you in the amount of one point three million dollars. And change. Five hundred thousand from his life insurance policy, and the rest from his various accounts."

Holy shit! The pen dropped from Rebecca's hand. She knew her father had a life insurance policy, and she knew he was well off, that he'd made sound investments that had survived the market crashes. Yet she'd never quite believed

Michael when he talked about her father being worth over a million dollars; she'd thought it was financial lingo, money *on* paper, not *in* paper, and when all was said and done, there would be around two hundred thousand or so left over.

"I called your home first," the lawyer said, "and Michael informed me you were away in Maine and would be there for a while. I'll need your address to overnight the package."

Her address. Rebecca raced outside and checked the front door. 44. "44 Elm Street, Wiscasset, Maine. I don't know the zip code. Oh, wait—Martin, you'd better send the package to the inn I've been staying at, just in case. I'm not sure if I'll be moving into the new place tomorrow or the next day." She gave Marianne's address.

"All set, then. If you could read over the documents and sign them and return them ASAP, I'll have them filed and you'll have your check within a couple of weeks."

My check. I'd much rather have my father.

Rebecca sat on the porch steps. "Martin, I need to know the truth about something. Are you familiar with the name Pia Jayhawk or Joy Jayhawk?"

He wasn't.

"There's nothing in my father's will about them?"

"No, nothing about a Pia Jayhawk or a Joy Jayhawk," Martin said.

She explained about her father's deathbed confession, about the letters, about finding Joy, about why she was in Maine. "So there's nothing in my father's accounting to indicate he paid child support over the years to Pia Jayhawk or set aside money in an account for Joy Jayhawk?"

Granted, Martin Fischer was her father's good friend, but he was also a good lawyer. Rebecca understood about confidentiality. Martin would tell her nothing, even if her father had told him about Pia and Joy. He would tell her only what was documented, what was legal. "No, none at all. There is no record of their names whatsoever."

How could that be? How could he not have sent Pia money, even anonymously? Had he really just turned his back so completely? Emotionally and mentally and physically, okay. Rebecca got that. But how could he turn his back financially? How could he not provide for the most basic of life's necessities: food, clothing, shelter? Joy was his child, whether he wanted her to exist or not.

Every birthday, he sat and wrote Joy a stupid, meaningless letter about himself, about what he was thinking and feeling, when what she needed, what she must have wished for every year, was an actual birthday card. Contact. A father.

Rebecca felt her stomach churn. Joy more than deserved her share of his money. And she would have it, too. Whether her *own* attorney approved or not. Not that Michael was really her lawyer. She'd never had reason for one.

She'd barely clicked off her phone when it rang again. Michael.

"Did your father's lawyer get in touch? He called a few minutes ago and I told him you were away, and then realized I didn't even know your address. Interesting, right, that I don't have my girlfriend's address where she's been for over two weeks."

"Why are you home at"—Rebecca glanced at her watch—"noon on a Monday, anyway? Are you sick?"

"Do you care?"

"I asked, didn't I?"

"I have the flu or something. I don't know. I'll live."

She loved how he managed to be such a drama queen when he was insisting he was the opposite. "Michael, you know I'm staying at an inn called Finch's in Wiscasset. Finding the address wouldn't be so hard."

She wasn't going to tell him about the new house just yet. He wouldn't understand. *She* barely understood. And it would only start an argument she wasn't ready to have.

"I assume Fischer is sending you papers to sign for the inheritance? It's over a million, right?"

"One point three," she said.

"You'll be set for life with that much money."

"Well, half of that much money."

Silence. Then: "Rebecca, you're not *seriously* going to give her half. She's *not* his daughter."

"We've had this conversation before. She *is* his daughter. She was denied his financial support. She deserved to *sue* for it."

"Why don't you let her know that, since you're so set on throwing your future away."

"I'm giving her half the money, end of story. I hope you feel better. Bye."

"Rebecca, *think* for once, okay? Just stop and think. You're an emotional mess right now—"

"Why, because I'm not doing what *you* want? What *you* think I should do? Because I have my own opinion on my *own* life? I have to go." With that, she clicked her phone shut and threw it into her bag, then noticed a little old lady staring at her from across the street.

She added another mental note to the list of thousands: Do not talk on the phone outside in a tiny town.

Rebecca went a little crazy in Bed, Bath & Beyond. Choosing a down comforter from a selection of at least twenty, with samples to feel and squeeze and varying warmth levels, had knocked her argument with Michael right out of her mind.

"Get the lightweight warmth," someone said from behind her. "I bought the second level and sweated to death last winter. Trust me."

Rebecca smiled at the woman and the little girl in her shopping cart. "I'll take your word for it. Otherwise I'll be here for hours."

She grabbed a big plastic-encased queen-sized comforter and put it in her own cart, then headed to the sheets department, where she chose a yellow duvet cover with tiny flowers. And matching shams. And soft cotton and flannel sheets. And between bedding and towels were rows of items that she couldn't resist, like a radio for the shower, so she could listen to Lady Gaga and Coldplay while shampooing her hair. She spent twenty minutes deciding on a vacuum cleaner (she wanted the Dyson, but couldn't imagine spending that much) and even longer on her china pattern. She selected soft lavender towels and a fluffy bath mat. Drinking glasses and a set of wineglasses. A corkscrew, too.

And a welcome mat.

When she checked out, she'd spent over eight hundred dollars on stuff for a house she didn't even technically have the rights to. She glanced at her watch. Only a little after two

o'clock. She'd go back to Marianne's, call the utility compa-
nies, order mattresses, and mentally decorate her new home
until Maggie came over.

All her packages barely fit in the little Honda. Maybe she'd
buy a Subaru like everyone had around here.

You are getting ahead of yourself again, she thought, annoyed that she was *not* stopping to think beyond the right now.
But who said she had to?

When Rebecca woke up the next morning, she eyed the
shiny silver key and lease on her nightstand and scooped up
Charlie for a hug. "We're moving tomorrow! And we have a
ton to do today to get our new home ready."

He licked her chin, which she took to mean he was happy,
too. She'd already told Marianne, who'd made her promise to
come talk over whoopie pies once in a while.

The whir of a power saw told her Theo was here. After a
quick shower and, granted, a bit too long choosing between
sweaters for someone who was "just a friend," she took Charlie
for a walk around the back.

Theo turned off the saw and lifted his work goggles.

"Guess what?" she asked.

He glanced up at the brilliant blue sky, then looked back at
her. "You rented that cute yellow house on Elm Street?"

"Good guess," she said, lightly punching his arm. "Talk
works fast around here. I'll have to remember that."

"Congratulations. I also guess that means you're sticking
around."

"Looks that way."

He smiled. "Let me know if you need something. Bookcases are my least favorite thing to make because they're so boring, but everyone needs them."

"I don't have any books. Yet, I mean."

"Now I know what to get you for a housewarming present."

It occurred to her that she *could* have a housewarming party. That she actually knew enough people in this town who would actually come. Like Ellie and Maggie. And Joy. Harry. Arlene and Matteo. Victoria and Victor. The Cutlasses. Marianne. And, of course, Theo.

As another guy with a toolbox came into the yard, Rebecca said, "Well, I'll let you get back to work. Come on, Charlie. Let's go clean our new house from top to bottom." She'd never been so excited to vacuum and spray lemon-scented Windex in her entire life.

When she returned to Finch's, exhausted and wishing she'd thought to buy rubber gloves on her shopping spree, there was a FedEx package waiting for her. She was about to drop it on the bureau to read later when she saw it wasn't from Martin Fischer, Esquire, but from Whitman, Goldberg & Whitman. Perhaps she was being officially fired. Or sued for abandoning her job. Or her boyfriend.

Inside was a letter attached to two sealed plastic packets each containing what looked like a Q-tip swab and another smaller plastic packet. On one of the many labels Rebecca saw the letters DNA.

What the hell was this? Rebecca sat down on the chair by the window and read the letter.

Dear Rebecca,

I don't know why this didn't occur to me before, perhaps because it's not Joy who's claiming to be your half sister or who's making any kind of claim at all, particularly to your father's estate. Regardless, who's to say she is, in fact, the child of Daniel Strand? A woman named Pia Jayhawk, with whom your father had an affair, told him he was the father. Who knows if she was involved with someone else at the time? Who knows who the father really was? She clearly didn't press the issue, did she? And considering the father was a successful New York City attorney, she likely would have—if he were Joy's father.

I highly recommend you and Joy provide a DNA sample herewith and return it to the laboratory (the return address label is on the packet). At least you'll know once and for all if you're throwing your life away (not to mention a great deal of money) to forge a relationship with someone who's not related to you.

Please note that I have enclosed a personal check made out to the testing company in the amount of $495. Enclose it with the samples and use the enclosed address label on the envelope. It's that simple.

Love, Michael

Good Lord. Could he be a bigger blowhard?

Rebecca had always known it was possible that Joy wasn't

her half sister, that Daniel Strand hadn't fathered Pia Jay-hawk's child. Of course it was possible. Highly unlikely, though. Rebecca had immediately discounted the idea that Joy wasn't his daughter. First of all, her father said he was the father. Second, Joy looked like Daniel Strand—had his eyes and his chin and that certain something in his expression. She was Rebecca's half sister.

But, it was possible that she wasn't. And years of working in the field of law did make some things black and white, either/or. Paternity was one of those black and white things. Father-hood, sisterhood, what constituted family—that was something else, that was shades of gray. But DNA and blood were abso-lutes.

Rebecca's stomach flip-flopped at the thought that she could possibly be chasing after a relationship with someone who wasn't her sister at all. There was that slight chance—and the *slight* was enough. Perhaps her father had been able to turn his back on Joy and Pia because he wasn't 100 percent sure he was the father. No—that was stupid. He could have easily taken a paternity test if he'd really wanted to know for sure. He *believed* he was Joy's father. Or . . . he didn't want to know for sure.

Rebecca let out a deep sigh and shoved the letter and packet back inside the envelope and put it on her bureau.

The only person who knew whether Joy was Daniel Strand's daughter was Pia Jayhawk. And if she wasn't so certain, well, maybe Joy would take the DNA test. Just to know. For sure.

And then what? What if Joy wasn't her sister? Did she pack up and go home? Back to her old life? Did this all just not happen?

How could she pack up and go home when she *was* home now? She'd rented a house. She had a thousand dollars' worth of stuff and her shiny new mattresses had already been delivered. And she wanted Joy to be her sister. Joy was her sister in her heart, mind, and soul. Period.

She didn't need to know for sure. Her father had told her Joy was his child and that was good enough for her.

But what if Michael was right? What if Pia had a few lovers that summer? What if she thought Daniel Strand was the father but he wasn't? What if she chose him because he was the best of the bunch?

Who the hell knew?

She thought of the Maury Povich show, which often showcased a question of paternity, a man and a woman on stage, waiting anxiously the return from commercial break when Maury would finally reveal the results of the DNA test. With the documentation in his hands, Maury would announce, "You are *not* the father," and the guy often strutted around the stage triumphantly, rubbing the mother's face in her lie—or her mistake. Or sometimes the guy dropped his head in his hands and cried.

Like Joy would take a DNA test.

Actually, she probably would. Joy liked facts, absolutes. She would know with certainty that she was Daniel Strand's child, and perhaps that would break down that wall Harry complained about. Perhaps she would finally be interested in reading the letters. In forgiveness. Or not. But at least Joy would *know* on the DNA level she insisted was all they had between them.

But if she asked Joy to take the test, that would mean something about Joy's mother. Rebecca wasn't so sure Joy would go there.

She had no idea what to do. If she should drop it. Pursue it. She needed to find a berry-bearing tree and fast.

That night, Rebecca knocked on Theo's door. She'd walked the stretch of beach with Charlie, hoping to find answers from the night sky or the quiet, but she still didn't know what to do. And she wasn't calling Michael—who'd called three times to make sure she'd received his package—so that he could scream his opinions in her ear.

Theo opened the door and smiled.

"You said I should knock if I needed anything. And I need something." But instead of explaining about Michael's letter and the DNA packet and the questions running up and down her brain, she burst into tears.

"Hey," he said, taking her hand and leading her inside. "What's wrong?"

She sat down beside him on his sofa, Charlie and Spock sniffing each other at her feet. She wiped under her eyes and took a deep breath, the story of the letter rushing out of her mouth.

"You could go to Pia outright and just ask her," Theo said, handing her another tissue.

"But Joy asked me not to tell Pia who I am. I gave her my word."

"Then the answer to your problem is closer than you

realize: Marianne. She's the keeper of all secrets around here. She's lived here all her life and has never left. I'm sure she knows Pia from twenty-five years ago. I think they're around the same age, too."

Marianne. Of course.

"I could kiss you, Theo. Thanks."

He leaned closer, and for a moment she was tempted to do exactly that, just kiss him already, but he got up. "Let me get Spock's leash and I'll walk you back. Marianne might still be up if you want to catch her tonight."

She leaned her head back and stared up at the wood-beamed ceiling. "I'm just so tired and talked out."

"I know. You're welcome to sit here and not talk as long as you want."

God, she wanted to hug him. His kindness, the ease of it, was becoming indispensable to her. She could sit on this sofa with him all night, content to be aware of him, to smell his Ivory soap, to feel his thigh just brush against her own.

"I'd better go, though," she said. "Marianne's an early bird."

"Like my grandmother. Bed by nine every night. C'mon," he said with a gentle tap on her thigh.

And as the two dogs scampered ahead, sniffing at leaves and each other, Theo tucked her arm under his, old-fashioned style, and walked her home without a word. As they arrived at Finch's, Rebecca sat down on the porch steps. "What if she's not my sister?"

He sat down beside her. "That's a tricky one. I'd say something corny about whether or not she's your sister in your heart, but based on what you've told me, you guys are at the starting point. If she's not your father's child, and you just met her a couple of weeks ago, you really can't just hand her a heap of money. You could ask her to take the test. Maybe she'd like it settled, too."

"I thought that, but now I'm not really sure. I'm not sure she cares. She didn't seem to want to know until I came up and threw her history at her."

"Everyone wants to know their history, the secrets of where they came from. They might not know they want to know or that they need to know. But they do."

Rebecca stared up at the stars. "If my father hadn't told me about Joy, I wouldn't be here right now. Wouldn't know you or any of the people I've met here. Wouldn't have Charlie. It's crazy. But if Joy's not my sister, then this whole life I'm living here is not really mine." She shook her head. "Forget it, that doesn't even make sense."

"It makes total sense. And this is your life, regardless of what happens with a DNA test, Rebecca."

"But I rented a house. I adopted a dog. This is big stuff, Theo. This isn't just some vacation. If Joy's not my sister, I don't really belong here, do I?"

"That's up to you. After a point, it's not only about Joy."

"This is so confusing! I don't even want to know if she's really my half sister or not."

"Yeah, you do. Because knowing and what happens next is *everything*."

"But what *will* happen next?"

He smiled and took her hand, and she stared at their entwined fingers. "You'll find out, won't you?"

•   •   •

Marianne was in the room she called her reading parlor, where she liked to serve afternoon tea. She sat on one of the overstuffed chairs reading a novel, the glow of the lamp on the table beside her practically the only illumination in the room.

"Marianne? Got a minute?"

"Sure," she said, and put down the book. She patted the chair next to her, and Rebecca sat down.

"Do you know Pia Jayhawk?" Rebecca asked.

"Joy's mother. Sure. I've known her forever—well, till she moved away some years ago. She was my younger sister's best friend, as a matter of fact."

Rebecca took a deep breath. "Marianne, just before my father died a few weeks ago, he told me he had an affair with a woman named Pia Jayhawk and that Pia told him she was pregnant and gave birth to a girl she named Joy."

Marianne gasped. "Is that why you came to Wiscasset? To meet your half sister?"

Rebecca nodded. "My boyfriend back in New York thinks I should make sure that Joy *is* my half sister before I get any more emotionally involved. And before I hand over half of my inheritance."

"My goodness," Marianne said. "I could understand that. I assume he wants her to take a DNA test?"

Rebecca nodded. "Which seems very intrusive on my part. Joy isn't asking for anything. She's the not one who came looking for me. She's not laying claim to anything. She's never even asked about what he left behind or if there was a will. I

can't even imagine going up to her and saying, 'Oh, and if you want half our father's money, I need you to prove that you *are* his daughter.'"

"Well, if it helps, I'll tell you what I remember from that time when Pia was pregnant. She was very broken up about the man she'd gotten involved with. I can't remember his name. It was, what, over twenty-five years ago?"

She nodded. "And his name was Daniel. Daniel Strand."

"Yes, Daniel. Now I remember. Oh, goodness, I just remembered something Pia said. She was starting to show, and Patty—that's my sister—asked her if she'd heard from him at all, and Pia said so sadly, 'He already *has* a little girl and a life.' And then she just stopped talking about him. I guess she was focusing on the baby and how to raise her without a father. She was madly in love with him. Patty and I got a glimpse of him once, and I was so surprised. Not that your father wasn't handsome, but he was just so . . . little. Pia was such a big personality, so full of big plans of taking over the art world and moving to New York to have her own shows. But she changed after he left and went back to his life. She just got quieter. She kept up with her painting, though, and has had quite a nice career up here. She shows in local galleries all the time. She even had a show in a Boston gallery."

Rebecca's heart squeezed at the thought of Pia and her broken heart, her dashed dreams. Of raising a child all alone.

"So it's highly unlikely that anyone else could be Joy's father, other than this man?" Rebecca asked.

"That I don't know. I think so, though. Pia was very beautiful when she was a young woman. She had men after her all

the time. I do know she was dating someone when she fell for her summer love. But she broke up with that guy."

"So Joy could be that man's child?"

Marianne grimaced. "I feel uncomfortable talking about this, to tell you the truth, Rebecca. I'm not close with Joy, but I have had nice chats with her, and her husband designed the work Theo is doing out back, did you know that? They're a lovely family. And Pia doesn't live in Wiscasset anymore—she's down in Portsmouth now, I think—but I feel wrong talking about their personal business. I've told you too much as it is."

"I didn't mean to put you in this position. I'm sorry."

Marianne squeezed her hand. "No, I didn't mean it like that. It's just the story is a sad one, and it has big consequences, consequences of now, I mean. I'm not just telling a twenty-five-year-old story, I'm saying something that will affect what you do now."

"I won't breathe a word of this," Rebecca said. "And I know what I need to do. I just need to tell Joy about Michael's letter, show her the stupid DNA packet, and see what she says."

Marianne nodded, then said, "I will say one more thing. Joy *is* a petite little thing, like you, isn't she. And Pia was taller than me and Patty, and we're both five feet six. I mean, that's why we were so tickled when we finally got a glimpse of her big summer love. He was so . . . *short.*"

Short. Joy was short like Rebecca and her father, despite having an almost tall mother.

A burst of relief flooded through Rebecca. She wanted Joy to be her sister more than she'd ever wanted anything. She'd

been her sister since the day before her father died. Weeks now. And corny or not, Joy *was* her sister in her heart. She didn't want DNA to say otherwise.

As Marianne headed into the kitchen to make them each a cup of tea, Rebecca kept her mind on how petite Joy was. Joy wore heels (she recalled now the clickety-clack of those red suede clogs), which was why Rebecca hadn't really focused on her height before. She didn't *look* tiny. But Rebecca was very glad she was.

fourteen

At the crack of dawn, Rebecca and Charlie drove over to the new house with her suitcases and the potted African violet that Marianne had given her the night before as a porch-warming present. When she opened the front door, she felt a burst of happiness. The sunshine lit the little foyer, and the living room gleamed with light. The colorful throw pillows brightened up the sofa, and the bowl of cinnamon-scented pinecones she'd placed on the coffee table made the whole house smell welcoming and delicious.

Charlie went off to explore, and Rebecca took her time putting away her clothes in her bedroom, the yellow room with the queen bed. Her new mattress had been delivered yesterday—they'd come within the first half hour of their delivery window—and was as comfortable as the 1-800-MATTRES lady had said it would be. Her cuddly flower-covered down comforter looked so inviting that Rebecca flopped onto the bed.

And she must have passed out, because when she opened

her eyes, it was almost nine o'clock and Charlie was nudging her arm with his nose.

She let him into the backyard and made a pot of coffee, the simple, everyday act so thrilling it reminded her of that scene in *St. Elmo's Fire* when Mare Winningham tried to explain to Rob Lowe how amazing it felt to make a peanut butter and jelly sandwich in her own place, her first apartment.

This wasn't Rebecca's first home away from her parents', of course, but there was something different about this one. She'd *chosen* this house. She'd fallen in love with it and chosen it. She *wanted* to be here. Whereas everywhere else she'd lived—from dingy walk-ups she couldn't afford with roommates she didn't want to the very nice nine-hundred-square-foot one-bedroom she shared with Michael, in a building with a friendly doorman and thirty-two floors—never felt like home. It was Michael's home, and she'd moved in. Just like she'd moved into her other apartments because of this or that. She'd never chosen a home simply because she loved it.

And she loved this little house.

After two cups of coffee, she finally picked up the phone and pressed in Joy's number.

"Hi, Joy, it's Rebecca. Do you have some free time today to stop by my new place? I have something really important to talk to you about."

"What is it?"

"It's the kind of thing we need to talk about in person."

Silence. Then: "Well, I can come over now, actually. I just dropped Rex off at preschool and am heading to my car right now."

"Great. See you in a few, then. 44 Elm Street."

Rebecca poured herself another cup of coffee and realized her hand was trembling slightly. To busy herself until Joy showed up, she made a fresh pot of coffee and took one of her pretty new mugs from the cabinet and set it next to the cof-feemaker.

And when Joy arrived, the first thing Rebecca noticed was how petite Joy really was. She glanced down at Joy's feet. She was wearing Pumas.

Joy was short—just like Rebecca. Just like Daniel Strand.

"You bought a *house*?" Joy asked.

"Renting on a month-to-month lease."

Joy just stared at her. "Oh. Is this what you wanted to tell me?"

Rebecca shook her head and gestured for Joy to come in.

"Cute place," Joy said, glancing around as she followed Re-becca to the kitchen.

"Do you remember that first day we met, when you came to find me at Mama's? I saw a painting of a little yellow house just like this on the wall, and something about it made me feel happy when I was so confused and didn't know what to do or where to go or how to feel. And then one night, I was walking Charlie—he's my new dog—and I saw this house. And so I rented it."

"Did all this stuff come with the place?" she asked, eyeing the retro toaster and the coffeemaker.

"All of the big furniture, like this table and the chairs. But I kind of went nuts in Bed, Bath and Beyond. Coffee? It's Suma-tra." She recalled Joy mentioning on both tours that it was her favorite coffee.

Stop trying so hard, Joy seemed about to scream. "Sure," she said, and poured her own.

They sat at the kitchen table, and Rebecca looked for her father in Joy's face. She caught it in expressions, like when Joy said, "Oops," after adding too much sugar to her coffee.

Joy Jayhawk-Jones was Daniel Strand's daughter. Rebecca had no doubt. Not in her heart. Not in her head.

"Daniel Strand was five feet four inches tall," Rebecca said. "Did you know that?"

Joy shot her a look that said, That *was random.* "I figured he must be pretty short. My mom is five seven. I'm five three."

"I'm five two."

"I guess neither of us would ever find a man shorter than we are," Joy said. "I once dated a guy who was five seven, and I thought *that* was short."

"Did you ever ask your mother about it?"

"About dating a short guy?"

"If your father was short, I mean. Did you ever ask her about him at all?"

Joy sipped her coffee. "The basics. When I was younger, I asked more. I remember asking why he wasn't around and what happened. She told me she'd fallen in love with someone who already had a family, someone who lived far away. And even though he wasn't in our lives, that didn't mean he didn't love me. Just that he couldn't be in my life." She snorted. "I believed that at six and seven. By ten, I called my mother on the bullshit."

"Did she change the story?"

"Nope. She didn't when I was sixteen, either. That's her story today, too."

Rebecca got up to top off her coffee. "It's a nice one for a child, I guess. I mean, it's the only one you could tell your child in that situation, don't you think?"

"I suppose. My mother loves me, which is why she came up with it. But Daniel Strand most certainly did not love me."

Rebecca took a deep breath and sat back down. Here goes. "Speaking of Daniel Strand. I heard from his attorney yesterday. His estate has been settled and he left me one point three million dollars."

"Holy shit," Joy said. "Are you serious?"

" 'Holy shit' is exactly what I said yesterday. I'm dead serious. And I want you to have half of it."

Joy stared at her. "What the hell for?"

"You're his daughter, same as me."

"Hardly the same as you, Rebecca. He didn't raise me. He wasn't my *daddy*."

"All the more reason, then, why you should have half."

She pushed the mug away. "I don't want his money. He's not my father, never was. Why would I want his money now that he's dead?"

Rebecca knew she could argue this till she was bright blue, and Joy would argue back the same thing. "You're being stubborn at your own expense. Literally."

"You sound like my husband. That's exactly what he would say."

"And? Maybe we're both right."

"Maybe you both aren't me. Maybe I have something called *pride*."

It was Joy's pride that would insist on the DNA test.

Rebecca got up and retrieved the package Michael sent and handed it Joy.

"What's this?" Joy said.

"Open it."

Joy pulled out the plastic bag, the letter from Michael still attached. She read it, her expression tightening with each line.

"I *believe* you're his daughter," Rebecca said. "My father believed you were his daughter. He wrote you letters on every one of your twenty-six birthdays. He believed you were his daughter and he turned his back on his most basic of responsibilities. Even if you aren't his daughter, by the slight chance, I think he would want you to have half that money."

Joy stared at Rebecca. "That's a mighty generous outlook you're ascribing to a man who *did* turn his back on his most basic of responsibilities. Don't confuse your own generosity with his, Rebecca."

"Okay, mine, then. I know you're his daughter. I know you're my half sister. I can see it in you, Joy. I can see it in your eyes, and the shape of your face and your expressions. But my father, this man I loved like crazy, *told* me that you are his daughter. Of how ashamed he was of what he'd done. He would want you to have the money."

Joy gripped the mug between her hands. Had it been a delicate teacup, it would have broken to bits. "Well, I'll tell you what *I* know. I know what my mother told me. Some I believe, some I don't. What I believe is that a man named Daniel Strand was my father. That's about it. She showed me the one picture she has of him, which she then painted and hung in our house. And when I looked at that picture, when

I look now at the painting, I don't think, *Oh, wow, that's my dad.* I thought and still think: *Oh, there's a stranger sitting on the beach, staring at the ocean.* Key word here is *stranger*, Rebecca. I don't want his guilt money. What I might have wanted from him is impossible to have now."

"I know," Rebecca said. "I understand that."

Joy picked up Michael's letter and then let it drop on the table. "So your asshole boyfriend thinks my mother was a whore?"

Whoa. "No. I mean, he just . . . he's a lawyer, Joy. A divorce lawyer at that. He's just being . . . a lawyer."

"Did you buy a pair of scissors on your shopping spree?"

"No. Why?"

She dug into her bag and rummaged around, pulling out a baggie full of pipe cleaners, plastic eyes, a glue stick, and a small pair of turquoise blue child's scissors. She took out the scissors and cut off a snippet of the bottom of her hair. "This enough?"

Rebecca stared at her. "I— Actually, you don't need a hair sample. Just a swab of your cheek. The lab analyzes yours and mine and they determine if we share genetic material."

"Fine," she snapped. She opened the plastic bag, took one of the long cotton swabs from its own protective wrapping and scraped it in her mouth, then sealed it. "Here. Send this to your fuckhead boyfriend. Let's find out if Daniel Strand is my father. If he's not, then the money is a moot point, isn't it?"

But then I will be, too, right?

Joy got up, slung her bag over her shoulder, and walked to the door. Rebecca followed her. "Joy, I—"

"What? *What?* First you come barreling into my life with a box of letters from my father, a man I've never met. Now I have to prove he *is* my father? What if he's not, Rebecca? Then I have to ask my mother who is. And then what? Then I'm left with the same nothing, except it's a new, even more *nothing* nothing." Tears filled her eyes and she wiped her hands across her face. "Call me when you get the results," she said, then turned and left, the screen door banging shut behind her.

Rebecca was soaking in a bubble bath when she heard the doorbell ring. She glanced at the digital clock on her new shower radio, which hung from the hot water knob. It was just after eight o'clock. Which meant she'd been soaking for over an hour. After Joy had left this morning, Rebecca had been an emotional mess and needed something to do, but the house was so clean that she headed outside and decided she needed to plant, to get down on her hands and knees and dig in the dirt. She'd driven to a greenhouse and nursery, asked for a quick course in Gardening 101, and brought home some bulbs—daffodils and tulips, and planted them in the front and backyard until her shoulders ached.

And then she'd gone into the kitchen and ripped open the other swab packet, scraped her own mouth, resealed it, and then read the fine print on labeling the samples and packaging and sending. With dirt under her nails and her hair in a haphazard bun on top of her head, she drove to the post office before she could turn around and dump the whole thing in a garbage bag.

Take it out of your hands, she'd told herself. *The truth is the truth*.

This was definitely a case of "it is what it is." Or "what will be will be." In eight to ten business days, she would know.

She wrapped herself in her white terry robe (Bed, Bath & Beyond truly did have everything), and her hair in a towel, and went downstairs to answer the door. She had a feeling it was Maggie, who'd said she'd try to stop by that night to see what Rebecca had done with the place.

It wasn't Maggie. It was Theo. She was suddenly self-conscious with her turban-wrapped towel atop her head and very fresh-scrubbed, completely unadorned face. Theo had never seen her without mascara and her trusty Clinique Black Honey lipstick. But at least she wasn't dirty and grimy and covered in soil like she'd been an hour ago.

He grinned. "Sorry to get you out of the shower. But there's something for you in the backyard."

"What is it?"

"A surprise," he said, and followed her into the living room, where sliding glass doors opened onto the backyard.

And there, by the fence he'd built, was a wooden doghouse, painted a sunny yellow like her house, the name Charlie painted in black, flanked by little white bones.

"Oh, Theo," she whispered. "What can compete with this?"

And before he could say anything, she grabbed him and kissed him. In their tangle of hands and heads and mouths, her towel fell off, her hair dropping in wet tangles around her shoulders. He untied her robe and his hands slipped around her waist, and then slid up her rib cage. They stood there, looking into each other's eyes, his hands just underneath her breasts. Without taking his eyes off her, he closed the curtains, then kissed her again.

"You are so beautiful," he whispered, snaking his hands through her wet hair.

And suddenly, they were on the fluffy yellow rug in front of the fireplace, where his clothes came off, her robe came off, and he made her forget all about cotton swabs and hair snippets and anger. All she felt was utter pleasure. And utter rightness.

He was gone. With the morning light streaming in through the filmy curtains, Rebecca woke up in her bed, where she and Theo had made love for the second time, and where they'd fallen asleep, her head on his chest, his arm across her stomach.

But he was gone. Disappointment hit her in the gut. And in the brain. Theo didn't strike her like a "love 'em and leave 'em" type. The type to skulk away at three in the morning while the woman lay sleeping.

There was a note on the pillow. Rebecca grabbed it and sat up.

> *Sleeping Beauty: Have to be at a jobsite at seven. Wish I could cook you breakfast. Until the next time, which can't be too soon.*—*Theo*

She pressed the note to her heart and closed her eyes, a burst of happiness exploding through her body.

fifteen

Too soon couldn't be that night, since Rebecca had a date with The Bitter Exes Club of Wiscasset. She was feeling anything but bitter herself. Her evening with Theo, during which very few words were exchanged (Rebecca realized she hadn't even thanked him for the doghouse), had crowded out most other thoughts, most other people.

Like Michael.

Her *boyfriend*, Michael. With whom she lived in New York City. With whom she worked. And from whom she was taking a sabbatical of sorts. But taking a sabbatical wasn't supposed to include cheating on him. Guilt grabbed her by the gut and wasn't letting go.

"Oh please," her friend Charlotte had said on the phone that morning. "Your relationship is in the toilet. What you did isn't so much cheating as it is self-exploration. How are you supposed to figure out how you feel about Michael and whether or not you want to come back to New York if you don't have some experiences that challenge all that?"

But wasn't that rationalizing the cheating? Was Michael supposed to be what Marianne's mother called "flexible"?

"Plus, he threatened you with a dangling cheat," Charlotte added. " 'If you don't come home right this minute, I'm going to kiss my gym crush.' Please, Rebecca. You really think he wasn't fucking her when he said that?"

Rebecca didn't know. Really. Michael was very into the letter of the law. She believed he'd break up with her before he'd cheat on her. Feelings for another woman would tell him what he needed to know, would be all the "self-exploration" he'd require. He'd told her, hadn't he, that there *might* be someone else in the event of their breakup.

"No, he told you there might be someone else if you didn't wush back and be his widdle girlfwend and pawawegal," Charlotte said, and Rebecca ended up spitting her coffee all over her cream-colored sweater. "Right, it's all your fault he's going to cheat on you." She'd snorted. "I'm telling you, Rebecca. You give Michael way too much credit. You always have."

Why had she called Charlotte? She could have been lying in bed, tracing the imprint of Theo's lips on her own, on every inch of her. She could have been reliving every moment of their magical night, which had been as sweet and tender as it had been hot, hot, hot. But then her gaze had slid over to the photo of her and Michael on her dresser (granted, it was sort of hidden behind the dancing ballerina jewelry box and she could see just part of Michael behind the edge of the box, but she could see most of herself). And so she'd called Charlotte and told her she'd slept with another man. Charlotte was a straight shooter.

"And I'm giving it to you straight, Rebecca. You're not doing anything wrong. You're just doing what you need to. You're not *married*."

But that didn't mean she hadn't cheated. She and Michael were in a committed relationship.

As Rebecca parked in front of Maggie's house, behind Ellie's black Toyota, she wondered if Michael's mother's wedding dress was still hanging on the back of her office door at Whitman, Goldberg & Whitman. But as she glanced up at Maggie's house, she suddenly thought of the first time she'd seen this tidy blue Cape, her first day in Wiscasset, when Joy had invited her on the tour and the orange minibus had pulled up in front. She smiled at the memory of Maggie announcing to Victoria that the Love Bus had arrived.

To ring the doorbell, she had to shift the huge tin of cookies in her arms, cookies she'd baked herself. She'd made chocolate chip and peanut butter chip, both Marianne's recipes, and they came out perfect.

"You're glowing," Maggie said when she opened the door. "Which means you're either pregnant or you had a facial or you got laid."

Rebecca laughed. "I'll never tell."

Rebecca was happy to see Maggie and Ellie—who was chatting with a woman on the sofa—casual for once. Maggie's shiny brown bob was in a cute low ponytail, and she actually wore jeans and a V-necked cable-knit sweater. Ellie's dark hair was loose, but she, too, wore jeans under riding boots and a floppy, dark green mohair sweater. She'd never seen these women *comfortable*; they always tried so hard to look sexy.

"Rebecca!" Ellie ran over and wrapped Rebecca in a hug. "You *are* glowing."

She glanced at herself in the mirror on the entry wall. She *was* glowing. Her brown eyes sparkled. Her complexion seemed clearer and lit from within. And she looked happier than she had in a long, long time.

"It's the house, isn't it?" Maggie said. "You're loving it?"

That and one perfect night with Theo. "I am. It already feels like home."

"I'm so glad you came tonight," Ellie said. "We need help. Serious help. Let me introduce you to everyone." She led Rebecca into Maggie's living room, a spotless rectangle with two white textured sofas that faced each other (you could tell Maggie didn't have children) in front of a fireplace. Next to a huge silver beanbag (upon which a man was sitting), there was a basket of yarn and two bamboo knitting needles with what looked like a baby blue blanket on it. Was the guy a knitter? "Over here is Lucy—she's the bookkeeper at my real-estate agency—who finally told her boyfriend that if he didn't propose by the end of summer, that was it. And it's almost October, and you'll notice there's no ring on her finger."

Lucy burst into tears. She was in her early thirties and had the particular type of short curly hair and appliqué sweater (little dancing moose) that made a woman look fifteen years older.

Maggie touched Lucy's shoulder. "Oh, honey. You're doing the right thing."

Ellie nodded. "Or you could be like me—and get the guy to

propose after whining and pleading and showing him pictures of diamond rings when he really doesn't want to, but then he does propose, because his father dies and he's low and you're suddenly his best friend, but then he gets his spirit back and he realizes you're really not the one. Or not the one yet."

"It's the *yet* that's the problem," Rebecca said, sitting down next to Lucy. "Because it's so hard to know what it really refers to. 'I don't know how I feel about you yet.' Or 'I'm not ready for marriage yet.'"

The man on the beanbag nodded. "And sometimes someone will go ahead and get married even though there's *still* a yet—on both counts. Because they want something else, like security."

"Oh gosh, I just realized I didn't even introduce you two," Ellie said. "Rebecca, this is Darren Doyle. He's the assistant manager at Rite Aid."

Darren waved. He was early to midthirties and wore a short-sleeved dress shirt and khaki pants. His light brown hair was close-cropped, like a soldier's. "I sort of told Ellie my life story when she came in one night to buy a roll of Tums. My wife had just told me on the phone that it was over."

"She said that on the phone?" Rebecca asked.

"Well, not for the first time. She told me a couple of weeks ago that there was someone else, but then she changed her mind, said it was me she wanted, but then she changed her mind again." His eyes pooled with tears, and Ellie handed him a tissue.

Maggie leaned forward. "Let me ask you this, Darren. Was she difficult when she was your girlfriend? Always breaking up with you and then reeling you back in?"

"How'd you know?" he asked before blowing his nose very loudly.

"I'm just thinking that we expect people to change when we get married. Like me—I really thought my ass of an ex-husband would change when we went from just dating to being a married couple. Like he'd suddenly stop being a mama's boy who expected the crust cut off his toast. Or that he'd stop staring at waitresses' cleavage. But nothing changed when we got married. Just my name. I'm changing it back by the way. If I had children I might not, but I'm taking it back. Maggie McDonald."

"Good for you," Ellie said, braiding her dark hair over one shoulder. "I'm not there yet. I *feel* like Ellie Rasmussen. Maybe because I wanted to be that woman for so long."

Tears pooled in Darren's eyes again. "Sometimes I wonder if my wife ever loved me at all. I don't know how she could have just suddenly fallen in love with someone else if she really loved me. But I don't know. I thought she did."

"It's such a hard question to answer," Rebecca said. "My father cheated on my mother. I *know* he loved her. But something was able to pull him away from her in that moment— when he met the other woman."

Maggie's hazel eyes sparked with anger. "But something *shouldn't* be able to. If you're committed, you're committed. Period. End of story." She glanced at Rebecca. "I don't mean anything against your father, hon."

Rebecca squeezed her hand. "It's okay. He did cheat. A vacation affair. But when it was time to go home, he just up and went back to my mother as though nothing happened. And something *big* happened. He must have fallen in love with the other woman to have the affair. But if he had been in love, how was he able to just drop her like that?"

"I'm glad to say I don't know," Darren said. "I've never cheated on anyone, girlfriend or my wife. And I can't imagine cheating."

Maggie patted his knee. "You're a good man. I wish there were more of you."

"Well, there can't be varying levels of 'committed,'" Ellie said. "At least, there shouldn't be. It's either/or. I'm the kind of person who honors a commitment, but I guess some people, like my own jerk of a soon-to-be-ex-husband just can't do that."

"You want to hear something crazy?" Lucy said. "My mother knew my father was having affairs from the time they got married until now. He was probably messing around with someone last night. But he came home every night, ever the loving husband, gifts for birthdays and anniversaries, was there for every-other-Sunday dinners with the in-laws. He'd never leave my mother and claims to love her. Is that still being committed?"

"That's a tough one," Darren said.

"Only if the wife doesn't know," Ellie said. "I mean, if she doesn't know, everyone's happy, right?"

Rebecca thought about that. "My mother didn't know. But even so, the marriage had to have changed, right? Wouldn't the affair have made my father a different person, even though it didn't continue? He'd cheated, he'd fallen for someone else. The dynamic between them must have shifted, even in small ways."

Maggie nodded. "I think the wife always knows. Because of just what you said, Rebecca—those subtle little changes. You *know*."

"I knew—suspected, anyway, until it was obvious," Ellie said. "But sometimes ignorance really is bliss. I'd have my husband. I'd have my marriage. I wouldn't know, so how am I hurt?"

"You're hurt because your husband is lying to you," Darren said. "About where he's going, what he's doing. He's living another life outside your marriage. And everything you think about him isn't the truth."

Ellie leaned her head back and sighed. "Oh, yeah. I forgot all that." She popped back up and grinned. "Don't worry, guys. There's no chance of me going back to Tim. Do you believe that my mother-in-law told me my expectations are out of whack? That it's *me* who has to change, not him?"

Maggie snorted. "Sounds like my former mother-in-law. 'Boys will be boys,' she told me. 'Remember that and you'll have a long, happy marriage.' Long, maybe, but unhappy is more like it."

"I just want to state for the record again that not all men cheat," Darren said.

Ellie winked at him. "We know there are some good guys out there. We're not *that* bitter."

"I'm a little worried I might be," Lucy said. "I feel like I cut off my nose to spite my face. And I'm not even sure I did the right thing. Did I? By giving John an ultimatum? Marry me or we're over? He says if I really loved him, I couldn't just end it. He's sort of right, right?"

"Does he not understand what an ultimatum *is*?" Maggie asked. "He sounds manipulative. 'No, stay and live my way, even though it's breaking your heart. Because if you really loved me, your broken heart would be okay with you.'"

Lucy nodded, but looked like she was about to burst into tears.

Ellie moved over to the other side of Lucy and slung an arm around her shoulder. "Rebecca says it's all about your breaking point, what's acceptable to you and when it stops being okay. She says only you can really answer that. Right, Rebecca?"

As if she were an expert on anything to do with relationships. The people in this room were the experts, the ones who'd been married, who *were* married, who'd been through the ups and downs, the thick and thin—especially the thin. "I do think it's true that only you yourself can know when you've reached your own limit. Sometimes it takes a while to realize that what your friends and family have been telling you is the truth. Short of an intervention, no one can tell you what's unacceptable to you. If I tell you, Yeah, you shouldn't feel or think or do X, Y, Z, it's not going to matter unless you believe that, too."

Lucy nodded again, her eyes tearing up. "I know he doesn't really love me, not *that* way. Not the way he loved his last girlfriend, the one he proposed to. She didn't want to marry him, though. I know he doesn't feel about me the way he felt about her."

"I'm so sorry, Lucy," Rebecca said. "I'm glad you found this group. I'm glad you all found each other. It helps just to talk about it, doesn't it?"

"It really helps," Maggie said. "You know what also helps? Tequila." She moved over to the buffet table by the window, where there were four bottles of tequila, a shaker, two bottles of triple sec and a bottle of lime juice. "Anyone not want salt?"

And for the next half hour, there was much drinking and crunching of nachos, piled high with beef, pinto beans, cheese, guacamole, sour cream, and salsa. The conversation turned to lighter, funnier subjects, such as the rudest customer at Rite Aid or the time Maggie found another Realtor having sex with a potential buyer in a house she was showing.

Ellie tinged the side of her glass with a spoon. "Okay, so now we're up to the burn-and-purge portion of our evening."

"Burn and purge?" Rebecca whispered to Maggie.

"Pure brilliance," Maggie said. "For our first meeting, we decided that we should all bring something that symbolizes our pledge to rid our asshole exes from our hearts, minds, and souls, and then we'll chuck that thing into the fireplace and let it burn to nothing."

Ellie walked over to the fireplace. "I'll go first." She took her wedding ring off and threw it in the fire.

"Did you really just do that?" Maggie asked, her mouth gaping open. "Did you just throw your wedding ring in the fireplace?"

"I did," Ellie said, slapping her hand over her mouth. "I can't believe it. Does this mean I really mean it?"

"You really mean it," they all said in unison.

Ellie bit her lip. "I'm signing the papers on Monday. To file for divorce. There are *actual* papers, with facts and figures and phrases like Rasmussen versus Rasmussen—that's how much I mean it."

"You're such an inspiration, Ellie," Lucy said. She pulled something from her purse and walked over to the fireplace.

"What is that?" Maggie asked.

Lucy held up a white box with multicolored lettering. "My birthday present from John. It's a box of alli. You know, the weight-loss supplement. If you cheat, you end up having rather embarrassing elimination issues."

Ellie's mouth fell open. "Oh my God. That's what he gave you for your birthday?"

Lucy looked like she might cry. "He said that maybe the reason he hasn't proposed is because I could lose a good thirty pounds, that he heard wives always gained weight after marriage, and then I'd really be a house."

"What an asshole!" Darren said. "You wanted to marry this jerk?"

Lucy burst into tears. "I deserve better than him. I deserve better than him. I deserve better than him."

"You most certainly do," Rebecca and Maggie and Ellie said in unison.

And into the fire went the box of alli. Lucy came back to the sofa with a look of determination on her face.

Maggie reached into her purse and pulled out a folded newspaper clipping. "This is the poor moron who married my ex-husband a couple of weeks ago. I cut her bridal photo out of the wedding announcements. I was actually studying her, trying to figure out what she had that I didn't, what was so special about her. And you know what? Yeah, she was the skanky bitch who stole my husband. But now she's just some idiot who's stuck with my jerk of an ex. She's no one to envy." And she tossed the newspaper clipping in the fire and they all watched it burn.

Darren stood and walked over to the fireplace. "I brought a letter my wife wrote me the last time she said she wanted our marriage to work. Should I read it to you?"

Everyone said yes.

He cleared his throat. " 'Dear Darren, I am so sorry for all the pain and suffering I've caused you. I was wrong about Vincent—he is totally not the man for me. And he's definitely not half the man you are. He was fired and was only pretending to look for a new job. Do you believe he was expecting me to pay his rent? Oh, Dar, baby, I miss you so much. I miss us. I love you, big bear. Tonight I'll show you how much. Love, Carrie.' "

"That's worse than the alli," Lucy said. "How transparent is she?"

"And I guess she went back to Vincent?" Ellie asked.

Darren nodded. "He got a new job."

"In the fire it goes!" Maggie said.

Darren crumpled it into a ball and threw it in. "That *did* feel good. Empowering."

"So what's going on with you?" Ellie asked Rebecca. "Did you make a decision about Michael? Are you and Theo seeing each other? What's the scoop?"

This wasn't the time or the place to start talking about how sometimes you did grow apart from someone, someone that maybe you did love once. But what you needed began to change, maybe. And suddenly everything felt wrong. And then you met someone else, and he feels just right, like the baby bear bed. Then again, maybe it was the time and the place. It was about hope, about possibilities. And Rebecca had just started discovering that possibilities were everywhere—if you went for them, if you insisted upon them.

"Michael and I are up in the air. My whole life in New York is up in the air. I am sort of seeing Theo. Trying to figure things out. Do you think that's wrong? To be seeing him while I'm still involved with someone else?"

"Well, you're living here," Maggie pointed out. "You've been here for, what, almost a month. You rented a house. You have a *dog*."

"It's not fair to keep the New York guy hanging on, if that's what you're doing," Lucy said. "I mean, I don't know the circumstances, though."

"Circumstances shouldn't make a wrong a right, though," Darren said.

"I don't know," Ellie said. "It's not like Rebecca's married. This is how and when you're supposed to figure out who you want to be with. *Before* you get married."

"I'll drink to that," Maggie said, raising her margarita glass.

Everyone clinked. But Rebecca knew that what she was doing was still cheating. Married or not.

Rebecca got the opportunity to properly thank Theo (for the doghouse *and* their incredible evening) later that night. And the next night. And the next. And on Friday, he was her official date to her housewarming party. Ellie and Maggie were there.

And Arlene and Marianne. (Matteo was trying to work things out with the girlfriend.) And Victor and Victoria, their hands seemingly fused together.

And an hour late, but bearing a beautiful orchid plant, were Joy and Harry.

Rebecca couldn't stop smiling like a fool. Joy was *here*. And not for any reason—such as to discuss something or because Rebecca had practically begged. She was here because Rebecca had invited her to her housewarming party. And she'd come.

After tour after tour of her tiny house (which now bore a few new vases, candles, and plants, thanks to her guests), Rebecca came back down to the living room to find Joy and Maggie deep in conversation on the sofa. Rebecca sidled up, ostensibly to remove empty drinking glasses from the coffee table.

"Oh, I wish I could, Joy," Maggie was saying, "but Ellie and I promised one of the members of our Bitter Exes Club that we'd take him to a comedy club tomorrow night."

"Well, I guess I can scratch Ellie off my list," Joy said, pushing her blond hair behind her shoulders. "Hmm. I've already asked Arlene and both my neighbors. No one's available. I wish someone would start a pinch-sitting service in town—'Need a babysitter at a moment's notice, call us.'"

"I'll do it," Rebecca said. *I'll babysit my nephew. And it'll cost you nothing.*

Joy stared at her.

Rebecca had to tread lightly here. She did have that one great morning at the library under her belt, but ever since the DNA argument, Joy had been very distant. "Rex does like my face, remember? And he knows me now—he's seen me a few times." *C'mon, say yes.*

"Problem solved," Maggie said, popping a Hershey's Kiss into her mouth.

"Problem solved," Joy repeated, eyeing Rebecca. "Well, if you're sure you'd like to, I'd really appreciate it." She hesitated, then whispered, "Harry and I are attempting a real date. Getting dolled up, going out to a fancy restaurant. The works."

Rebecca beamed. "That's great. What time should I be there?"

"Six would be perfect."

"Six it is, and you get home when you get home. No set time."

Joy let out what Rebecca knew was a sigh of relief. "Thanks."

I have a nephew, Rebecca thought for the hundredth time since she'd first seen Rex Jayhawk-Jones. The wonder of it never abated, though, never seemed anything less than magical. She had a sister and a nephew when a few weeks ago there had been no one.

Rex was too adorable. Rebecca understood why this three-foot-tall little bundle of energy made Harry want to be a better person. Rebecca hadn't spent much time around little kids—any kids, really. She'd had no idea just how funny and clever and interesting three-year-olds were. Rex wanted to be a cloud for Halloween, which he pronounced Hah-EEN. His favorite food was an apple slice, but maybe a chocolate brownie, or, no, "strawbry" ice cream. His favorite color was orange. His favorite person was Elmo—and his mommy and his daddy.

She looked for Grandpa Strand in Rex's face, and even though Harry's coloring dominated—the brown hair, the hazel eyes, Rex had the Strand round eyes, the Strand nose, and the Strand chin.

You are my nephew, Rebecca thought, watching Rex stack multicolored blocks on top of each other for the door of the fort they were building in the family room. She felt a surge of emotion in her heart for this little boy—because he was her nephew? Or because she knew the story of his parents, how much this child meant to them, and they meant something to her?

"Wanna color wid me?" he asked, and they moved on to his collection of coloring books. He chose the robots, and for the next half hour, they colored five robots each, then Rebecca hung his little masterpieces up on the clothesline of artwork hung across the wall.

Seven o'clock was his bedtime. And so they headed upstairs for teeth brushing and pajamas (footies with clouds and lightning bolts) and Rebecca read him three stories, all about pigs, but "none with wolves cuz they're not so nice." She was almost done with the third when she realized he was asleep, his little mouth open, one hand flung up on his forehead.

God, he was precious. Rebecca didn't have baby fever yet, but she could imagine having a little Rex of her own. She turned off the lamp and tiptoed out, leaving the door slightly ajar, then headed back downstairs, her heart full to bursting.

Rebecca was reading one of the magazines on the

coffee table when Joy and Rex returned home. Harry barely said hello before stomping downstairs to his half-finished basement.

Uh-oh.

Joy burst into tears, and Rebecca took her by the hand and led her to the couch.

"Everything okay with Rex?" Joy asked, sniffling.

Rebecca nodded. "He's an angel."

"I'm just going to check on him. I'll be right back." She returned a minute later and sat down, tucking her legs underneath her. She didn't look at Rebecca, didn't say anything.

"Joy?"

Joy leaned her head back against the couch and stretched out her legs. "We just can't get past the same old argument. I don't know how we're ever going to get past this. It's *my* business. Why can't he understand that? Why can't he understand me?"

"About your father?" Rebecca asked.

"That and everything else. I finally told him about our conversation, about the money and the DNA test, that I don't even want the money, and he flipped out. So I accused him of wanting the money, of only caring about that, and he got so angry and insisted we leave."

"Do you really think he only cares about the money?" Rebecca didn't know Harry well, of course, but she'd spent the weekend with him in that lodge and she'd bet anything he didn't care about the money at all. He cared about Joy.

Joy shrugged. "It'd be nice to have, wouldn't it? I *get* it. I just . . . I don't know. Do you and Harry really think I don't want half a million dollars? Six hundred and fifty thousand dollars? Rex's education will be assured. Our home can be paid for in full. We can buy a new car instead of constantly dumping money into the old one just to pass inspection each year. And I could do fewer tours. And Harry could take a vacation instead of working twenty-four/seven. And my parents could finally retire if they want. Yeah, the money would be nice. But it doesn't feel like *mine*. It doesn't feel like it belongs to *me*. I hate that there's nothing behind it, nothing attached to it. That's what Harry doesn't get."

"But there is something attached," Rebecca said gently. "The letters Daniel Strand wrote you. Maybe it would help if you read them."

Joy shook her head. "I don't want to read them. Harry doesn't get that, either. He keeps saying I'm emotionally blocked and this is the sterling example."

He has a point, Joy, Rebecca thought. There would come a day when she and Joy would be able to argue and bicker like sisters did, when Rebecca could say what needed to be said, and she wouldn't have to worry that Joy would slam the door. Because that's what sisters did—they argued and bickered and then made up, because they were sisters. The door was always open.

"I don't know how you'll feel about this suggestion, Joy, but would it help if you talked to your mom about all this? Maybe what she has to say would somehow loosen all this for you a little."

Joy let out a deep breath. "Maybe it would. I don't know that, either. I never talk about it with her. I will, though, if the

DNA test confirms that your father is definitely my father. Otherwise, like I said, the money is a moot point if he's not."

"Moot or not," Harry said from the doorway, "we need some help." He came into the living room and sat across from them. "Rebecca, I want to hire you as a mediator. I think Joy and I need to sit down and really talk this out with someone impartial guiding us, leading us back to center when things get heated."

"She's hardly impartial," Joy said.

"Why not?" Harry said. "You're the one who keeps calling her a stranger."

Touché, Harry.

Joy was silent for a moment, then turned to Rebecca. "What would it be like? The sessions, I mean."

"Whoa," Rebecca said. "I'm not a marriage counselor. I'm not even a trained mediator. I don't have a degree in counseling or a certificate in anything. I'm just a paralegal in a divorce mediation firm. *Was.*"

"We've seen you in action," Harry said. "You're good at this. I don't want to go to some marriage counselor who has no idea who we are. I can't stand the idea of starting at the beginning when we're in the middle."

"I can understand that," Rebecca said. She turned to Joy. "Are you okay with it? If you're game. I am."

"What will it be like?" she asked again. "How does it work? He says his piece and I say mine? Is it just arguing back and forth?"

"What I'd try to do is limit the arguing. Yeah, Harry says his piece—but you listen. Then I ask both of you questions about it. If there's arguing, I change tacks. And then you say your piece, and Harry listens. And then I ask you both questions about it. And somewhere in there, both of you start to hear each other a little better. And hopefully, you start seeing things from the other's perspective. You take some time with it. And you mix all that together with how much love there is between you, and things start to change."

"That *does* sound good," Joy said. "You can really accomplish that?"

"Not so much me. *You*. And you," she added to Harry. "I could come here, if you'd feel more comfortable on your turf, or if you want a neutral zone, you can come to my house."

"I'd prefer here," Joy said.

"How about Monday at six p.m.," Harry asked.

"Monday at six, it is," Rebecca said.

Joy reached into her purse and pulled out some bills and held them out to Rebecca. "For tonight."

Rebecca shook her head. "I won't take money for tonight. And I won't take money for the sessions. Take it or leave it."

Harry smiled. "You drive a tough bargain."

"You're used to that," Joy said with a smile, and Rebecca knew her work would be difficult, but not *that* difficult. This was not a divorcing couple. This was a couple with much, much more than a flicker of love.

This was a couple *deeply* in love, truly committed to each other, yet having some serious problems in hearing each other, compromising, accepting.

And bringing them back together would be Rebecca's greatest pleasure.

• • •

The chimes of Rebecca's cell phone woke her up. She glanced at the clock on her bedside table. It was after two in the morning.

Michael. "So I think you should know that my relationship with my new friend has progressed to something slightly romantic."

Rebecca leaned back against her pillows. "Did you just leave her apartment or something?"

"I'm home now. Sitting on the sofa and feeling like shit."

"I'm dating someone, too," she said softly.

"Great, so we're seeing other people. Or did we break up and someone forgot to tell me?"

She didn't know what to say to that, so she said, "I sent in the DNA test. I'll have the results by the end of next week. It was nice of you to enclose the check, by the way."

"I thought you might need it, if the test proves she's your sister and you hand her seven hundred thousand dollars." At her silence, he added, "If she *is*, are you going to stay up there? Permanently?"

She got out of bed and walked over to the windows and sat on the little padded bench. She looked out into the inky darkness. There were no stars twinkling tonight. "I don't know, Michael. I really don't know. I just feel like I'm between two worlds right now, and right now, this is where I need to be."

"Where you *want* to be, Rebecca."

"Where I want to be, then."

"How much longer do you expect me to give you? This indefinite crap is wearing thin. Or are you saying it's up to me? That if I want to call it a day, all I have to do is say so, and you'll hang up and go screw your new boyfriend."

She went back to her bed and slid under the comforter, pulling it up to her chin. "I suppose it is up to you, Michael. I don't know for sure how I feel about anything right now. I know that there was once something incredible between us, but that it's been gone for a long time."

Silence. And then: "Do you think we can get it back? It was weird being with someone else, Becs."

It wasn't for me, though, she thought. Should it have been? Did that mean she really didn't love Michael? Why didn't she know? "Do you think we can?"

"I don't know. But I know we can't while you're living more than three hundred miles away."

"I can't come back right now."

"You've said that over and over, and I still don't know why. Is it the guy?"

"He's part of it," she said. "But I felt this way before we became involved."

"I'm sick of talking about this," he said. "Nothing changes. Am I supposed to give you an ultimatum? You'll just choose to stay there and give me the same answer, that you're not ready to come home. I'm not going to be here indefinitely, Rebecca. I'm sure you're aware of that. So let's just hang up. There'll come a point when this will be intolerable to me." *Click.*

She put the phone back on her bedside table, and opened the drawer where she'd put the photo of herself and Michael. Why wasn't she ready to let go of him? If her father was still alive, she'd still be living with Michael, still be working at

Whitman, Goldberg & Whitman. Still be living the same old life. And if her father had died without telling her about Joy, it would be the same still.

Why was *knowing* the difference?

Maggie's words came back to her: *"He was telling you he wasn't leaving you all alone in the world, that you didn't have to marry Michael."*

He was telling her she had family out there, that if Michael wasn't really family, if he didn't feel like family, she could go find family somewhere else. And she had.

sixteen

The next morning, Rebecca sat under a tree in the little park near the center of town, the brilliant red of the leaves reminding her just how long she'd been here. Long enough to send Michael to his gym rat.

As if she were any different. She'd developed a crush on Theo from the moment she saw him.

Rebecca leaned her back up against the tree and stared up at the cottony white clouds moving through the bright blue sky.

"Hey."

Rebecca was startled to see Joy Jayhawk standing on the path. Her blond hair was in a low ponytail and she wore a dark denim jacket, another reminder that late summer had turned into fall. Rebecca was surprised that Joy had called out to her; Rebecca's eyes had been closed and Joy could have hurried past without being spotted. But she'd chosen to say hello.

That was something.

"I wasn't sure if you were asleep," Joy said, stepping onto the grass and walking over to where Rebecca sat. Charlie came running over with his little squeaky toy, and Joy petted him on the back and threw the rubber cat, sending Charlie scampering after it.

"Just thinking about some stuff," Rebecca said, squinting up at Joy in the bright sunshine. "I've got some relationship woes of my own."

Joy glanced over at Charlie, who was racing back with the rubber cat. She threw it again, and Charlie went running. "The boyfriend back home and the new guy?"

Rebecca nodded. "Michael is basically telling me he's not going to wait much longer, and I understand that. I'm leaving him hanging and . . . then there's Theo."

"So things have progressed between you two?" she asked, sitting down beside Rebecca. She plucked out a long blade of grass.

"Seriously progressed." She closed her eyes again. "I wish I knew what to do, how I felt. Michael and I have been together for two years. He's been with me through some very hard times. He was there when my dad—"

"Died," Joy finished.

Rebecca glanced at Joy. "He arranged the funeral for me. He did everything."

Charlie ran over and dropped the toy by Joy's knee, then chased after a white butterfly. "And yet you're seeing someone else."

Guilt crept up along her spine. "Michael's a good person, but things between us have been so . . . wrong lately. I used to think we were just going through phases, since we've been living together for a year and we sometimes get on each other's nerves. I mean, that's normal, right?"

"Normal enough that my husband is living in the base-ment," Joy said, then suddenly stood up as though she realized the conversation was getting too personal. Too . . . sisterly. And outside the context of Rebecca as mediator. "I have to get going. Preschool pickup. See you Monday night," she said, then walked back to the path, stopping to pet Charlie.

Rebecca watched Joy until she disappeared around a bend. This was the first time they'd talked about *her*, about *her* trou-bles. The way *sisters* did. It didn't answer any of her questions about Michael and Theo, but it sure made her feel better.

"You don't *understand*," Joy snapped at Harry for the tenth time. Or was it the eleventh?

Rebecca had been sitting on the Jayhawk-Joneses' love seat for twenty minutes, Joy and Harry on the sofa across from her, each on an opposite end, Joy completely rigid like a marionette with an imaginary string holding up her body with perfect posture, and Harry sprawled out as though trying to take up as much room as possible. Joy would say her piece, and Harry would listen with gritted teeth, looking as though he might ex-plode any moment with "What kind of idiot are you?" And Joy, who'd ever so slightly pause at his every sigh, raised eyebrow, and head shake, would stop midsentence and say, "What's the point?" and cross her arms over her chest. Then Harry would say his piece, and Joy, looking like she might cry or storm off, would either say "That's not fair" or "You don't understand."

"No, *you* don't understand," Harry said for the tenth or possibly eleventh time. And then, for the very first time, he stood up and walked out of the room. Rebecca heard a door slam, then a car starting and backing out of the driveway.

Joy, her brown eyes a mix of fury and hurt, stalked up the stairs. Rebecca heard another door slam.

Oh no, oh no, oh no. Why had she thought she could help? She wasn't a mediator. She wasn't a marriage counselor. She wasn't *anything*, and she was fooling around with someone's marriage. Not just someone's—Joy's.

In divorce mediation, the end result was all about avoiding a battle, a trial, the back and forth of costly attorneys. What you needed to get the couple to agree to was fairness—and what was fair to each depended on everything from one or both of the spouses' moods in that moment, to black and white numbers, to inventory, to *stuff*.

But saving a marriage wasn't about what was arbitrarily fair. It was about love.

Maybe she'd given them too much open air time, too much freedom to say their piece, something they'd been doing on their own. She'd need to come up with a different approach for them. An approach based on the heart, not the bottom line, even if in this case the bottom line *was* saving the marriage.

She went into the kitchen and wrote a note on the refrigerator magnet pad:

Joy and Harry, please don't be discouraged by tonight.
The first time is usually the hardest. It can seem like you're

getting nowhere, but you're both blowing off steam and
getting started in listening. I'd like to try again ASAP.
—Rebecca

She imagined Joy coming downstairs in the middle of the night, unable to sleep, finding the note and crumpling it in a ball and stuffing it down the garbage disposal.

"What you need is one of my world-famous massages and perfect hamburgers," Theo said.

She'd called the minute she flung herself inside her car outside the Jayhawk-Jones house, her heart heavy, her shoulders slumped, her mind a jumble of worries. And out came the entire story in a rush of details, details she hadn't shared with Theo because she'd thought they were too personal to Joy or to both Joy and Harry, but she realized how central *she* was to the details right now—the DNA test, the inheritance.

"See you in twenty minutes," he said.

"I hope your massages aren't *that* well known," she said, but he had already hung up.

His massages *should* be world famous. Between his warm hands and the delicious-smelling Kama Sutra oil, which apparently heated on contact with skin, she completely relaxed. She lay facedown on her bed, and he kneeled over her, kneading, pressing, smoothing, rubbing. Every now and then he would whisper something sweet or naughty in her ear, but he never took off his own clothes, never touched anything but her back and her feet and her shoulders. He disappeared for a few agonizing moments to draw her a bubble bath, then continued pressing those strong hands of his into her until he whispered, "C'mon," and led her by the hand into the bathroom.

"I cook, you soak."

He was the perfect man. "Thank you, Theo."

And twenty minutes later he appeared with a towel and took his time drying her off and dusting her with his special powder, which apparently was edible. She smelled so good she could eat herself. Which was a good sign: She was hungry. She'd gotten back her appetite just in time for dinner.

She came downstairs to find Theo lighting the candles on the kitchen table, two plates with burgers (and she could see they were topped with the works—lettuce, tomato, onions, pickles) and sweet-potato fries, which she loved.

"Is there anything you can't do?" she asked, biting into the burger, which was as perfect as he'd proclaimed.

"I can't draw a straight line," he said. "Which is why I'm not an architect. I also can't make a decent pot of coffee."

She smiled. It was true about the coffee.

"And I can't go around pretending to be a marriage counselor," she said, pushing her fries around on her plate. "Michael was right. I'm not a mediator."

"Michael your boyfriend," he said.

"Michael the something," she said, instantly regretting it. What was she *doing*?

He eyed her, then uncapped the two bottles of Shipyard beer and poured them into the beer mugs she'd thought to buy during her shopping spree, despite never drinking beer. "Joy and Harry are talking, which is always good. Bad is when people retreat but don't talk, don't communicate at all. From what you said, they're still on the same old argument, so that's nothing new. Which means you didn't make things worse. They're just the same. Comfortable and familiar in an unfamiliar area—them talking to you. They're both new at that. So you're on the right track."

The glow of the candle cast shadows on his handsome face. "How'd you get to be so smart about all this? And how'd you learn to cook so well, anyway?"

He smiled. "I like working with my hands."

She grinned. "I see. I'm happy to have been the recipient more than a few times. Charlie, too. He loves his doghouse." She upped her chin to look out the window, where Charlie's little black and white form was curled up on his round bed, his little head hanging over the edge of the bed out of the doghouse.

They ate, listening to Johnny Cash, who Theo insisted was soothing to the mind and spirit, and Rebecca had to agree, though she wasn't sure if it was Theo, the massage, the bath, the food, or all of the above that had wrapped itself around her like a hug. It started to rain, and Charlie came running to the sliding glass doors to be let in. She loved the sound of rain against the window and the roof when she was cozy and warm inside—even after Charlie shook his wet fur all over her.

With their beer and two cupcakes that Theo had stopped at Mama's to buy, they sat on the couch in the living room, Charlie curled up at their feet.

"Better?" he asked.

"Much better," she said. "I owe you in a big way."

He shook his head. "Nope."

She took his hand and held it. "Maybe a requirement of talking to anyone about their marriage should be being married. What the hell do I know about being married? What that kind of commitment is like? I have no idea what really goes on in a marriage."

"You don't have to be the thing to do the thing. You just need insight and feeling. And you have both. Given that it was the first session, they probably expected too much—he probably expected her to suddenly understand his side, she expected the same from him, so they both dug in their heels even more." He leaned down to scratch Charlie behind the ears. "It's a tough situation because they're both right."

She stared at him. "You think so? I think Harry's more right."

"Of course you do. You want what you want from Joy. So does Harry."

"All I want from her is to be my sister. He wants quite a bit more."

"No, not really. He wants what you want: Joy to open up, be emotionally present for him one hundred percent. That's what you want. You want her to be your sister in the true sense of the word."

Out of nowhere she felt the prick of tears. "You're right. That is what I want. That's all I want. It's a lot, isn't it?"

He nodded. "She met you, what, a few weeks ago? Yeah, it's a lot. Harry's been working at getting Joy to open up for years, Rebecca."

She hadn't looked at it that way before. "You're right again. It must seem like a lot of pressure. A sister barreling into her life out of the blue, asking for a relationship based on nothing more than a father she never met."

"What if it turns out that she's *not* your sister? What then? Are you prepared for that?"

"No. I'm not going to prepare for it because I know she is my sister."

He raised his eyebrows. "You know one hundred percent without a doubt?"

"Well, not without a shadow of a doubt. But I'm ninety-nine point nine percent sure."

"And if that teeny percentage point says she's not your sister. What then?"

She looked away from his intense hazel eyes. "I don't know. Go back to New York? I don't know." And she really didn't know. Could she stay here, build a life here when the reason she came stopped existing?

He stiffened. "You mean go back to Michael?"

"No. I mean I don't know. I don't know."

He put his glass down on the end table. "So this thing between us is what? Just something you're doing while you're here?"

"No. I didn't mean it that way." What was this? Since when did Theo pressure her to know how she felt, what she felt?

"Then . . . ?"

"I don't know, Theo."

"When you rented this house, I thought you'd made a decision. I thought you were *here*. But what you're saying is that you don't know what you're doing with me. And 'the something' in New York is on hold. Do I have that right?"

Her shoulders slumped and she nodded.

"What, I'm a guy so I'm supposed be fine about this? I'm not looking to get my heart smashed again, Rebecca. Been there, done that, long enough for me not to make the same stupid mistake twice."

"I didn't know you got your heart broken."

He stared at her. "You haven't really asked, have you? We've been mostly talking about you."

"I guess we have. My life is crazy right now."

"I know. But that doesn't give you the right to run roughshod on me—or the guy in New York."

"I just know that I want to be with you, Theo."

"While you're here, you mean."

"No, I mean—" What *did* she mean? Always? Maybe. That was how she felt. But being here felt like some kind of limbo state. Limbo depending on six more business days.

He stood. "Come to me when and if you're free and clear, Rebecca Strand."

She jumped up. "Theo, please. Don't do this. Don't take yourself away from me."

"Sometimes it's easier to figure out what you want when you're not right in the middle of something," he said.

"So that's it? Either I break up with Michael or that's it?"

"Rebecca, this is junior high stuff. Yeah. That's what I'm saying. Me or him. Not both. Does he know about me?"

She nodded.

"And he's okay with it?"

"He's willing to give me time to figure things out."

He opened the front door. "Well, he either really loves you or he's an idiot."

"What about you?"

"I'm not an idiot, that's for sure."

And with that, he was gone.

Rebecca took Charlie for a long walk down side streets she hadn't yet explored, hoping the rain would pelt her on the head with the answers to her five thousand questions. Including: How had her massage and the perfect hamburger ended that way?

Now suddenly Michael was the flexible one, the one willing to give her time and space? How had they flip-flopped?

Not that Theo was wrong.

Or Michael.

She lifted her face up to the stars, the gentle rain feeling good against her skin. "What am I supposed to do, Dad?"

She wished he was here. Whenever she was really low, broken up about something, she'd go see her father, and he'd take her out for Chinese, and they'd order five dishes, but always two of the sesame chicken, and he'd offer so much wisdom. He'd say just the right thing without being preachy, without uttering a single platitude or cliché.

"I miss you," she said, and felt tears prick her eyes. The only thing she really had of him was the box of letters, but she'd stopped reading them because they seemed so exclusive of her, even though her father went on and on about her in several she had read. They were Joy's letters, *for* Joy. And when Rebecca came up here and met Joy, the letters seemed like something that should be private, between Daniel Strand and the daughter he'd never known.

She supposed she could read a few more, just to hear the sound of her father's voice. Several of the ones she'd read didn't contain much more than *"Dear Joy, you're seven now. I'll bet you received your very first Barbie doll today. Rebecca loved Barbies when she was seven and eight."* Hardly personal. Yes, she'd go home and read a few more of the letters, just to spend some time with her dad, and perhaps it would be a comfort.

She let Charlie lead the way home, let him stop and sniff every leaf and blade of grass that he wanted, and for a good five minutes, she stood in the drizzle and chatted with a woman she often saw in the little park with her pug.

Once they were back home, Rebecca stretched out on her bed with the letters and read them one by one, starting with the first, but she began skimming them, since they truly were mostly about what he assumed Joy was doing, what Rebecca had done at that age. There was very little about himself and what *he* was doing, how *he* felt, what *he* had missed.

How had he expected Joy to know him from these letters? Or perhaps that hadn't been his point. She'd hoped the letters would *explain* more—why he had cheated, *how* he'd been pulled away from the woman Rebecca had heard him describe many times as the love of his life. And how he had lived every day with what he'd done to Pia and Joy. But there was no explanation, nothing that made sense of it. Just the stupid seaweed and the rock and chemistry on a beach when he'd had a bad day.

So why had he written the letters? Just to mark the day with something? Had he really intended for Joy to read them one day? Perhaps he had no intentions. Perhaps he just made a ritual of the letter writing, something he did by rote, yet something ever-changing with the year, with the times.

She wished she understood.

She skimmed through *"Dear Joy, you're twenty-five, a quarter of a century,"* blah, blah, blah. And then she took the last letter from its envelope. It was dated six months ago.

Dear Joy,

I was diagnosed with pancreatic cancer thirteen days ago. I haven't told anyone yet, not even Rebecca. But I'm telling you. If I die tomorrow, Joy Jayhawk, I want you to know that I did love you in my heart. You probably don't think that's possible. But I've loved you from the moment I heard about you, even though you'd never know it.

You can love someone and not be able to be with them. You can love someone and never meet them. The idea of someone, even. If you want to know how I know this is true, how I know it's possible, it's because I have experienced it. I feel it.

You're twenty-six now and probably hate the idea of me. But I do love you, Joy. I always have. Not everything can be explained—and explained easily. I don't know if you'll ever forgive me for turning my back on you and your mother. I hope you can. I wasn't your father and there's no

*way to give you that back. So I guess there are two things
I want you to know: The first is that I'm sorry. I am, Joy.
Very, very sorry. And the second is that I do love you.*

*There's something that has been on my mind these past
couple of weeks, and now that I'm probably not going
to be around too much longer, I'd better do something
about it. It's the only thing I can do. One of the worst
repercussions of what I did was I denied a pair of sisters.
I don't know if you have any brothers or sisters, but
Rebecca is an only child. She always wanted a sister.
She's been asking for one since she was five years old.
And she always had one. The two of you are completely
innocent bystanders in all this. And if you could find
your way to each other out of nothing, wouldn't that be
something?*

—Daniel Strand

Tears streamed down Rebecca's cheeks. *Yes, Dad, it would
be something.*

She should have thought of reading the last letter first, but
she doubted it would have been exactly what she needed before now.

And exactly what Joy needed.

Rebecca knocked on the Jayhawk-Joneses' door at ten fifteen, but there was no answer. Both cars and the Love Bus
were in the driveway, so Rebecca knew they were home. This
late, Rex had to be fast asleep, so Rebecca gave the doorbell a

quick press, hoping it wouldn't wake the little guy. She carried the box of letters, just as she had the first day she'd arrived in Wiscasset.

When Harry opened the door, she said, "I thought you and Joy might want to have another session."

Joy appeared behind Harry. She looked more surprised than bothered. "Now?"

"Now," Rebecca said.

Harry stepped back to let Rebecca in. "She's here, and we're here, so we might as well."

"Can I make a pot of coffee so I have something to do other than sit and be uncomfortable?" Joy asked, eyeing the box of letters.

Rebecca smiled. "I'd love some coffee."

Harry sat across from Rebecca at the kitchen table. "Thanks for your note, by the way. I think we were a little discouraged."

"I don't see how this will be different than last time," Joy said, pressing the red button on the coffeemaker.

"It's different because I have two rules," Rebecca said. "It's the No Saying 'Yeah, But' rule, which in your case means no saying 'You don't understand' or 'You never listen.' In fact, neither of you is going to respond to what the other says. I'm going to ask you each a question. You're just going to listen to each other. And then I'm going to read you something."

Joy sat down with a slight scowl and wrapped her hands around her empty mug.

Here goes everything, Rebecca thought. "Harry, what do you want Joy to know most of all?"

"Most of all?" he said, running a hand through his dark hair.

"Most of all," Rebecca repeated.

He stared at his wife. "That I love her to death."

Rebecca smiled to herself. She was hoping he'd say that. No, she *knew* he would say that. She turned to Joy. "Joy, what do you want Harry to know most of all?"

Joy looked from Rebecca to Harry, biting her lip. "That I love him, too. And that I miss him. A lot."

Harry's hands covered Joy's. "I miss you, too."

Rebecca let out the deep breath she'd been holding. "I want to read you the very last letter my father wrote to you, Joy. On your twenty-sixth birthday. Is that okay?"

Her expression hardened, but Harry squeezed her hand, and she said, "Okay." Whispered it, but finally said it.

And so Rebecca sat there and read the letter, and when she finished, there was dead silence, until Joy broke it.

"I don't forgive him," she shouted. "I don't and I can't. I don't care if he says he loves me. I needed a *father*. And now I'm twenty-six years old and I'm supposed to be over this, not crying about it like a loser. I always thought that someday I would get to meet him, get to ask him *why*, and punch him in the face or something, but now he's dead, and I don't know how to get over *that*, the end of this stupid dream I've had for as along as I can remember." Tears fell down her cheeks. She leaned into Harry and sobbed into his shirt. "I don't know how to get over any of it."

"It wasn't a stupid dream," Harry said, stroking her hair. "And I'll help you work through it. You just have to talk to me like you're doing right now."

She nodded into his chest.

Harry let out a deep breath. "Thank you," he whispered to Rebecca.

Thank you, Dad, she whispered silently to the ceiling. In the end, their father had said the right thing, the right way. At exactly the right time.

seventeen

When she turned her car onto Elm Street, she saw that someone was sitting on her porch, on the steps next to the ceramic pot of African violets. A man. Was it Theo? Her heart thudded in her chest—she couldn't wait to tell him everything that had happened, tell him she was sorry, tell him she just needed some time. But as she pulled into the driveway she realized it *wasn't* Theo; Theo was taller and lankier and wouldn't be sitting on her porch at eleven at night wearing a business suit. He also didn't have a maroon sedan, which was parked in front of the house. She sat in her car for a moment, wondering if little Charlie had it in him to bust through windows and attack if need be, and then the man stood up and she saw that it was Michael.

Michael?

"You bought a *house*?" he asked in exactly the tone Joy had as Rebecca came out of the car and walked toward him. Charlie was barking like crazy inside the house. "And you have a dog? When the proprietor of your bed-and-breakfast gave me this address for you, I assumed it was another little inn, since that other one was closed. But this isn't a hotel, is it?"

She forgot how good-looking he was. How his dark blue eyes were like the color of the ocean on certain stormy summer days. How his thick brown hair sometimes fell in his eyes, and how he'd run his hand through to shove it back. It was good to see him, truly good, in a heart-and-soul way. He was familiarity and comfort and everything she'd left behind in New York, and here he was in Maine, in his suit and expensive black shoes.

She couldn't take her eyes off him. "I'm renting the house on a month-to-month lease. But the dog is mine."

He stared at her, and she expected him to say he thought they'd discussed that they wouldn't have pets, that pets shed and puke and pee all over the place. But instead he said, "You look pretty."

She smiled. "You too."

"Is the dog going to try and kill me?" he asked. "Dogs hate me."

That was true. Every dog they met in New York, from their neighbor's yippy terrier to friendly golden retrievers chasing Frisbees in Central Park, growled at Michael.

"You're safe," she assured him. "Any friend of mine is a friend of Charlie's."

"So is that what we are? Friends?"

She dodged the question by unlocking the door. As he walked in behind her, Charlie got between them and flattened his little ears and growled in as menacing a way as Charlie could.

Michael scowled at him, then glanced around. "You bought all this stuff?"

"It came mostly furnished," she said, pulling open the sliding glass doors to let a still suspicious Charlie out into the backyard.

Michael sat down on her red sofa, against her pillow with the embroidered sunflowers, and he suddenly looked so out of place that anyone doing a Guess What Doesn't Belong in This Picture would circle Michael Whitman immediately.

"Did you fly up here?" she asked. "And rent a car at the airport?" She couldn't imagine Michael driving seven, eight hours from New York City to Maine after work. The flight was only an hour.

He nodded. "I left work late as usual, but I just couldn't bring myself to go home to an empty apartment again. Every night I leave work without you, I go home without you, and you *never* come home. That's a lot of space to think in."

She sat down next to him. "And what have you been thinking?"

"That I miss you. That I'm not really into Lena. I want you to come home, Becs."

Oh, Michael, she thought, keeping her sigh to herself.

She stood up. "Do you want something to drink or eat? I have some amazing fried chicken in the fridge. And I have some Shipyard beer. I'll bet you'd like it."

"They have Shipyard beer in New York, Rebecca."

"Oh."

"I don't want anything to eat or drink. I want an answer. I want you to come home. I'm here, asking you to come home."

It cost him, she knew, just to fly up here and tell her this. He wasn't a "big gesture" kind of guy, and this was a big gesture. Her heart surged with emotion for him, and she wished she could just walk up to him and hug him, but she couldn't, so she stayed rooted in her spot, frozen.

"I see us married one day, Rebecca. I see us in that three-floor Perry Street brownstone we always used to talk about. I know we have to work things out. But we both know how to accomplish that. That's what we *do*."

She sat back down. "We don't see eye to eye on some very important issues, Michael."

"About your inheritance?"

"About that, about Joy and what she means to me, about my being here."

"I assume you didn't get the DNA results back yet?"

She shook her head. "I can start checking online the day after tomorrow to see if the results are listed."

"I've been thinking about that," he said. "From your perspective. And if she's your sister, it would be very generous if you gave her ten thousand."

Was he kidding? "*Ten thousand?* That doesn't even begin to add up to child support, based on my father's income, for ages one day through eighteen. That doesn't come close to paying off her student loans, either."

"Okay, so twenty-five thousand. Fifty thousand, even. That would be very generous, Rebecca."

Generous, her ass. "I'm not interested in generous. I'm interested in appropriate. I'm giving her half."

He shook his head as though this was his decision to make.

"Half is our future, Rebecca. It's the down payment on our brownstone. It's our children's college education. It's the summer house in Montauk that we used to talk about. We could even rent a ski house up here."

She didn't ski. She didn't particularly want to ski.

"Anyway, why are we arguing about this now?" he said, leaning closer to take both of her hands in his. "Let's talk about this when the results come in. Fly back with me tomorrow morning. You can check the results online at home."

She pulled her hands away. "You haven't really listened to one thing I've said. You don't hear me at all."

"Rebecca, I hear you loud and clear. I just think you're making a mistake and I'm trying to stop you from doing it. Once you throw away the money, it's gone."

He was infuriating. Was this the way things always were between them? His way was the only way? His thoughts and beliefs the *right* ones? "I don't think I'm making a mistake at all. And I'm done discussing it with you."

He let out a frustrated breath. "Why are you so fucking stubborn?"

"Did you fly up here to curse at me? To call me names?"

"I flew up here to talk some sense into you."

She stared at him, then sat back down. "Michael, what's the one thing you want me to know—most of all."

He looked annoyed. "That you're making a big mistake, that's what."

"By giving Joy the money? By not coming home? Which one?"

"Both. They're connected, aren't they?"

She looked at him, at this man she'd been with for two years, who'd comforted her through her father's death, who'd made the funeral arrangements, who'd held her for those nights when she'd just cried and been unable to speak.

"Do you love me?" she asked.

He stared at her. "Do you love me?"

She was tempted to say "I asked you first," but she suddenly knew what the problem was between her and Michael. The real problem, the problem of all problems: They didn't love each other anymore. They had once, and there was still feeling there. Fondness. Tenderness. But not love. And certainly not the kind of love that made for marriage. He cared about her and he wasn't ready to let her go, just like she hadn't been ready to let him go. He wanted the money for the vague future, so it would be there like a concrete thing for them. But he didn't love her, and she wasn't so sure the mighty, smart, insightful Michael Whitman even knew it.

He held her gaze. "I care very much about you, Rebecca. And I think we can work things out. I want to work things out."

He did know. He knew and he wasn't ready for it. She felt another surge of emotion for him. A purge of emotion, maybe. *She* was ready to let go.

"I care about you, too, Michael. And I think we did love each other in the beginning, but somewhere along the way we stopped, but we're both too *something*—I don't know what, exactly—to acknowledge it, so we just forged ahead, living together, working together, our lives entwined. We care about each other, but we don't love each other."

He stared at her, then let out a harsh breath and kicked one of Charlie's rubber chew toys against the wall. He closed his eyes and dropped down on the sofa, his head in his hands. "I do care about you, Rebecca. More than you think, maybe."

"It's the same for me, Michael."

"So this is it?" he said, glancing up at her. "This is the end? Just like that?"

"It's not 'just like that,' though, is it? We've been heading to this for a while," she said gently.

He nodded and leaned back against the sofa, staring up at the ceiling. "Well, it sucks."

She bit her lip. It did suck, but it was the *truth*. Black and white, no gray areas.

"Okay, Rebecca," he said, getting up. "Good luck with everything," he added, and then walked out the door.

She was not free and clear, not really. As she lay in her bed, Charlie's warm body beside her, she longed for Theo, longed to be wrapped in his arms, longed to be underneath him, on top of him, to be fused with him. And she longed to just look at him, to have those intense dark brown eyes warm and sweet on her. But he wanted her free and clear, and she wasn't either.

Because Michael was a part of it, but not all of it.

Regardless of the results of the DNA test, perhaps she should go back to New York and see how things felt there, how she felt. That was her home, wasn't it? Where she was born, where she was from, where she and her family had lived intact before Wiscasset and a woman named Pia Jayhawk had entered their lives, without two of them knowing it.

But in the past few weeks, Rebecca had made Wiscasset her home.

What do you want most of all? she asked herself.

She wanted to know where she belonged. And she wanted the results of the DNA test—if Joy was definitely her sister—to mean something to Joy. She wanted the word *sister* to be backed up with sisterhood.

And if she wanted Joy to be her sister in the ways that mattered, she needed to let her go, too. Let the relationship settle some, give Joy space, time. And the freedom to make the choice to come to Rebecca.

Two days passed, and Rebecca had heard from no one. She could be dead in her kitchen, having slipped on her freshly mopped floor (she was in a cleaning frenzy again from the angst of waiting—waiting for the DNA results, waiting to be free and clear, waiting to understand *something*), and they'd find her with poor, starving Charlie resting his head on her chest.

Great, now she was sounding like her late grandmother Mildred.

She hadn't heard a word from Joy or Harry about how things were going, if they wanted another mediation session, if they needed one. She hadn't heard from Ellie or Maggie. She hadn't heard from Theo, of course. And it would be a while before Michael would contact her about packing up the stuff she'd left behind. She'd call his mother once some time had passed and say she would have otherwise loved to wear her beautiful wedding gown, and that some other woman would be lucky to walk down the aisle in it.

She'd thought about calling Joy and telling her about what happened with Theo and then with Michael, how suddenly she went from two boyfriends to none. But she felt like she'd be pushing herself on Joy at the wrong time, demanding she be her sister and bring over a pint of Ben & Jerry's and a box of tissues.

She would just love that.

"It's just you and me, Charlie," she said. She glanced at the clock. It was eleven thirty at night. She'd take Charlie out for his last walk and then she'd try to go to bed, but she knew she wouldn't sleep.

She put on a sweater and let Charlie lead the way along the path of the beach. This was Charlie's favorite walk, and if she happened to run into a gorgeous man named Theo Granger, well, that was life in a small town. And when Charlie began tugging on his leash to get away, his tail wagging, she knew his best friend, Spock, was close by.

As Charlie pulled her around the dark curve of the evergreens, her heart started beating like crazy. And then there was Spock with his pointy ears. A moment later, Theo appeared in the shadows. He looked so handsome, so . . . conflicted, she thought. Or maybe he was just pissed off that she'd engineered this possible run-in down by his end of the beach.

She barely got the opportunity to say hello when her cell phone rang. Theo nodded at her and began walking away. "C'mon, Spock," she heard him say, but of course Spock wouldn't budge; he was busy chasing Charlie's tail.

Maggie's name appeared in the tiny screen. At almost midnight? "Maggie?"

"Rebecca, you've got to come! I'm at Ellie's—maybe you can talk to her. She says she's going to kill herself. She locked herself in her bathroom. She's drunk off her ass."

What? Oh God. "Theo!" she shouted, her voice shrill in the still night air. "Maggie says Ellie's in trouble, that she's drunk and threatening to kill herself." She said into the phone, "Maggie, we'll be right there."

He rushed over to her. "My car is closer. Let's go." They ran to his house, a quarter of a mile away, her legs a rubbery mess, her heart thudding. He put the dogs in the yard, then they jumped into his car, and within seconds they were at Ellie's house.

Maggie had left the door open for them. She stood, hands braced against the bathroom door, ashen-faced and red-eyed. "Ellie, honey, please, just let me in." She turned around when she heard Rebecca and Theo enter. "She's been in there for a half hour. I'm getting really scared."

Maggie whispered the story. Ellie had signed the divorce papers and had brought the envelope over to Tim's mother's garage apartment, where he was living. Apparently, Tim signed the papers right then and there with an "I guess it's for the best" and handed the document back to Ellie, then said, "So, you wanna do it one last time?" Ellie got all nostalgic and misty, but Tim had been unable to "perform," and so Ellie had gotten on her knees, but that hadn't worked, either. And then Tim said, "I guess you don't do it for me anymore, babe. But that doesn't mean we can't be friends. In fact, I guess it means we should be."

Ellie had punched him hard in the stomach, and because Tim hadn't been expecting it, he tripped over some beer bottles and fell and hit his head on the corner of his dresser, and there was blood, and then his mother came in to see what the commotion was, and accused Ellie of trying to murder her "precious boy."

"At least she thought to grab the signed divorce papers," Maggie whispered.

And so there had been an emergency meeting of the Bitter Exes Club, and Ellie had been very down. After a few hours of talking and crying and eating, Lucy and Darren reluctantly left, Maggie assuring them she'd stay the night with Ellie. But then Ellie began drinking heavily, downing shots of tequila despite Maggie's insistence that she stop and have coffee instead. Ellie started crying and couldn't stop, and when Maggie went to make a pot of strong coffee, Ellie disappeared. Maggie discovered she had locked herself in the bathroom. And then Ellie said she wouldn't come out and stopped answering. Until she finally called out, "Maggie?"

Maggie, who'd been sitting by the door, jumped up. "Yes, sweetie? Honey, open up so we can talk face to face?"

"Mags, do you think my pink razor would be sharp enough to do the job? Or should I just use the little scissors in the medicine cabinet? That's so gross," she slurred. "Tim used to use those to cut his nose hairs. Maggie, can you call Darren and ask if he knows if Rite Aid brand razors are sharp enough? I was trying to save money so I bought the generic kind, but I'll bet Bic or whatever is sharper."

Maggie had raced for the phone and called Rebecca.

"I could just swallow all these pills," Ellie said now on a wail. "Between the Tylenol and the Midol, there's enough."

Rebecca and Theo and Maggie stared at one another, all of them going white.

Theo knocked on the door. "Ellie, it's Theo. Will you open up? I really want to talk to you. Give you the guy's perspective, okay?"

Yes, that was good. That would likely work. Ellie was obsessed with the guy's perspective. According to Maggie, she'd taken armfuls of books out of the library this past week, from *Men Are from Mars, Women Are from Venus* to *How to Heal a Broken Heart In 30 Days* to *Divorce Is Not the Answer*.

Hurting yourself wasn't either.

"Men suck shit," Ellie slurred. "You all suck. I hate you."

"She's so drunk," Maggie whispered.

Theo sat down against the wall next to the bathroom door. "See what you can do," he whispered to Rebecca.

She sent a silent prayer up to the ceiling and pressed her hands against the door. "Ellie? It's Rebecca. Honey, please open the door. Please. Let me talk to you."

"Hi, Berecca." She laughed. "Hey, did I say that backward?" She started to cry, loud sobs, then stopped suddenly. "I'm so drunk."

"That's okay, Ellie. Sometimes you just need to get smashed. But you've got three people out here who care about you, and we want you to come out and talk to us. You've been so strong, Ellie. Come on out, okay?"

"I'm so comfy, though," she said. "Well, not that comfy." She laughed, then wailed again. "I'm so tired. Did you hear I killed Tim?"

Rebecca's heart squeezed in her chest. "Theo saw him going into Mama's an hour ago with a Band-Aid on his temple. He's alive and eating pizza."

Sobs from the bathroom. "I hate him so much. And I hate his stupid mother."

"Ellie, come on out, and you can lie down on the couch. We'll stay with you, okay?"

There was a moment of silence. Then another wail. And then some thudding sounds, then a click, then the thud again. Had she opened the door? Rebecca and Theo locked eyes, and Rebecca tried the doorknob. It turned. She let out a deep breath and gently opened the door. Ellie lay in the empty bathtub with a towel covering her up to her chin, mascara running and smeared all over her face. The empty bottle of tequila was on the bathroom floor. And Ellie had vomited near the toilet.

"I just want him to love me," Ellie said, pulling the towel over her head. Pieces of her straight dark hair were splayed against her mouth, and Rebecca pushed them aside. "Why doesn't he love me? Why? Theo? Are you still here?"

Theo came into the bathroom and sat down on the rim of the tub. "I'm here."

"Why doesn't he love me?"

He took her hand and held on to it. "I can't answer that, Ellie. But I do know it's not because you're not beautiful. And it's not because you're not wonderful. It's not because of you at all."

"Then I can't do anything about it," she said, and burst into tears again, pulling the towel over her face. Her sobs racked her slight body.

Theo picked her up out of the tub and carried her to the black leather couch. He lay her down and covered her with a throw and stroked her hair. "Ellie, honey, it hurts like hell, but you've got family and friends who love you and who will see you through it."

Ellie cried and turned to face the back of the couch. Maggie stroked her hair, and in a few minutes, she was so quiet that they realized she'd fallen asleep.

Maggie let out a very deep breath. "She's going to have some headache tomorrow."

Theo slid down on the floor, his back against the couch, his face pale.

Maggie handed him a cup of coffee. "This should help." She headed back into the kitchen and brought another cup for Rebecca, her hand shaking. "I think she'll see my therapist now. I couldn't convince her to make an appointment before, but I bet she'll go now. Thank you, guys, so much for coming. I was so scared. I'll stay the night with her."

Rebecca rubbed Maggie's shoulder. "I'll stay here with you."

Theo downed his coffee, then headed into the kitchen. He returned a few minutes later with a bottle of Pine-Sol and Ellie's Swiffer WetJet and a roll of paper towels and went into the bathroom. When he came out, he said, "Much cleaner in there now." He put away the mop and cleaning supplies. "Okay, I'm gonna go. If you need me, call." He locked eyes with Rebecca for a moment, then left.

"He's gold," Maggie whispered. She turned out the lights and lay down on the floor, her head on one of the floor pillows.

Rebecca found a linen closet near the bathroom and took out two cotton blankets. She covered Maggie with one, then lay down next to her and stared up at the sliver of moonlight on the ceiling for a long while before she finally fell asleep, the sachet-scented blanket no match for the smell of Pine-Sol.

In the morning, Ellie did have a killer headache. She was also mortified. She swore she wasn't serious about killing herself, that she'd hit rock bottom and had no where to go but up, right? She'd even called her mother, who'd called Ellie's four aunts, who'd called their daughters and daughters-in-law, and they were all coming over at nine to take care of their girl.

When the very loud group of women arrived—there were at least ten of them—talking over themselves, shrieking, grabbing Ellie into fierce hugs, "That lying, cheating loser of a wuss doesn't know from blood!" was among the bits and pieces Rebecca was able to make out.

Ellie had family. And she had friends. And they would all make sure she was okay.

Once Rebecca and Maggie had Ellie's sworn vow to call Maggie's therapist that morning, Rebecca and Maggie finally left. The cool morning air was like a rejuvenating blast, but Rebecca still felt shell-shocked. And her back hurt like hell from sleeping on the floor.

"I think she scared the bitter right out of herself," Maggie said as they walked to her car. Maggie looked exhausted, dark circles and puffy bags under her usually alert hazel eyes.

"And she's not even an ex yet," Rebecca said. "I'm worried."

"She'll be fine. I'm sure of it. I've been there. Not quite as bad, but worse in other ways. We just need to keep a close eye on her for a good while. Plus, she's got all those women to rally around her, too. She'll be okay."

With thanks and more assurances, Maggie dropped off Rebecca at her house. Rebecca took a quick shower, then fell asleep until the phone woke her up.

Theo. His voice was like a soothing balm. He asked after Ellie, said he'd drop off Charlie, fed and walked, in her backyard sometime this morning, then hung up. But he'd called her, when he could have called Maggie or Ellie directly. He could have just told her to pick up Charlie from his yard.

He cared. And for right now, that was good enough.

eighteen

It was Business Day Eight. Which meant the results of the DNA test might finally be available online. Rebecca had checked yesterday, and the day before. And the day before, but she hadn't really expected the findings to be posted. Today was the earliest the information packet had said to expect results.

Rebecca brought her laptop to the kitchen and set it on the table next to the vase of sunflowers that Ellie had brought her yesterday as a thank-you. She stared at the little boxes into which she was supposed to type her name and password. *Just do it*, she told herself. But she couldn't. Now that the results *could* pop up, she was overtaken by fear. What if Joy wasn't her sister? What if?

Which meant it was a perfect time to take Charlie for a walk or scrub the spotless white enamel of the sink again. She chose Charlie. And after an hour-long walk off the beaten path, she was back. And there was her computer.

She hadn't really thought much about the what-ifs because she did believe, heart, mind, and soul, that Joy Jayhawk was her half sister. But the shadow of a doubt did exist, and shadows were creepy things. And now, for the first time, the shadow was scaring her.

She took a deep breath, feeling exactly as she had the day she'd typed Joy's name into the Google search engine and then deleted it five times. This time, though, Charlotte wasn't here to take over.

Okay. *Just do it!* she yelled at herself. And so she logged on, entered the password, and then held her breath and closed her eyes.

She opened them to see a jumble of words: *half siblingship DNA testing . . . genetic link strongly supported—conclusive . . .*

Rebecca jumped up. "Thank you, universe!"

She printed out the page and drove over to Joy's house and knocked on the door. "Please be home," she said to the door.

No answer.

She rang the bell again. And again.

The door opened, and there was Joy, her hair in a ponytail, her feet in the same red fringed clogs she'd worn the first day Rebecca had seen her.

"You're my sister," Rebecca said, clutching the printout.

Joy stared at her, then grabbed the paper and scanned it. Her hand flew to her mouth. "It's so . . . official," she said. "Right there in black and white."

"I never had any doubt. You *feel* like my sister, Joy."

"It doesn't really change anything, though. I've always known who my father was. I really didn't need a test to confirm it."

God, she was tough.

"But doesn't it make it just a tiny bit more real?" Rebecca asked.

All of a sudden, Rex in his Superman cape came barreling over and snaked around Joy's legs. "Hi, Becsa! Read me story?"

Joy bit her lip and closed her eyes for a moment, and Rebecca knew she had her. The wall already had a big crack in it and now it was starting to crumble.

"Honey, I don't know if Rebecca is able to stay for a story," Joy said to Rex.

"I can stay for a little while. If it's okay with your mom," Rebecca said, her eyes on Joy.

Rex grabbed Rebecca's hand and tugged. "Come on! I want to show you what I made in school today. It's pipe wieners."

Rebecca laughed, and Joy stepped aside, her expression tight. But still, she'd let Rebecca *in*.

At six o'clock that night, Rebecca arrived at Joy's bearing a loaf of Portuguese bread. After Rebecca had left that morning, after only twenty minutes—Joy had interrupted the building of a tower of blocks by insisting it was Rex's naptime—Joy had invited Rebecca over for dinner "to talk." It was a start.

Rebecca wanted to bring wine, but she wasn't so sure if Joy would think of the results as a cause for celebration or an "It is what it is." Yet when she followed Joy into the kitchen, there was a bottle of white wine and two glasses on the table.

Joy poured, then held up her glass. "To learning how to be sisters."

Rebecca's heart flip-flopped. She held up her glass, and they clinked. "I will drink to that."

Joy grinned. "I might have to drink the whole bottle to that.

Like I said, it's not like I needed anything confirmed. I always knew you were my half sister. I just couldn't deal with it, with what it meant. What it means."

"What does it mean to you?" Rebecca asked.

Joy took a sip of her wine. "It means I have to finally deal with the fact that my biological father turned his back on me, didn't want me, wasn't interested in me. My mother used to tell me that, impossible as it seemed, I shouldn't take it personally because it wasn't about me at all—it was about him. But how's a kid supposed to do that?"

Rebecca nodded. "I've thought about that a lot since my father told me about you."

"And then—*wham!*—one day you show up with the news that he's dead and that you're my sister, and everyone's expecting me to welcome you into my life with open arms. No."

Rebecca ripped off a piece of the crusty bread. "I completely get that. I guess I had this fantasy fairy tale in mind that you would."

"Yeah, I've noticed," she said, then laughed. "You do try hard, don't you, Rebecca?"

She smiled. "Guess so."

"My son sure likes you."

"That goes back double for me."

Joy let out a deep breath and leaned back, her blond hair falling over the edge of the straight-backed chair. "So I have a sister. Huh."

"And we have, what, the next seventy years to figure all this out." Maybe she shouldn't have said that. That was a lot of pressure.

But Joy just smiled. They were family. And not just because the results said so. Because *they* said so. Because Joy was *finally* saying so.

Over Pasta Primavera and Rebecca's Portuguese bread, Joy said, "I still don't feel comfortable taking the money, but I will. What a hardship, right? To save my marriage, I have to accept over half a million dollars." She shook her head. "It's so crazy. I can't even believe this has become my biggest problem—a fortune dropping into my lap."

"I'm relieved you've made peace with it," Rebecca said.

"I do think Harry's right—the money is symbolic of my accepting what is and getting over it." She bit her lip and glanced at Rebecca. "And I want you to know that I'm glad you stuck around, stuck it out. Stuck *me* out. I know I'm not the easiest person to get to know. A teacher actually wrote that on my second-grade report card: 'Joy isn't very easy to get to know, but once she opens up, I'm sure her personality will shine.' She was always pissed at me because I never brought in anything for show-and-tell. Some people just don't want to bring something from home and tell twenty blank faces all about it, you know?"

Rebecca laughed. It was one of the first personal things Joy had said about herself. "I have one of those report card zingers, too."

Joy glanced at Rebecca for a moment. "So, I've noticed that you've seemed kind of down lately. Man trouble?"

Rebecca almost burst into tears—at the sisterliness and at the thought of Theo. "Theo broke up with me because I was still with Michael, and I broke up with Michael because we don't belong together anymore, but I don't know if I messed up too much with Theo. I miss him so much, but I don't know if he'll take me back now."

Joy topped off Rebecca's wine, and it was as good as Ben & Jerry's and a box of tissues. Better, actually. "Why don't you go find out? You're good at not giving up, remember?"

Rebecca laughed. "I am, aren't I."

"Oh, I almost forgot," Joy said. "I have something for you." She pulled out a brochure for the University of Southern Maine. "I took Rex to one of the kiddie shows at the planetarium in Portland today, and since it's right on the USM campus, I stopped in the admissions office to ask for brochures on counseling programs for you. Did you know they have several types of programs? You could become a therapist, a marriage counselor, anything you want. You should look into it."

Rebecca couldn't remember the last time she'd been so touched. And not just because Joy had thought of her, but because she was very clearly telling her that she should continue to stick around these parts. "Thank you."

"This seems the kind of thing a sister would do, right?" Joy asked.

"It does," Rebecca said, feeling like she might cry.

By the time Harry and Rex came home, Joy and Rebecca were marveling at how they had absolutely nothing in common (except for certain foods, like pizza and peanut butter and jelly sandwiches) and would have to just come up with things neither had done so they could discover together whether or not they liked them. Like fishing. And knitting.

"Mommy!" Rex said, flinging himself at Joy. She scooped him up into a hug, and he stared at Rebecca, his tiny dimples popping. "And hi, Becca!"

"That's right, I'm Rebecca," she said with a smile and a tickle on Rex's smiley face T-shirt. Rex dashed over to his little table, upon which was half a Lego tower, and he began stacking the brightly colored blocks.

"That's your nephew," Joy said. "I'll start using the words *aunt* and *sister* in relation to you, and he'll just pick it up naturally."

Rebecca looked over at Rex, *her* nephew, and again felt that surge of emotion for him. She felt it for everyone in the house, including her father, whose heart—a piece of it, anyway—had been captured and hung on the hallway wall.

"And you've got yourself a brother-in-law," Harry said, coming into the room. He poured a glass of wine for himself and raised it Rebecca. "I don't want to get too heavy into a discussion while Rex is still up, but I've been thinking about everything, too, Joy. If you want to turn down the money, I'll understand. We don't have the money now and we can't miss what we don't have. This is your history and your past, and maybe I've been trying to get you to think and act in a way that would make life easier for me. That's not fair. So I want you to take me out of the equation about the money. You do what seems right to you."

Joy jumped up and hugged him. "I already told Rebecca I'll accept the money. I'm going to give my mother half. I think that's fair." She paused, then said. "Do you?"

Harry wrapped his arms around her. "Yeah. More than fair. I love you."

"I love you, too," she said.

All this love was making Rebecca miss a certain tall, blond, and handsome man. "I think that's my cue to go. Thanks for dinner, Joy. And thanks for . . . everything."

Joy walked her to the door and held it open. "Oh, and I'll take that box of letters. I'm not so sure I'll read them right away. But I'll be ready to one of these days."

Hear that, Dad? Rebecca said silently. She felt something ease inside her chest, something she hadn't realized was still there until the dull heaviness of it was gone. She touched her hand to her heart and smiled. "I'll bring them by tomorrow."

"Or, I could get them when I come pick you up the day after tomorrow to show you the farm I'll be working at starting next Monday." Joy's brown eyes lit up. "I've signed on for two mornings a week while Rex is in preschool. I'll be grooming the Beltie bulls and starting on something of an internship program."

"Congratulations!" Rebecca said, thinking she'd finally have a good use for her cowboy boots.

"Not that I'm parking the Love Bus for good or anything. I'll be doing a tour a month for the Bitter Exes. Unfortunately, that club is going to keep me in business. Pick you up at nine, nine fifteen?"

Rebecca thought of Ellie and Maggie and Lucy and Darren. Exes, but not bitter. Just some wonderful people trying to make sense of something that involved the heart and the head—and every other body part. Just like *everyone.* "Nine-ish

the day after tomorrow is perfect," she said, then headed down
the impatiens-lined path. As she was about to get into her car,
Joy called her name.

"Welcome to the family, Rebecca."

Rebecca smiled. "You too."

Rebecca went straight to Theo's, but the house was dark.
She sat on his porch steps for at least an hour, but he never did
come home.

"I'm free and clear," she said to the stars. "So where is he?"

Please don't let me be too late, she prayed to the universe.
Please, please, please.

She sat there for another twenty minutes, feeling like a
stalker, then walked over to Mama's, where he often took his
grandmother for the Early Bird special, even though it was
past ten and Mama's was closed. Arlene sometimes stayed
open late for her regulars. But Mama's was dark, too.

When her doorbell rang the next morning, Rebecca rushed
to answer it, then realized it wouldn't be Theo. He wouldn't
come to her. He'd made that clear.

She opened the door to find Joy and her mother standing
there. Rebecca gasped; the two of them on her doorstep was
just so unexpected. Pia Jayhawk smiled as if she understood
and extended both hands, and when Rebecca put out her own,
Pia clasped them. For a split second, Rebecca saw Pia as she
must have been twenty-six years ago, alone and pregnant on

the beach in her fingerless gloves and shredded layered tank tops, clutching the rock that had started it all. But it was truly momentary; when Rebecca blinked she saw a beautiful and strong woman who'd raised a child alone.

Joy, who looked happier and lighter than Rebecca had ever seen her, said, "Rebecca, this is my mother, Pia Jayhawk Montenegro. Mom, this is Daniel Strand's daughter, Rebecca."

"Hello, Rebecca," Pia said, her voice full of warmth. "It's very nice to meet you. I know we met at Joy's the other weekend, and believe it or not, my first thought when I came upon you looking at the painting of Daniel was that you were his daughter. But then I said to myself, 'Don't be silly, Pia, what would Daniel Strand's Rebecca be doing in Joy's house?' I mean, what was the likelihood of that, even though I saw the way you were looking at the painting of him. But between that and the way you were watching me—and the strong resemblance, of course—I truly wondered."

Rebecca smiled. "I had a feeling you knew, but I wasn't sure." She opened the door wider. "Would you like to come in and have some coffee?"

"Actually, we're running a bit late for my appointment for my dress fitting for my vows renewal," Pia said. "But when Joy told me everything late last night, I wanted to stop by and see you first thing. Just to tell you how very glad I am that you came into Joy's life. It's something I've always hoped for."

"My father, too," Rebecca said. "I hope that's all right to say."

Pia nodded. "Of course it is. Joy shared his final letter with me. I was glad to know that. Very glad."

"Good," Rebecca said, letting out a deep breath. "This is all so new for all of us."

"Maybe you can meet us for lunch in town later," Joy said.

Rebecca beamed. "I would love to."

After a very lovely lunch with Pia and Joy (they'd talked about the upcoming vows-renewal ceremony, the second-honeymoon plans, and current events—there had seemed to be an unspoken understanding that they had all the time in the world for discussing the one big thing they all *did* have in common), Rebecca picked up the makings of Theo's favorite dinner—he loved a good tuna steak—and rushed home to doll herself up. Her grand plan was to arrive unannounced at his door with her bag of groceries and an apology and an "I love you."

Because she did. Of all the things she knew for sure, she knew that most of all.

Not that she had any idea if he'd be home tonight. Or if he was with one of those women he'd mentioned he saw from time to time. Or if she'd ruined things between them.

She put on her red wrap dress and black T-strap heels and a light spritz of Chanel N° 19, then grabbed her bag of groceries, promised Charlie a doggie bag, and headed out the door.

Straight into Theo Granger's chest. He stood on the porch, looking gorgeous as always, his dark brown eyes intense on her.

Second gasp of the day.

"I was just going to see you," she said, clutching the brown paper bag.

"And here I am. My busybody neighbor, Mrs. Finnegrew, told me that a young lady was sitting on my porch for hours last night. You?"

"Me."

"That's a long time to sit on a porch. You must have had something important to tell me."

"I did. I do. I'm free and clear, Theo." She gasped for the third time. *That* was what she knew most of all. She was free and clear.

He smiled that smile that had taken her breath the very first time she saw him. "I'm very glad to hear that, Rebecca."

"And since I'm going to buy this place, I was wondering if I could hire you to build a small deck."

"On the house." He took the bag of groceries and set it down on the little rocking chair, then picked her up in his arms and kissed her in the glow of the pink and red setting sun.

READING GROUP GUIDE

• • •

THE SECRET OF JOY

MELISSA SENATE

BOOK SUMMARY

In Melissa Senate's sweet and sentimental eighth novel, twenty-eight-year-old Rebecca Strand is about to lose her father and be left alone in the world without a family. But her father makes a confession on his deathbed—that he had a secret affair twenty-six years ago and Rebecca has a half sister named Joy that neither she nor anyone else has ever known about. Shocked by her father's infidelity and secrecy, Rebecca is determined to find her sister and make up for Daniel Strand's abandonment of his second daughter. She leaves New York City, her job, and her boyfriend behind and heads to Maine to track down the only family she has left. But when Joy doesn't exactly welcome her with open arms, Rebecca must look within herself to discover the meaning of the word *sister*, and to figure out what she wants out of life and where her future lies.

QUESTIONS AND TOPICS FOR DISCUSSION

1. Is sharing the same DNA enough in and of itself to make someone family, or do words like *family* and *sister* hold meaning that goes much deeper than genetics?

2. Rebecca makes a lot of major decisions without really thinking about them—going to Maine, getting a dog, renting a house, giving up half her inheritance. Why do you think she is able to make these decisions so easily and confidently, even while acknowledging that she doesn't really know what she's doing?

3. On page 121, Maggie suggests that Rebecca's father told her about Joy to let her know that she's not alone in the world, that she doesn't have to marry Michael "just to have someone." Do you agree with that idea? Do you think Rebecca's father was worried that she felt like she needed to marry Michael to keep from being alone?

4. Rebecca gives a lot of thought to faithfulness in relationships as she struggles to understand how her father could have cheated. Is her relationship with Theo really cheating? Does not being married make it any less wrong?

5. How do you feel about Marianne's attitude toward her husband's infidelity? On page 211, she talks about the woman her husband had his second affair with, saying, "He was carrying on a sexual affair, and she thought she was having a love affair." Can you really differentiate between the two? Is one type of affair more forgivable than the other?

6. It seems clear to everyone but Ellie that Tim is a total jerk. Why do you think she clings to her marriage so strongly when it's obvious that she'd be better off without him?

7. Why do you think Joy keeps the painting of her father hanging in her house when she seems so opposed to talking about him and acknowledging his role in her life?

8. Rebecca feels a lot of guilt and sympathy for her father's abandonment of Pia and Joy, but she doesn't seem to be very angry with Pia for getting involved with a married man. Were Pia and Daniel equally wrong in their situation, having both known all the details? Or is Daniel more at fault because he was the one who was already married?

9. Why do you think Daniel Strand never tried to contact Pia or Joy, even after his wife died? How do you feel about what Rebecca decides to do with her inheritance? Would you have done the same thing?

10. Is Michael being selfish in telling Rebecca that her inheritance is their future, their down payment on a home, their kids' education? Do you think he is more concerned about securing his own future than he is about helping Rebecca make the right decision for herself?

11. Had Daniel told his wife about the affair when it happened, Rebecca's life could have been completely different. Should she be at all grateful to her father for preserving her happy and stable childhood? What do you think would have been the right thing for him to do?

A CONVERSATION WITH MELISSA SENATE

How did you come up with the idea for *The Secret of Joy*?

My own life provided the inspiration (truth is stranger than fiction). Out of the blue several years ago, I received an email with the subject header: I think you might be my half sister. Whoa. I've had no contact with my biological father or any member of his family since I was eight years old, but I've always known I had a half brother, who was born when I was seven. And now here the half brother was, making contact. You can imagine the soul-searching, the questions I asked myself: Who is this person to me? A total stranger or a family member? What does the word family mean, exactly? How do I feel about it all? I had so many questions and no answers. And that's one of the gifts of being a novelist; I could pose that question on paper, create a fictional scenario (using real life as a basis), a fictional character, and have her help me find the answers. And to make things more interesting for myself, I flipped everything: a half sister instead of a half brother. And I made the main character the one who grew up with the mutual father—that was very revealing for me.

You've written about sisters before, but in different capacities. Do you have a sister of your own? How did your experience of growing up either with or without siblings shape your understanding of what it means to be and have a sister?

Sisterhood is such a powerful word, such a powerful concept. That shared upbringing, that shared female experience. I love exploring the ways in which sisters can be raised in the same home by the same parents, yet have such different experiences, be so different. I do indeed have a sister of my own, two years older, and though we haven't lived in the same state since I was sixteen, I've always felt very close to her. In The Secret of Joy, *there are two sisters with DNA and a father (barely, for one) in common, but nothing else to bind them together—no shared upbringing. How do they forge a relationship? Especially if one isn't interested? There is so much to delve into!*

In your own life, you moved from New York City to a small town in Maine for what you call a "quality of life experiment." Was your move as impulsive as Rebecca's? How did that move affect your life and inspire your writing?

It was as impulsive—and yet, not, at the same time. I have long-known that my gut instinct serves me well, and when it said to move from the Upper East Side of Manhattan, where I'd lived for fourteen years, in the apartment of my dreams on the twenty-third floor with a balcony and a tiny-but-there view of the East River to a small town in Maine with one (unnecessary) traffic light, I listened, despite. *Despite leaving my family, my friends, and my beloved New York City itself. What I needed was quiet—though I didn't realize then that the quiet I sought was an internal thing, not an external thing. When I did move to Maine and got the external quiet, I could hear myself think and slowly realized that the peace and serenity I sought did not come from long stretches of grass and blue ocean and the lack of honking taxis and eight million people, but that peace is something you have to find within yourself, not from your surroundings, though your surroundings can certainly have a huge effect. Ah, life lessons. The good news: I love Maine. And I do appreciate the quiet! As for how the move affected my writing, I've discovered that all of my adventures, big and small, have found their way into my novels in ways even I can't identify sometimes.*

Are any aspects of *The Secret of Joy* at all autobiographical? Are any of your characters ever loosely based on friends or acquaintances?

See question number one! Interestingly, though I love to borrow from my own life for the premise of my novels, I never, ever base, loosely or otherwise, my characters on anyone in my life.

I am nothing like Joy Jayhawk, for example. Or Rebecca. I do like to take situations from my own life and turn them around to explore them in fiction, though. I've done that in every book. A serial dater in NYC—check. A single woman who gets pregnant two months into a new relationship—check. A wedding that isn't quite what you envisioned—check. A half sibling who "knocks" on your door one day out of the clear blue sky— check!

What are some of your favorite places in Maine? Have you ever been to Wiscasset?

The sign welcoming you to Wiscasset announces that it's "The prettiest village in Maine." I was so charmed by that and had to see for myself if it was true. And it is! The drive into Wiscasset is all part of the pretty—blueberry stands dot the countryside, and there are beautiful old farms and grazing horses. And the town is picture-postcard lovely. Many of Maine's towns are so pretty and charming, but also bustling at the same time. I particularly love Camden and Kennebunkport. And my own town is pretty cute, too.

How did you come up with the idea for Joy's singles tours?

I saw a glossy advertisement for a pricey singles bus tour of California's wine country, and I wondered what happens when that bus leaves the station: Are singles checking each other out? What if you're not attracted to anyone—do you want your money back? Or is it about the adventure? What if two singles are vying for the same person? What if, what if, what if? But I immediately envisioned that weird little yellow minibus from Little Miss Sunshine, *not a real bus with air-conditioning and a bathroom, and that strange little minibus began informing the kind of people who'd be on the tours — people on the quirky side. Seeking not so much romance, but acceptance, connection. It's so interesting how ideas take root.*

Many of the characters in this novel experience heartbreak at one point or another. What was your motivation for creating so many troubled relationships?

I didn't do it consciously! I think I wanted to explore what the word family *means to many different kinds of people in different stages. Including . . . myself.*

Rebecca is pretty confident all along that she and Joy really are sisters. As you were writing, did you ever waiver on your decision of what the blood tests would say? Do you usually know how a story is going to end when you start writing it?

I always write to a last sentence, actually. Does that sound strange? I always knew what I wanted for Joy and Rebecca at the end, and I wrote to that ending. I wasn't sure exactly what would lead them there, the twists and turns, the ups and downs; the characters take over to tell their own stories. But I knew before I wrote a word that these two women were sisters, in every sense of the word.

How did your work in publishing help prepare you for life as a writer? Is it helpful having been on the other side of the book business?

You know, it's hard to answer that question, because I don't know what it's like to be an author who wasn't an editor first, who wasn't working in the New York City publishing world. I started out in publishing as a twenty-two-year-old editorial assistant at a fiction house and left as a thirty-four-year-old senior editor. I feel like I grew up in the editorial world. The one thing I am sure of about publishing is this: it's a business. It's vital to remember that and probably the one thing that has been the most helpful to me these past ten years that I've been a full-time writer. But just as vital to remember is the fact that the creation of books, from the author who writes to the publishing house who produces, is a labor of love for everyone involved.

What's up next for you?

I am hard at work on my next women's fiction novel for Downtown Press. It's set in an Italian cooking class and involves the tiniest bit of magic and a lot of romance. My working title is The Love Goddess's Cooking School *and it will be published in 2010. I'm also very excited that in May 2010, my second novel for teens,* The Mosts, *will be published. Though set in the high school world (and mostly on a farm in Maine!), I explore my favorite themes: acceptance, family, relationships, and self-discovery.*

ENHANCE YOUR BOOK CLUB

1. Marianne isn't the only one famous for her whoopie pies—they're a Maine tradition! Order some of these delicious desserts from Labadie's Bakery in Maine at www.whoopiepies.com, or try making them yourself. Go to www.epicurious.com/recipes/food/views/Whoopie-Pies-107615.

2. Do you have a sister? Or maybe a best friend who feels more like a sister? Bring a photo of the two of you to your book club and talk about how the word *sister* defines your relationship.

3. Joy's singles tours were more than an opportunity to meet one's match; they were also a great opportunity to see some of Maine's beautiful attractions. Take advantage of your home state, too! Look up local attractions and consider hosting your book club somewhere outside the living room this time!